Check out the complete Aubrey Dark collection:

His

Mine

Yours

His Gift
His Ransom

Mr. Black's Proposal

-

Bad For Me

A Billionaire Romance Novel

By

Aubrey Dark

PROLOGUE
Rachel

I'm pinned on my back, my dress pushed up to my hips, two hundred feet above the streets of New York City. The floor underneath is all glass: if I crane my head to the side I can see the streets below, the cars moving like blinking white and red ants. It's almost midnight, and I feel like a lightning bug being held inside of a glass jar, suspended among the stars in the air above the sleepless city that I shouldn't love, but do.

Terrified. Thrilled. Electric with sensation.

It's the first time I've ever had a man's body pressed against me like this, the hard muscles against my soft curves sending all sorts of strange signals through me. And his one muscle, *there*, hard and insistent against my inner thigh. The music in the air is loud, filling my ears with a beat that almost matches my pounding heartbeat. It echoes through me, and I feel hollow, needy.

I shift, and his body shifts with me, pushing us even closer together.

"Rachel."

The music dissolves in my mind, and I hear his voice under the thrumming bass notes. A growl in my ear that sends bolts of desire shooting through me down to my toes.

He has me tied up with sashes, floating in the air, and he's floating with me, his sculpted body arched over mine. A red sash around my ankles, two more sashes knotted around my wrists. I'm supported in a dozen places by soft fabric stretched taut under my body, but the only sensation I care about is that muscle, hard and throbbing between my thighs. He *wants* me.

If you had told me a month ago that Clint Terrance would *want* me, I would have laughed myself silly. But nothing is silly now. I'm melting with every second that passes, every drum beat that stretches out time. I never want this to end, and we haven't even started.

When he threads his fingers through my hair, I moan. He's not touching me where I need it most. I ache for him in a way I never knew was possible. I ache for the kiss he hasn't given me yet. I ache for his hands on my body. I ache for him, *him* most of all, him inside of me, filling me the way the music fills my ears.

The tattoo peeking out from under his white jacket is a splash of musical notes, and for a brief moment I want to reach out and touch it with my fingertips, to try and read the music that's written all over him. I can't move my arms, though. The sashes are taut around my wrists. I bite my lip in frustration, and he sucks in a tight breath.

"Rachel. Tell me you want this."

I looked back up to see his dark desirous eyes above me, and I'm scared to think about what will happen if I say *yes*. My whole life has been a careful, sheltered existence. And now he's asking me to give it all up. Give up my family. Give up my life.

For *him*.

The sky is glass, the floor is glass, and all of a sudden I'm scared that we'll shatter everything if I let him take me now. I'm not supposed to be here, not with this man. I'm not this kind of girl. I never have been.

He's waiting for my answer, tense and ready, holding himself back even though I can see it kills him to do it. And as the music plays, I know that I'll never be ready, not really. There's never going to be a perfect time, a perfect place. There's only here and now, and I won't ever know how to fly until I let myself jump.

His lips are close to mine, so close that I am sure he can feel my breath, even if the word is lost in the music.

"Yes."

CHAPTER ONE
Clint

Goddammit. I'm such a fuckup.

I didn't mean to get into a fight at the studio. I swear I didn't. But trouble seems to follow me around like a band of underage groupies.

That night, I burst into the studio after-party already buzzed. The show had gone perfect—I couldn't wait to hear what my pops thought—and I'd been swimming through hot chicks on my way out of the stadium. I hoped Piers had brought an extra limo to hold all the girls.

Something bugged me, though, and I didn't know what. I was the lead singer of a hot rock band on the biggest tour of my life. Life was good, and tonight was the peak of it all.

Then why did I feel like something was missing?

The music blared from the speakers, but the crowd was so loud that I could barely hear who was playing. I scanned the mob of people, my eyes passing over girls in tiny skirts and men with fading tattoos poking out from their suit sleeves.

They'd turned the soundboard counter into a bar, and Piers looked like he was getting a kick out of playing bartender for the night. The studio was jammed from wall to wall to celebrate our last run in New York. There were probably a dozen platinum records sitting at the makeshift bar.

Three years ago, I would have been drooling at the opportunity to network with the big names in the biz. But tonight, after a killer show at Shea, I just wanted to find a girl to take home. Maybe two, to get rid of this bug up my ass.

Hell, maybe three.

Pops wasn't there yet, but his latest girlfriend was leaning over the bar, helping herself to a bottle of Jack Daniels Black Label.

Figures. Sherry was poison, and it was probably her that made me feel something in the air wasn't right. Oh fucking well. A drink would fix everything.

"Shots on me!" I yelled, and the crowd roared their approval. I motioned to Piers, who quickly yanked the bottle of Jack Daniels out of Sherry's hand and flipped it over the counter to me.

"You know what I like, Piers," I said, ignoring Sherry's dirty stare. "You in the weeds yet?"

"If I wasn't before, I am now. This place is a bloody madhouse," he said, in such a proper British accent I couldn't help but chuckle. Piers wasn't really into music—I don't think he'd ever sat through one of my concerts in its entirety. But chicks dig accents, and Piers played it up whenever he came out after one of my shows.

"Hey, you wanted to be the bartender."

"You kidding? I can't tell you how much shit I've overheard already. If I wanted to blackmail someone in the music business, I'd be all set."

"Remind me never to get you mad."

"Don't worry. I think the tabloids have already printed every picture of your bare ass in existence."

"Not bare anymore."

"You finally got that tattoo?"

"Bet your bare ass I did! Wanna see it?" I started to unbutton my jeans, but Piers held up his hands.

"Whoa! Later, big boy. Don't want to scare away all the ladies with your *derriere*."

"Scare them away? I'll have you know that girls fly across the world to get to see this."

"Humor me and keep your pants up for the first hour of this party, Clint. You showed up before most of the security guards."

"Fine," I said, tucking my shirt back into my jeans. "Wouldn't want to start a riot, I guess."

"Thank you for not flashing everyone in here. Trust me, it's a great kindness."

"You're *so* welcome."

I leaned back against the bar, looking out over the crowd again. Still no Pops. And Sherry was flirting with some other producer, I forget his name. What a bitch. My fingers itched at my side, and I tapped out a beat on my knee.

"How was the show?" Piers asked, interrupting my rhythm.

"Huh? Oh, great! We all kicked ass."

"So?"

I looked up, unscrewing the cap off of the bottle. Piers was already stacking shot glasses in a pyramid on the bar top. I stole a glass and poured myself one.

"So?"

"So why does your face look like you just licked a sour pussy?"

"Fuck, I dunno," I said. He gave me a look that said he wasn't going to give up that easily. I'll give Piers one thing—he knew how to read people. Especially me.

I leaned over the bar so that I didn't have to yell. I was trying to figure out what had gotten into me, to put it into words.

"It's like… it's all the same shit."

"The same shit," he echoed.

"All the music and the shows and the girls."

"Uh huh. And? Your problem is?"

"I dunno, Piers. The music world moves so fast, man. But we're still playing the same shit we played three years ago."

"Well. That's what people want to hear. The hits, yeah?"

"Yeah."

But that's not what I want to play.

I didn't say it. I had it good. Talismen had been my dad's idea, and he knew best. He was the one with the big office, the platinum records, the number one hits. He'd built this recording company from the ground up. If he told me to get up on stage and play *Row Row Row Your Boat* with a harmonica and a cowbell, I'd do it and I'd like it.

"Look at me," Piers was saying. "You think I *like* doing reality TV?"

"You *don't?*" I let sarcasm drip over the words. "How could you not love *Secret Baby Bachelor?*"

Piers rolled his eyes at me.

"You know, I came over to America to be a news reporter."

"That would be something else." I tried to imagine Piers behind a news desk, talking about... Syria or something? I didn't have a clue what news people talked about.

Piers slammed an empty shot glass down onto the bar.

"But people don't want news. They want Paris Hilton and Kim Kardashian clawing each other's eyes out over which shade of lipstick is better."

"So what do you do with that?" I asked. I already knew the answer, but I wanted him to say it.

"Fuck it. You do what you have to do."

"Do what you gotta do."

"That's how we're on top, right? Fuck it."

"Fuck it," I echoed, and slammed down the shot. The whiskey burned hot in my throat, but then it was down and a warm fuzzy feeling swept back whatever it was that had me feeling like shit.

"Hey, I got something for you tonight."

"Yeah?"

"Yeah. Her name's Roxie." He nodded over to the far corner of the studio. I looked over and saw what he was talking about: a buxom chick with fiery red hair lounged around in a skin-tight silver dress, a pouty expression on her face. "Pour these shots. People are getting restless."

"You *do* know what I like." I grinned and flipped the bottle, pouring the shots expertly over the pyramid of shot glasses. The sweet amber liquid flowed over the top glass and into the others in a fountain of whiskey.

The first shot was taking hold, and with Roxie on the horizon, my mood was rising already. Nothing was missing. Everything was perfect. I hummed a couple bars of an old timey song I had stuck in my head, nothing like the rock that was actually playing overhead.

In the big rock candy mountain, you never change your socks,
And little streams of alcohol come a-tricklin' down the rocks.

Along with whiskey and wine, redheads were a weakness of mine. Always had been. Not that this Roxie chick was a natural ginger—it looked more like she had dipped her head in candy apple dye. But fake was fine; nobody in this city was real, anyway. I winked at her as I finished the pour, not wasting a single drop. She bit her lip and tossed her hair over one shoulder.

It was gonna be a wild night, I knew it.

"Ladies and gents, drinks are served!" Piers started passing out the shots down the bar. I took a few for myself and retreated through the crowd, still humming as people clapped me on the back in appreciation.

There's a lake of stew, and of whiskey too,
You can paddle all around em in a big canoe
In the big rock candy mountain.

As I finished with a whistle, I caught a glimpse of someone over by the recording room. "Hey, Danny!" I called to one of the security guards. "That asshole over there leaning on the glass—"

"Got it," Danny said, snapping his fingers. He moved toward the recording room. I'd personally overseen the remodel of the studio, and I wasn't about to have some drunk rocker fall through the plate glass window between the two rooms.

"Killer set, Clint, absolutely killer!" my tour manager cried out.

"Thanks," I said, handing him one of the shots of whiskey.

I was about to head over to Roxie to share a shot with her when it happened. I could already imagine the way the night would go: we'd share a shot, then we'd share a kiss, then we'd share a bed. She'd get a cab ride home by herself, of course, but first we'd have a night of crazy hot sex.

Then something caught my eye.

A woman at the end of the bar shook her head, her light blonde hair falling in long waves down her back. Not really my type, but that wasn't why I was looking at her anyway.

It was the guy sleazing out all over her that drew my attention.

I didn't know who he was or what record company he was with, but he looked like every stereotype of an old-school rocker gone bad. A black leather jacket with patches all over it and metal studs around the neck. Three days' worth of patchy scruff on his cheeks. A gold chain around his stringy neck. It was laughable.

The guy had his hand around the chick's midriff. She leaned away from him, but he didn't get the hint. Instead, he pulled her away from the bar.

I moved closer as he began to tug her towards the exit. Some sort of stupid instinct that draws me toward trouble instead of keeping me away from it.

"Come on baby, let's go," he was saying.

"But I don't want to go," she said, her voice rising above his. "I didn't even meet him yet!"

I headed between them and the exit door. Yeah, I'm the kind of idiot who doesn't know when to mind his own fucking business. But I figured it was my name on the studio door, and my reputation on the line if some girl got treated bad at a studio after-party.

"You can meet him later."

"But I want to see him now!"

She was shouting by now, causing a commotion at the end of the bar. Not even the music could drown out her high-pitched shouting.

I stepped in front of them and put my shot glasses down on the bar. The guy leered at me from under his greasy, slicked back hair. I had no doubt that I was doing the right thing.

"Move, buddy," he said.

"Is this guy bothering you?" I asked the girl. Not a girl, really, but a woman. She was older than I'd thought, maybe thirty-five. Too old to be wearing a fake leather miniskirt or bright red lipstick, that's for damn sure.

"Oh my god. You're Clint Terrance." Her mouth dropped open.

I nodded.

"I was supposed to come here for an audition!" She couldn't stop gushing, and every sentence coming through her fire-engine red lips was an exclamation. "I love your studio's music! This is like fate! Me meeting you here!"

"You're the Terrance kid?" the guy asked. His leer turned uncertain. I could tell he knew who I was. My name was a weapon, and I didn't use it unless I had to. Usually I didn't need to.

"An audition?" I focused on the woman. She licked her bottom lip and I realized her pupils were dilated from some designer drug. She wasn't awful-looking, but I'd seen too many of her type. Bleached blonde wanna-be rock stars who had gone past their prime.

All coked up with nowhere to go.

"Where is he?" she asked. Her hand clawed around my wrist. "Can I see him?"

Him? Who the hell's she talking about?

"Come on, sweetie," the sleazeball said, yanking her

away from me. "Let's get you out of here."

"Hey!" I said, planting myself firmly between them and the door.

"You don't want to interfere here, kid," he said. The warning was in his tone and in the way his arm clamped even tighter around the woman. She barely seemed to notice. All of her desperation had turned to me, and she was waiting for me.

"I'm not a kid to anyone but my dad," I said.

"Whatever, kid," he said. "Come on, we're leaving." He tried to push past me with the woman.

"Nobody messes with the girls in my studio," I said, pushing him back.

"Not your fucking studio, *kid.*"

Fuck that. I wasn't going to let this guy push me around. The whiskey was boiling in my blood, and the security guard was over on the other side of the room.

I clamped one hand on his shoulder and shoved him back against the bar.

"Hey!"

He winced and let go of the blonde. She jumped away from him behind me, putting her hands on my back.

"My savior!" she cried. Way too melodramatic. I could smell the alcohol on her breath as she pressed her fake tits against me.

"Fuckin' stop it, kid—" the guy started to say, but I didn't wait to hear him. My arm was already in the air, and the punch landed right across the guy's ugly face.

"I'm not. A fucking. Kid." My face was inches away from his, and I could smell the blood that was already dripping from his lip.

"Goddamn lunatic!" He tried to shove me away, but now I was burning mad. "You have no idea what the fuck you're doing."

"Yeah? When has that ever stopped me?"

"Listen—"

"Shut the fuck up, asshole." The whiskey spun my

brain, and the energy of the crowd around me gave me another burst of energy. I grabbed him by the collar and lifted him off the ground. He kicked at me, sending a jolt of pain through my leg.

The fuck! Who kicks me? Who kicks Clint-fucking-Terrance?

I punched him again, and my fist cracked across his nose. Behind the bar, Piers was yelling and waving wildly for security.

"Nobody calls me a kid," I said. "No-fucking-body, no fucking way! You get that?"

I mashed a finger into his bloody face, right on his nose. He squealed like a slide guitar.

"Clint, stop!"

My tour manager's voice buzzed in my ear, and someone was tugging at my shirt. I heard it rip as I pushed forward, shaking the smarmy bastard in my grip. He twisted in my hands, his eyes filled with terror. Some people were yelling, and I could hear Danny coming through the crowd behind me.

I gave the asshole one more shake and raised my fist again.

"Please don't," he said, only with his broken nose it came out as *Preese dunt.*

"You fucking sleazeball," I said. "You goddamn—"

"Stop."

The voice behind me wasn't a shout, but it boomed across the crowded studio as loud as if it had come through a megaphone. The crowd went silent.

I dropped the guy back against the bar. He whined softly, slithering back away to a safe distance from my fists, and I turned around.

My dad stood in the middle of the studio floor, looming over the crowd in his dark navy business suit. Moses himself couldn't have parted a crowd like my dad did. They fell back in waves. He cleared his throat and adjusted a silver cufflink at his wrist.

"Get your ass in here, kid. Now." He turned his back and stepped into the recording room without waiting for a reply.

"Sure, Pops," I said under my breath, gritting my teeth and turning back the bar. Piers glanced over at me, but I didn't meet his eye. I threw back one shot, then the next, without taking a breath between. So much for sharing. The party—and Roxie—would have to wait.

CHAPTER TWO
Rachel

I step forward on the stage. The lights are so bright I can't see the crowd, but I can hear them cheering for me, calling for an encore. I take a deep breath, the song already rising in my throat, and—

"Where's your mother?"

I spun at the question, my long tangled braid flying over my shoulder. My dad was standing alone in the middle of the room, streaks of dirt down his face. I looked to the corner of the living room. My mom's chair...

My mom's chair was empty.

Her knitting lay abandoned on the patterned floral upholstery of the big armchair. The small TV on the side table was still playing her lunchtime soap opera.

Panic bolted down my spine. The plate I was holding clattered to the bottom of the sink.

"Mom?" I called, my voice already trembling.

"Charlene?" My dad called out, a little louder.

"She was just in her chair. I was doing the dishes—"

I cut myself off. I hadn't just been doing the dishes, had I? I'd been daydreaming again. I hadn't been paying attention.

Quickly, I strode toward the back door, the planks creaking underfoot. My hands wrung the bottom of my apron, drying off suds automatically.

I wasn't paying attention.

My dad was right behind me.

"I'm sure she's fine," he said, but I heard the worry in his voice. He would never let himself get worked up emotionally, but after so many years I could sense the undercurrents of his mood. I could tell by a twist of his upper lip that he was upset, or by the way his sentences went flat. Now, I could sense his worry, and it made me even more anxious.

The screen door banged open and a gust of November wind blew through my thin dress.

"*Mom?*"

My eyes scanned the yard, not lingering on the chestnut oak, the fields of alfalfa beyond the old wooden fence. Cows stood flicking their tails lazily in the pastures, no human form among them. Behind the alfalfa fields, cars zoomed down the two-lane highway that cut through the farmland. Overhead, the clouds pressed down in a gray haze.

On the other side of the highway was a half-acre of corn that we hadn't harvested yet; could she have wandered off there? A shiver went down my back as I thought of her crossing the highway.

No, she would never do that. She hated cars.

Just then I heard her voice humming a melody. It was coming from around the side of the house. I flew down the steps.

"Mom?"

Relief swept through me at the sight of her. She was in the blackberry bushes. Her gray dress was caught up on the thorns of the bush, but she didn't seem to notice. Holding a wicker basket in the crook of her elbow, she reached out with both hands into the blackberry bush. Her long gray hair flowed loosely down her back into the folds of her dress.

She looked like a princess—a princess with gray hair and wrinkles, but a princess nonetheless. That's how I'd always thought of her, back when I was smaller than her.

Back when it wasn't dangerous to daydream.

I hurried to the bushes and picked my way through to where she was standing. She was still humming as she turned her face up to me, a blissful look on her features.

"Mom!"

"Rose?" she asked. A flicker of confusion in her eyes.

"No," I said, my heart contorting in my chest. She never forgot my twin sister's name when she came home to visit, but she mixed me up all the time. "No, Mom. It's Rachel."

She didn't respond when I corrected her. She rarely did. Being corrected made her irritable, and she was very good at ignoring things that made her irritable. Maybe she wanted to pretend that I was, in fact, Rose.

The other daughter. The better daughter.

"I thought I'd pick some blackberries," she said. Her lips pulled her thin skin taut over her cheekbones, the wrinkles of her smile making her look strangely younger. "Wouldn't you love a pie for dessert tonight?"

"It's not summer anymore, Mom," I said.

"Not summer?"

"It's November. There aren't any blackberries."

She turned to the bushes, a confused look on her face. Her hands splayed out over the bushes where only a few browned leaves still hung, searching for something that wasn't there. Behind me, my dad sighed.

"Mom."

I took her hand and held it. It trembled slightly, like a dying bird. Her eyes were the same faded gray-brown of the dead crops in the fields.

"I wanted to make a pie," she said. "But... the berries..."

"We can go get berries from the store," I lied. Blackberries in November were six dollars a pint, but I would have promised her the world to get her back in the house. Back to safety.

"I want to pick berries."

"It's freezing out here, Mom. We have to get you inside."

Her eyes refocused then, and she *saw* the bushes, really saw them for what they were. It was as though she'd been walking through the sunshine, through green bushes and plump berries, and my words took it away from her.

Goosebumps rose on her arm, and I saw the shiver go through her body as the cold finally hit her.

Pain thudded through my body, landed in a well-worn spot in my heart.

I'd taken the sun out of her eyes.

"Come on, Charlene," my dad said.

"I'm coming," she snapped. Her beatific smile turned into a frown and she shook my hands off of her arm. "You don't need to help me. I can walk just fine."

Sure, you can walk just fine, I wanted to say, irritation mixing in with my relief. *You can walk anywhere, walk until you're lost.*

But I didn't say anything. I was relieved, after all, that she hadn't gotten far. That we had found her.

She clamped her dress up in her hands and shuffled out of the blackberry bushes. My dad held out his hand, but she only huffed past him. We both followed her to the back steps of the house. He wiped his hand across his brow.

"I'm sorry," I whispered to my dad, as the screen door banged shut behind her. "She could have gotten lost again. I should have paid better attention. I should have—"

"You're doing too much already," my dad said. Weariness tugged down the sides of his face, and his eyes flickered back to the fields. I knew he had to get back to the cows. "There's no two ways about it."

"I wish I could do more."

"As soon as we can afford the help—"

"As soon as we can afford the help, we're getting a hand who can do some of the milking," I interrupted. "That's what we really need."

"Yeah," my dad said, after a pause. "You're right."

My dad had been up since four thirty that morning. Apart from working the milking center, he had to herd the cows into the next pasture today. Even with a smaller herd than last year, it would take until sundown.

Last year, I'd been able to help with the herding. This

16

year, though, I had to stay in the house. Rose was in her senior year of college, and she couldn't spare any time to come home and help look after Mom.

And she really did need someone looking after her. Even going out to check the mail took too long to be safe.

Anything for Rose, I thought bitterly.

A college education was more important than the farm, as my dad never hesitated to remind us. But Rose was the only one in college, while I was still here.

We had gotten our acceptance letters on the same day when we were seniors in high school. Rose raced back from the highway mailbox, ripping her letter open as she ran. I'd walked slowly behind her, feeling the heft of the envelope in my hand, opening it carefully and reading through it not once, but twice.

Congratulations, Rachel Ritter, it started. I scanned down the letter, looking for the financial aid statement. There it was, on the back page. A five hundred dollar stipend for artistic merit. Five hundred dollars. My heart crumpled in my chest.

Congratulations.

A hollow victory. It was as good as a rejection, and I knew it. I put the letter back in the envelope, folded the envelope in half.

I came in the door as my mom was hugging Rose tightly, not knowing what they were celebrating but celebrating anyway.

"A full scholarship! Can you believe it!" she shrieked. Any flicker of happiness I'd had at being accepted disappeared when I saw Rose beaming in my mother's arms. She'd done it again, managed to take the spotlight.

"Oh, Rose!" my mother cried out. "Rose!"

Oh, Rose.

The envelope burned my fingers. My dad, sitting at the kitchen counter, stood up when I walked in. I crossed the room quickly and tossed the letter in the trash.

"Guess I'm staying on the farm," I said.

"I'm sorry, baby," he said, patting my hand. He didn't even hug me. Why would he? I never needed anyone to comfort me. I was strong.

And the thing was, he *wasn't* sorry that I was staying. The look of relief in his eyes was palpable. In a small way, I felt better knowing that he needed me here. Even as he protested, telling me to apply to other schools, I knew that I wasn't ever going to leave.

So I had stayed, and did what I was good at: herding cows, working the milker. Taking care of my mom.

Except today I'd failed even at that.

My mom was already back in her chair, knitting furiously. She didn't lift her head up to look at us.

"I worry…" I said, trailing off.

"Rachel, Rachel. My little worrywart," my dad said, patting me on the arm. He was big, bigger than even me, his gnarled hands twice the size of mine. I thought for a moment that he might draw me into his arms, that he might kiss me on the top of the head like he used to do when I was a little girl.

But of course he wouldn't. He hadn't hugged me for years. He was as stoic and unemotional as every other dairy farmer in New Jersey. The best I could hope for was a crooked smile, maybe a high five. Now, though, he looked completely blank, his mind on other, more important things. Four days of gray scruff stood out on his chin. He shook the thought away.

"That's what I count on you for," he said.

"For worrying?"

"Yep. You worry enough for the both of us." He clapped his hands on his thighs and smiled at me, as though it wasn't him who had found Mom missing in the first place. As though I hadn't failed us, again. "I've got to grab lunch and head back out to the pasture."

"Still herding?"

"The dogs can't do it alone."

"Lunch is on the counter," I said, gesturing to the

brown paper bag I'd made up earlier that morning.

"What would I do without you?" he asked.

There was no answer to that. I had to stay here. I went back to the sink and picked up the half-washed dish, standing sideways so I could see my mom's chair.

My dad went over to her and knelt down. He looked like an ogre kneeling before the princess.

Too bad I'd inherited the ogre half. I'd always wanted to look like my mom, but fate had given me an extra foot in every direction as I grew into my awkward body. If Rose looked like a model for Victoria's Secret, I was a model for *Shrek*.

Twins... yeah, right. If they had told me I was adopted, I wouldn't have been surprised.

"I'm going out to the pastures, Charlene," he said. His rough hand brushed back a silky strand of gray hair behind her ear. Her knitting needles went *click click click*. He was gentle with her, so completely gentle. It always surprised me when his voice went low and kind like that.

"Charlene?"

She looked up at him, and worry flashed across her face. A knack for worrying—maybe that was the one thing I'd gotten from her.

"You be careful with those cows, John," she said. "They'll kick you if you pull their udders too hard. Will you be careful?"

"I'll be careful," my dad said. It had been five years since we'd hand-milked any of our cows, but he didn't say anything about that.

He stood up slowly and kissed her forehead, caressing her hair. There was so much love in his eyes that I turned away, embarrassed. It was the only time he showed affection, and Mom couldn't even remember who he was half the time.

I never wanted to be like my mom, but I envied the love my dad gave her.

"I was thinking of baking a pie for tonight," my mom

said, her voice happy and clear as sunshine. "Will Rose be home for dinner?"

I picked up the plate from the sink, biting my tongue.

"Maybe, Charlene."

The plate wasn't cracked, not at all, even though I'd dropped it hard in the sink. I picked up the scouring rag and turned the water to scalding. The steam rose white and hot over my arms, and I focused on the soap and the dish and the knitting needles going *click click click* behind me, focused intently on everything that was here and real and not a daydream at all.

CHAPTER THREE
Clint

My pops pulled me into the recording studio and closed the door. This part of the studio was soundproof, and the music cut off abruptly as he closed the door. I saw the people dancing and yelling, but I couldn't hear anything through the plate glass that separated the two parts of the room.

"Was that woman looking for you?" I asked.

"Never mind her. Come do a line with me."

He plopped down on the black leather couch and motioned down to the coffee table. There were three small neat lines of white powder on the glass table, and a few traces of the coke that he'd probably already snorted.

I sucked in a breath. I hadn't done that shit in a while.

"Pops…"

"She was a bitch, okay? Only wanted to get with me to do an audition. Just like the rest of those gold diggers."

"So that guy—"

"I told him to get rid of her. And then you had to come along. Stop punching people for no reason, kid."

I clamped my lips shut. Man, I'd fucked that up. But how was I supposed to know?

"Sorry, Pops," I said finally.

"That's okay, kid."

"You know, Sherry was out there talking with some producer. Flirting."

"Fuck Sherry. She can flirt all she wants. They're all gold diggers."

I wasn't going to argue with that. My dad flicked a business card at me.

"Go on, do a line. I gotta tell you something."

I glanced through the window at Piers, who was busy serving out the last of the shots of Jack Daniels. He didn't see us. I hesitated, not sure if I should.

But I was still feeling weird. And I knew that coke was one thing that wouldn't just get rid of that hollow feeling inside of me; it would *obliterate* it.

"What are you waiting for?"

Without another thought, I bent over the low table, out of sight of the partygoers, rolling up the business card that said *SKULL TERRANCE, CEO* in raised gold lettering. The line of coke disappeared, burning my nostril as it went.

The coke hit my bloodstream like a rocket booster. Spikes of energy pumped through me and I forgot all my previous anxiety. I shook my hands out, cracking my knuckles.

"You feel good?"

"Yeah, yeah. Thanks, Pops."

Good? I felt fucking *awesome*. I could party until sunrise. I'd forgotten how much coke could help when you were stuck on some bullshit worry. Look at all those people in the studio. They were all here to celebrate Talismen. They were here to celebrate *me*.

I was pumped up and ready to take on the world. I didn't even mind that my knuckles were cut from punching out that guy.

"Hey, listen. Listen."

My dad was talking, and I shook my head to regain my focus. Only my father would give me coke and then expect me to listen to him ramble. I shifted anxiously in my seat, eyeing the two remaining lines of coke on the table.

"Sure, Pops. What's up?"

"We need a new act."

"A new act?"

"You listening to me? Quit jerking around. Yes, a fucking new act. You've been slacking."

My fingers danced on my knee. I clenched my leg and

tried not to fidget.

"We're not slacking, Pops! We just did two sold out concerts at Shea."

"I'm not talking about Talismen. Talismen is shit. You know it, I know it."

"Sure, sure," I lied, frowning.

I had no fucking clue what he was talking about. Talismen had been our band from the start, and it had done better than even I had expected. When my dad started managing us, he created our brand as carefully as Johnson and Johnson creates diaper branding. And it hit hard.

The music had gotten worse with each album, but when had that ever been an issue? My dad swore by record sales, and by that metric, we were killing it. We had the radio stations in our pockets. Featured singers were lining up to do tracks with us. We'd gotten three number one singles out of our first album, a Europe and an East Asia tour. We'd been living the rock star dream for the past three years.

"Talismen is dead. *Rock* is dead," my father said.

I twitched, and it wasn't from the coke. I didn't know where he was going with this rant.

"We're doing fine, though, aren't we?" I asked.

"Fine isn't good enough. You really want to take over the company?"

"Dad, come on."

He slammed his hand on the table, and the neat lines of coke collapsed into a messy pile.

"I'm serious. I'm not gonna be around forever."

"You won't if you keep doing coke every weekend, that's for damn sure!"

"Fuck, that's nothing. It keeps my heart pumping fast. Don't worry about me."

He waved a hand in the air, and I noticed his hairline. He'd been dying his hair forever, but at the top of his forehead was an undisguised line of white. I wondered how long he'd had white hair.

"Sure, Pops. Whatever you say."

"I'm serious. I want you to take over the business, kid."

I sat up straighter, my senses all on high alert. He'd been mentioning retirement for a while now, but never seriously.

"When?"

"When you prove to me you're not a one-hit wonder. I want a new act."

"You're saying you want me to start a new band?"

"That's not what I'm saying. Pay attention. Do you see me flouncing around onstage like some teen rock star?"

I squinted.

"Look at me. How am I dressed?" He didn't wait for me to answer. "Like a businessman. And this is a business. You've done a good job with Talismen, kid."

I beamed. The coke was spreading through me, throbbing in my veins, and a good warm feeling rushed through me at his words.

"Thanks."

"But it's time to move into your proper role if you want to head the studio. Leave the music to the creatives. Creatives get paid shit. We run this like a business. Look at me."

I snapped to attention, but was struggling to keep up. The coke had me twitching, looking away to the silent party through the glass, wondering if Piers knew what we were up to back here, wondering if that redhead was still sticking around.

"You don't want me playing in a band?" I asked.

"Playing. Exactly. That's fucking play. It's time to work. Get it?"

"Got it," I said, although I didn't. "So you want me to find someone to front a new band?"

"I want you to do what I did with Talismen. I made you a star."

I licked my lips and nodded, uncertain. Was that what

he had done?

"Find a singer. Someone we can brand."

"Just a singer?"

"You don't need a band. We can get studio musicians to back the tracks, it'll be faster. Cheaper. I want a hit album you can put out by the end of the year."

This year? That was, like, two months from now. But I nodded vigorously. Maybe it was the intense vibe he was putting out, or the drugs in my blood, but I was pumped to try my hand at doing some real studio work.

Even with the energy from the coke, that nagging feeling reared up at the back of my mind. It sounded like I wasn't going to play any more music. Part of me recoiled at the thought of giving up guitar, giving up singing. But if that's what my dad wanted me to do so that I could run the studio, then I had to show him I was ready.

I had to find a singer.

"So I should talk to the talent scouts, then?"

"Fucking talent scouts," my dad scoffed. "What have they brought in? That folk group? Pfft." He shook his head dismissively. "Show me something I haven't seen. A new act. A new hit. Something to get us back in the game. A real star."

A star. I nodded again. I had to find a star. My mind spun with coke and possibilities.

"Good, I know you'll do me proud, kid. Now get your ass back in that party and get rid of that bitch for me," my dad said, as he leaned over the table to do another line.

CHAPTER FOUR
Rachel

I tucked the covers up to my mom's chin for her nap. It was getting late, and I hoped that I would have some time to steal away to the barn before dinner. My mom blinked softly, and I could tell she was trying to remember my name.

"Rachel," I said. "It's me, Rachel."

Her face twisted into a grimace, like she hated me for having to remind her. She plucked at the covers with her thin fingers.

"Do you want anything before your nap, Mom? Water?"

"Sing for me."

I sat down on the bedside. My bones ached with exhaustion, and it was lovely to sink into the soft bed. On the farm, I was always weary, but in my mom's room at least I had somewhere soft to rest. It made me feel guilty to think that I wanted to get away and be alone with my daydreams. She wanted me here, and I shouldn't be thinking about anything else. I smiled at her with all the energy I could muster.

"What do you want me to sing?"

"Sing about the bird."

The bird. It was always that song. Little more than a nursery rhyme, really. When I had been a little girl, she had sung it to me. I supposed that it made sense, in a sad sort of way. Now that I was taking care of her, I had to sing the lullaby.

When had the switch happened? When had I become the parent? It had been so many years, I didn't even remember.

I began to sing softly, almost in a whisper.

Long ago, so long ago, a young bird left her nest,
And flew for miles and miles and miles, without a thought of rest.
Searching for a tree of thorns, oh why? She could not say.
Something deep inside her sent her winging on her way.

Fly, little bird,
Fly until the break of dawn.
Fly, little bird,
Fly on, fly on.

My mom closed her eyes.

"Thank you, Rachel," she said.

I stroked her hair, gray and smooth against the pillow. It almost hurt, how much my heart swelled when she remembered my name.

She moved her mouth with me as I sang the next stanza:

The nightingale was born to sing, the clouds were born to rain
The young bird found the tree of thorns and did not mind the pain.
The thorns impaled her downy breast, the thorns pierced through her heart
But she would never stop the song that made her pain depart.

Sing, little bird,
Sing until the break of dawn.
Sing, little bird,
Sing on, sing on.

The story was a Celtic legend, my mom said. She'd learned about it from a novel first, a book she'd read when she was a girl. It seemed gruesome to me now that I was the one singing it. The bird dies, for goodness' sake, with a thorn stuck right through her! What kind of a song was that to sing to a baby?

The whole world listened to her song; God smiled from heaven's eye
She traded her life for that one song and gave it to the sky.
And so you trade your pain to sing, struggle to find the way.
But the sweetest song will always cost the dearest price to pay.

I supposed there were lots of nursery rhymes about death. Humpty Dumpty, for one. Rock-a-bye baby was about a baby falling out of a tree. And wasn't Ring around the Rosie supposed to be about the black plague?

My mom always sang that one to Rose, because it had her name in it. Rose was special. There were tons of songs about Rose. I couldn't think of a single song with my name in it.

Just another way Rose was better than me.

By the end of the song, my mom was already dozing off, her breaths even and regular. But I finished the song for her anyway, lilting the last chorus in a voice that was so soft it was almost invisible.

Fly, little bird,
Fly until the break of dawn.
Fly, little bird,
Fly on, fly on.

There. She was asleep. Her breaths were shallow; her chest rose only slightly under the covers. I looked at her with a mix of emotion, then stood up. Was this how mothers felt towards their babies? I never wanted to leave her. I wanted to keep her safe. And yet, something inside me pulled away, wanted to be by myself. Wanted to be alone to daydream.

She was sleeping now, and I didn't have to feel guilty, but I still tiptoed out of the room, trying not to stir her sleep. I'd be back before her nap was finished. When she woke up, I would be there for her. As much as it took out of me, as much as it hurt sometimes, especially when she forgot. None of that mattered.

I would always be there for her.

I stole away to the farthest barn. It was where we kept the stores of hay for winter, and it still smelled like summertime, even in November. One or two cows gave me a halfhearted *moo* as I walked through the pasture and to the big red barn. I didn't mind them. Rose had given the cows names, but I knew better than to do that. They weren't pets, not to me. Every season a few of the dairy cows died or got sick and had to be put down. I couldn't give out my heart to all the creatures that depended on me. It was too much.

Inside, I clambered awkwardly up to the top of the hayloft. When I was a kid, I'd been a scrawny little bean with two thick braids keeping my hair tidy. Now I was twenty-two, and each year had added padding to my hips, my thighs, my chest. Still, I was strong enough to climb up to the rafters, where I pulled out the wooden box from my secret hiding spot.

I settled back on the prickly hay and opened the box.

The red dress was still in its plastic bag. I slid my hand inside, letting my fingers run along the satiny fabric. It had been an impulse purchase, the one time I'd visited New York to see Rose at college. I'd gone out shopping on my own and found the red dress hanging up in the clearance section of a store. I'd bought it with the last of my spending money and skipped lunches instead. To me, it was the quintessential New York dress. Sexy and slinky and oh-so perfect.

It was a waste of money, too, for I'd never worn the dress. One day, maybe I would. But not today. Not on the farm. This was the opposite of a farm dress.

Clasping the dress against my chest, I stood up on the

highest bale of hay. I looked around, imagining myself standing on a concert stage.

The rafters turned into a ceiling shimmering with lights. The hay stacks turned into throngs of cheering crowds. I was the best singer in New York City, and I was going to perform for all these people.

I stepped up to the imaginary microphone. In my mind, I was wearing that slinky red dress, and everyone quieted down to listen to me. What song would I sing? I had a perfect song in mind for tonight, after singing that Celtic song to my mom.

"Welcome, everyone," I said in my best sultry voice. "Thank you for coming. I'm sure most of you will know this next song."

I cleared my throat and began to sing as loud as I could. That was the beauty of the empty barn—nobody came back here but me. Me, and the imaginary crowds listening to me sing.

Oh Danny boy, the pipes, the pipes are calling
From glen to glen, and down the mountain side

I sang my lungs out, loud and clear, to any cow who would listen.

The summer's gone, and all the roses falling
It's you, it's you must go and I must bide—

"Rachel?"

I snapped back to reality at the sound of a man's voice. In shock, I clapped my lips together. My dad never came out here looking for me. Who could it be? I quickly stuffed the red dress back into the wood box. As I heard footsteps coming through the door, I kicked the box back into the hay bale and spun back around.

"Oh, it's you!"

Derrick stood in the middle of the doorway, his arms

31

wide open. He looked like a high-powered financier in his navy blue business suit, or at least I thought so. I breathed out a sigh that he hadn't seen me pretending to wear the red dress. I didn't feel confident enough to let anyone know what I'd really been dreaming about, especially him.

"It's me!" he said, kicking a tuft of hay aside as he came into the barn.

"Wait down there," I said. "And turn around! I don't want you looking up my skirt while I climb down!"

He laughed and turned, leaning against the barn door. His lean silhouette was dark against the light gray sky. I quickly pushed the wood box back into its hiding spot and scuttled down from the hay loft.

"Cow karaoke?" Derrick joked, as I came forward to hug him. I flushed. How long had he been out there, listening?

"Yeah, something like that."

"I'm glad you're keeping busy."

"What are you doing here?" I asked, still a bit breathless from being caught mid-song.

"Well, isn't that a nice question? Shouldn't you be happy to see your future husband?" He put on a fake pout and I laughed lightly, touching his shoulder. He took my hand in his and we began to walk back to the house.

"I mean... you just normally don't come until the end of the month."

Derrick worked in New York City. We'd known each other forever, but after we'd gotten engaged, he'd gotten an offer from one of the actuarial firms in the financial district. It was a great start to a career in finance; he would have been stupid not to take it, really. And he came back to the farm once a month—he always insisted on giving my dad a hundred dollars or so for bills. He said he would be able to give more once he was promoted, but right now anything extra was a gift from heaven itself.

"Lacey asked me to drive down tonight and get you, so I drove down with Rose."

"With Rose?"

A pang of jealousy pierced my heart, and I looked straight ahead as we walked, trying not to show it. Thinking about her spending time with my fiance made me feel weird. I didn't know why; Derrick wasn't the kind to cheat on me. But she hadn't come back in so long, and now she was here with Derrick?

"She drove us down, actually. Didn't want to let me drive my own car."

"I believe it," I said, forcing a chuckle. "What do you mean, Lacey wanted you to get me? To go where?"

His shoulders shrugged back and he looked at me with a tilted face that said: *Really?*

"To New York City, you doof," he said. "She said it was important for you to come tonight."

"But... but why?"

"It's a music opportunity, I think. That Jake guy she's with knows someone in the music industry."

My pulse quickened.

"Why didn't she call me to tell me about it?"

"You know exactly what you would have said if she called. The same thing you say when I invite you to come visit New York. *There's so much work to do on the farm...*"

"There *is* so much work to do here!" I protested.

"See?" He laughed. "She knew that nothing short of a kidnapping would work."

"So that's why you're here? To kidnap me?" I ran a teasing finger down his arm, but he didn't respond. "What else did Lacey say?"

"I don't really remember," he said, shrugging.

I could have ripped his head off! He hadn't bothered to get any of the juicy details from Lacey. But I supposed I would see when I got there. But...

"My mother," I said. "I can't leave her."

"Already planned for that," Derrick said, looking pleased with himself. "Rose said she had a slow week before her midterm exams, so I convinced her to come

33

and take care of her."

I thought of Rose taking care of the farm. Taking care of Mom. Could she handle everything?

"I don't know…"

I looked out at the pastures as we walked closer to the house. I was in charge of making sure the cows were milked properly. And even though she had given them names, Rose hadn't ever bothered to learn how to work the milking machines.

"It won't be for long. Just a few days. A week at most."

"But—"

"No buts. Lacey was adamant. And your sister will do fine. It can't be that hard, anyway."

"It's not—"

"Stop. Hush. Rachel. You are coming to New York City. The world won't end if you're there for a week. End of argument."

They'd thought of every possible objection. I felt cornered. And, in a strange way, excited. I'd only ever been to New York City twice before, once to see Rose and once when I was a small kid. It was silly, really—it was only a few hours' drive. But to me, it was as thrilling as if I was flying across the world to Dubai.

"When were you—uh, we—planning to leave?" I twisted my fingers together.

He looked at me like it was the most ridiculous question in the world.

"Now."

CHAPTER FIVE
Clint

"What do you mean, you need me to help you find a singer?"

Piers leaned back against the wall. It was past three in the morning and most of the party had disappeared, but I was bouncing off the walls. My dad had given me another line of coke, and after he left, I'd jumped behind the soundboard to help Piers "clean up the bar." Which, of course, really meant cleaning out the rest of the Jack Daniels. The whiskey and coke mixed together to give me a rabid energy.

"I need to find a singer."

"A singer?"

"For the studio. A star, a fucking star!" I pounded my fist on the bartop, rattling the empty bottles.

"You need to calm the fuck down, is what you need to do." Piers leaned back against the wall, the perfect image of British cool.

"I need this, Piers. I need to reinvent myself. And the studio needs a new singer."

"What you need is a fuck and a drink. Not necessarily in that order." He reached for the bottle of whiskey, but I pulled it away from him.

"No. No more drinking," I proclaimed. "It's time to work."

"At three in the morning?"

"New York never sleeps. And I need to find a singer. How do I find a singer? Can *you* sing?" ·

"Are you high?"

"Yes. No. Just a couple lines."

"Your father gave you cocaine? I *knew* something was

up. Clint—"

"Don't fucking preach to me, Piers. You're not one to talk."

"Oh?"

"I'm not the one who's facing charges for underage sexual misconduct."

Piers grimaced.

"Thanks for bringing that up. Really. Thanks."

"You're welcome. So tell me, Mr. Unethical Misconduct—"

"First off, it's been two years. Second off, it's not like I wanted a seventeen year old to throw herself into my bed wearing a minidress made out of plastic wrap! *She* was trying to seduce *me!*"

"So you're saying she's nineteen now? She's legal now? Is that what you're saying?"

"Fuck, Clint. You're my best friend. You know how entertainment works."

"Enlighten me."

"You get these girls, these groupies, they all want in your pants. You want to find a singer, just snap your fingers and they'll come throwing themselves at your dick."

"I don't want them on my dick. I want them on my records."

"What's the difference?" he smirked.

"Any girl can suck cock. I want them to be able to hit a top-octave C note."

"You want a bird with a deep throat and a talented tongue."

"And good lung power. Wide range. And enunciation."

"I didn't think you knew two-bit words like that, darling."

"Neither do the teenagers you bang."

"Ouch. You know how to throw a punch, Clint."

"Did you want to see my tattoo?"

Piers burst out laughing. He knew that I could never stay focused on anything when I had done a line or two.

"I never want to see any of your tattoos, Clint. Save it for your groupies."

"Fine, fine. But what about the singer? How do I get a singer?"

Piers paused in thought. I tried to wait him out. The silence only went on for a few seconds, but to me it seemed like an hour. Finally, he snapped his fingers.

"How about this. I have an idea."

"Shoot," I said.

"Okay. We'll do a reality TV show."

"Get serious, Piers."

"No, no, no! Hear me out!"

I crossed my arms and looked narrowly at him.

"You need a singer," he said.

"A *star*."

"You need a star. And what would be more perfect than a reality TV show to pick America's next big star?"

I squinted, thinking about the idea.

"It's been done. Hasn't it?"

"Not by a studio. And who cares if it's been done? There's nothing new under the sun. But you and me hosting a show—"

"Wait, what? Me on TV?"

"—We'll round up a bunch of sexy birds—"

"*Chicks*, Piers. In America we call them *chicks*."

"Chicks?"

"That's right."

"Chicks are baby birds. That sounds like pedophilia."

"You would know." I shrugged. "That's what we call them."

"Put all the birds—I mean, *chicks*—in the studio penthouse—"

"You mean *my* penthouse?"

But Piers was already rolling, and he wouldn't stop.

"We do it all in two weeks. Like, five, maybe six rounds

of elimination, and a final bracket—"

"Like basketball?"

"Basketball? What? No. I don't know. Who watches basketball? No, like every other fucking reality TV show there is. Pay attention, Clint."

"Okay, okay."

"Cash prizes along the way, and by the end of the two weeks, you have three finalists. Pick the hottest one, get her in the studio and work your magic, bam! You've got yourself a star!"

I nodded. It made sense. It sounded good. Granted, I was high and drunk and hopped up on two lines of coke, but I didn't know what could go wrong.

"I've been trying to think of an interim series before the next *Bachelor* starts up. This is perfect. Bloody perfect."

"When do we start?"

"Now."

"Now?"

"Tomorrow. Ask Jake to open up one of his clubs for three hours of auditions, and spread the word. A hundred dollars to audition."

"Tomorrow? Isn't that too soon?"

"Are you kidding? Everybody in this goddamn town thinks they're a star. And everybody and their mom wants to be on TV. They'll be busting down the doors to audition once they hear the final prize is a record contract."

"A record contract?"

"Yes. With the infamous Clint Terrance! Who could resist?"

A smile crept up on my face before I even agreed. He was right. It was a perfect idea. Soon I'd show my pops that I could run the studio. *And* I'd have a half dozen girls to choose from. I couldn't wait to get started.

CHAPTER SIX
Rachel

"Now?"

My pounding heart skipped another beat.

"Of course," Derrick said. "Rose will stay here and I'll drive you up. Lacey told me I could drop you off at her apartment whenever."

"I'm staying with her?" I frowned. "Why not with you?"

"This week is crazy at work," Derrick said, shrugging again and tossing back his perfectly tousled chestnut-brown hair. He took my hands in his and held them lightly. "I could barely get away tonight. And I thought you would have more fun with your friends. I normally fall asleep by ten."

"Ten PM? Really?" I didn't remember his schedule being that bad when he was first starting out.

"...*and* I wake up at four to start studying. But I'm sure I can make some time to hang out later in the week."

Oh, right. The tests. There was always another test, and whenever one popped up, Derrick would pop away. He'd seal himself up in a room and study for hours on end, not wanting any distractions.

I felt guilty for not remembering this test. He'd mentioned it a couple times, now that I thought about it.

"This is an important one, right?" I asked.

"Hmm? Oh, the test. Yes. This could be the last step before they promote me to junior actuary."

"Derrick, that's great!"

He beamed, and I beamed back, happy that he was making headway in his career. I worked hard on the farm, but nowhere near as hard as Derrick did at the actuarial firm. I couldn't understand half of what he did.

"Okay, then," I said, trying not to sound as nervous as I felt. "Give me two minutes to get a list of chores together for Rose, and—"

"Rachel!"

Rose popped into view in the door frame as we walked up. She pushed the screen door open and came forward to hug me.

Rose and I were twins, but nobody even pegged us as sisters. Rose had darker hair and my mom's slim figure. People always asked her if she was a model. But me? There was no mistaking me for anything but a farmer's daughter. I didn't even bother to try and compete on Rose's turf; when she tried to put makeup on me, I protested. If I didn't try, I couldn't fail, right?

"Hey, Rose," I said, plastering a bright smile on my face. "How's college?"

"Great!" she said. There was a strange look in her eyes. I wanted to ask her what it was, but not in front of Derrick. "So are you ready to take over New York City?"

"I don't know. Are you ready to take over Ritter Farm?"

"Oh, you're so silly! Come on," she said, tugging my arm. "Let's pack!"

"Hurry up," Derrick said. "I need to get back as soon as we can."

"I'll be ready to go in two minutes," I told Derrick.

Two minutes turned into an hour as I ran around the farm getting things ready. I kept thinking of things that Rose needed to know, and by the time I was ready to go I had six sheets of checklists for her. I worried that my dad would have a hard time without me, but he assured me that he could manage for a week or two without me, especially with help from my sister.

Still, I worried and worried, even as I hugged my mom and dad and Rose goodbye. I worried all the way down the driveway to Derrick's car. He'd bought a Lexus last year, and it was probably the prettiest car I'd ever seen. But my anxiety ran so high that I found myself furrowing my brow as we put my suitcase in the trunk, trying to remember if there was anything I'd forgotten.

"Hey."

I looked up to see Derrick watching me. I erased the frown from my face, but I couldn't get rid of my worry. It had been years since I'd left my mom for more than a day or two. I hoped they would be okay without me. I hoped I would be okay without them.

"Hey. This is going to be fun."

I nodded, and he kissed me lightly on the lips. I ached for more, to have him take me in his arms and kiss me, really *kiss* me! But he was already opening the car door for me. It wouldn't have been proper anyway, to kiss like that when my parents were watching.

I slid into the black leather seat and buckled up, and Derrick closed the door firmly behind me. The car was pristine. Its interior was black and slick and every inch of surface looked like it had just been polished.

"This is going to be fun," I echoed, but the words melted away as I looked out the window back at the small house and my parents.

The roof shingles of the house were glued on with black patches of tar. The deck was bleached from the sunlight, and even the old chestnut in the front yard seemed to droop under the pendulous weight of old age. I missed it already. My mom used to say that every child was born into Eden, and I never knew what she meant until now. This was my *home*, this was my paradise, and it terrified me to leave it, to leave them.

My mom was in the front yard, waving her handkerchief and crying. Rose stood right next to her, and as I watched, she put her arm around our mother's waist. Tears pricked the backs of my eyes. My mom turned to my dad and I could see her eyes frowning, questioning, already faded again to that dim brown-gray of the hoarfrost in late fall.

Who's going away?

Winter was close, and all the pastures were fading, fading away.

I blinked, and the tears were there, dripping down onto my cheeks. Maybe that's why it was so hard for me to leave the farm. That was my fear. I didn't want her to forget me.

And I worried that she already had.

My fingertips brushed my cheeks dry before Derrick slid into the driver's seat. I made a long show of looking for, and not finding, something in my purse. When I sat back up, my eyes were clear as the sky. I looked forward, through the windshield, as we drove out of the farm, onto the highway, through the country until the chestnuts and sedge were lost far behind us.

I'd managed to sneak out and get the red dress from the barn, packing it into my suitcase without Rose seeing it. I didn't know why I wanted to take it with me so badly, but when we passed over the last hill and saw New York, I was glad that I'd packed it.

The city rose out of the water, and from far away you couldn't see the crumbling bricks and mortar, just soaring lines of steel and glass sparkling with light. It was more beautiful than any other city, and a spark of hope began to kindle in my chest as we raced over the highway toward the New York skyline.

I'd been on the farm for so long that I had started to think I couldn't live anywhere else. I belonged on a dairy farm. But with a red dress in my suitcase, the idea pricked over and over in my mind, until it became a hope that I couldn't ignore.

Maybe... maybe I could belong there.

By the time we arrived in the city, I was as nervous as a cow going through the milking chute for the first time. Derrick dumped me off unceremoniously on the sidewalk in front of Lacey's apartment, promising that he would come and see me tomorrow. One quick kiss, and he was gone.

I stood on the corner, struck by how crowded New York was. Nobody seemed to ever run into anyone else, but the whole street was full of a hundred near-collisions. Dogs yanked at their leashes, bikes whizzed by through narrow lanes, and cabs honked at stopped traffic. The air was filled with the good smells of cooking food and the bad smells of overflowing trash cans. And it was so *noisy*.

I stood for a moment on the street, listening to all the different voices. The rapid-fire tangles of Spanish, the beautiful slurred Slavic languages, and a dozen varied dialects of English that were equally exotic as any foreign tongue. Even so late at night, the streets were humming with noise that sounded like music in my ears.

I wondered if the kids who grew up here thought it was paradise. I wondered if I could ever manage to think of it as home. Rose had moved here. Was all of this as familiar to her as the cows and chestnuts? I couldn't believe it.

"Rachel!"

I turned around to see who had called me, and almost ran into a jogger. He didn't even blink as he skipped around me on the sidewalk.

"Up here!"

I looked up and saw Lacey leaning out the window.

"Hi, Lacey!" I called, waving with my free hand.

"You're so late!" she yelled down. "We have to leave now! Get up here!"

"Leave for what?"

"The open mic contest! Get your ass in gear!"

"Contest? Derrick didn't say anything about a contest—"

But she had already snapped the window shut.

After that, it was a mad scramble to throw on my red dress, which was tighter than I remembered it being in the dressing room. Lacey did her best to put makeup on me, all the while reminding me that she was a tomboy and never did "that makeup stuff."

"If Rose were here, she could handle it," I said, strapping my feet into heels while Lacey brushed out my hair. "How is she doing, anyway?"

"I don't know," Lacey said, her eyebrows furrowing into a knot on her head as she smeared lipstick across my bottom lip. "I tried to hang out with her a few times, but she's always busy."

"Hmm. Probably busy doing college stuff." I had no idea what "college stuff" entailed, but Rose was studying science, so I imagined it was pretty hard work.

"Alright, you're as good as you're going to get." Lacey checked the time. "Dang! We have to get out of here. We have fifteen minutes."

We rushed out the door and jumped into a cab. I looked in the rearview mirror to check out my makeup.

"I look like a hooker!" I cried. The cabbie eyed me in the mirror and nodded in mute agreement. Dark eyeshadow made my eyes pop out of my head and my hair was a brushed-out mess. I tugged my hair back and started to braid it down.

"What are you doing? Stop that!" She swatted my hands off and fluffed the mess of hair back out with her fingers. "Your hair is fine. You look like Julia Roberts."

"Like, 80s-style Julia Roberts in *Steel Magnolias,* maybe. And this lipstick is like a fire engine!"

"It matches your dress. Anyway, it's a singing competition, not a beauty competition."

The cabbie watched me, and I could swear he was suppressing a laugh. Whatever. I didn't look any weirder than any other New Yorker, I bet.

"What kind of contest is this, anyway? Derrick didn't tell me anything."

Lacey shrugged. "No idea. Jake just told me that his friend was looking for singers, and I thought of you. I guess you'll have to sing something, but I don't know any details."

"So this was just an excuse to get me to come visit."

"Are you mad? I thought it would do you good to dress up and get out. Plus, I need you to meet Jake."

I ignored her, peering into the rearview mirror to check out my eyelids.

"No wonder you do graffiti. All these bright colors—"

"Ahem! It's called street art. And I think the colors look good on you." She eyed me critically. "Although maybe I did overdo the gold eye liner."

"Lacey, I love you, but I'll never let you do my makeup again."

"Cosigned. We can get Steph to do it for the party tomorrow."

"Party? What party?"

"My boyfriend is throwing this dinner party thing."

"That's the other thing! Since when did you get a boyfriend?" I felt like I had been thrown into a tornado of activity. Was this how New York was? It was thrilling and scary all at once, and I felt a rush of adrenaline as we drove down the crowded streets into downtown.

Lacey chattered on and on about her new boyfriend Jake. He was a rich guy, apparently, so rich that he was the owner of the club we were going to. And she couldn't stop talking about his eyes.

I couldn't imagine feeling so crazy about a guy. I mean, I loved Derrick, but I wasn't going to gush about the way his irises glowed in the dark and his eyebrow arched *just like that*.

"You want me to tell him that we're on our way? He's helping judge the singing competition."

"What? I don't want your new boyfriend to *judge* me! And here I am dressed like *this*!" I started to freak out. I didn't want to meet Lacey's new boyfriend dressed in this sexy red dress and so much makeup. "Please don't tell him. It wouldn't be fair to the other singers, anyway. *Please*!"

45

"Okay, okay. I won't tell him it's you. Wow, you're a ball of nerves tonight, aren't you? Oh, here it is!"

The cab jerked to a stop and we scrambled out. There was a line out the front door, and another sign pointing to a side entrance that said *CONTESTANTS*. I stopped in front of the sign, my chest seizing up in terror. This was it. I was here, and I was going to sing. Now that it was all happening, I was shaking in my heels.

"Oh my Lord."

"Don't worry. You'll be fine. I'll see you inside, okay?"

"Okay. Okay." I took a deep breath. *Fine*. I would be fine. "I can do this."

"Of course you can. Now hurry!" She gave me a hug and slapped me on the butt to get me moving.

"I'm not a horse, Lacey!"

"Go on! Git!" She smacked me again.

"Ahh!"

I strode quickly around the sign and into the doorway. As I walked, I muttered to myself.

"I can do this. I can do this."

I picked up the pace as I came into a hallway. I could see the stage inside past a crowd of dancers, and a woman sitting at a table by the stage with a sign that said "Contest Entry."

"I can do this. I can do this."

As I walked faster, the music growing louder, she stood up and yanked down the sign.

No! I wasn't going to be late. I began to jog in my heels, raising my hand so that she would see me coming. It was hard to run fast on the concrete floor in these shoes, but I wasn't going to lose my one chance.

"Wait!" I started to cry, but as I ran out of the hallway into the club, a man stepped out into my path. A huge man. He took up the whole entrance of the hallway. I couldn't veer around him if I tried.

Unable to stop myself, I skidded on the slick floor. With a shriek, I slammed right into his chest.

It was like running into a cow. His barrel chest knocked the wind out of me, and I fell backwards, losing my balance. He grabbed me by the waist, keeping me from falling.

I gasped for air and looked up into a frowning face.

My first thought, though, was simply: *Wow*.

He must have been a bouncer. A male model-turned-bouncer. He had a black leather jacket over huge arms, the top edges of a tattoo peeking out from the top of a white shirt that was so thin it was nearly transparent. As he looked down at me, his dark hair fell into his face, framing eyes as black as coal. He was so huge that I couldn't help but be intimidated.

I tried to find my breath but couldn't, even though my lungs were drawing in gulps of air. It was like the whole room was a vacuum sucking the oxygen away from me. His fingers pressed into my hips, and I realized just how close we were to each other.

My hands came up to his chest, pushing back, but it was like pushing against brick. I twisted to get out of his grip, but his hands were vises locked on my hips. Instead of letting me back away, he pulled me closer to him.

I could smell the sharp scent of his cologne, the salt of his sweat mixed with leather. His expression softened a little, his eyes moving down my body. I could *feel* his eyes on me, like fingertips moving inappropriately over my curves, my cleavage.

I shouldn't have worn this dress. I shouldn't have let Lacey put any makeup on me. I shouldn't be here.

Only a moment had passed, enough time for him to step away from me and let me balance myself. But he didn't. Even though we were only twenty feet away from the crowd of the club, I had the distinctly strange feeling that we were completely alone, that he would keep me here for as long as he wanted.

And, even stranger, I *liked* it.

I should have screamed, pulled away, but I didn't. His

eyes transfixed me, like twin dark pools hypnotizing me into stillness. His arms were hard around me, and although every rational thought in my mind was yelling at me to escape while I still could, some deeper instinct in me spoke in a quiet voice, almost imperceptibly, under the panic: *You're safe with him.*

He leaned down and pressed his lips close to my ear. His body towered over mine, and before I could even think to wrench myself away, I felt his breath against my skin. I shivered as he whispered to me, his hands releasing me, sliding further down my hips.

"Hey, sugar," he said, his voice rumbling thick and low through my body. "Where do you think you're going?"

CHAPTER SEVEN
Clint

I leaned back on the couch, sinking into the black leather. The girl on stage was shrieking out a Lady Gaga song to a mob of people who sang along for the choruses. I could barely hear her over the racket, but I knew one thing: she wasn't going to be a finalist. I sighed and took another sip of whiskey. I'd promised myself that I would stop at three drinks, but that was before I heard anyone audition.

"I can't believe you talked me into doing this," Jake said. He looked around at the crowded club full of young people dancing. It was obviously not the usual crowd for this place.

Piers threw up his hands in defeat.

"We filtered through the girls in the line," he said. "At first, anyway."

"Your filter must have a hole in it. This is worse than the worst karaoke night ever."

"The crowd doesn't seem to mind," Piers noted.

"This isn't high class," Jake said, his voice rising. "My clubs are high class. This is Friday night in downtown Manhattan. And do you *know* how many people have ordered bottle service tonight? Nobody. *Nobody*!"

"I ordered a bottle of whiskey," I protested, pouring out fresh shots for everyone.

"We'll make it up to you," Piers said, picking up his shot.

Jake crossed his arms.

"Yeah? How?"

With a worried look, Piers downed the shot and, biting his lip, gestured over to me with his empty shot glass.

"Clint will make it up to you," he said.

"What! Me?"

"You're the one who needs a singer," Piers said.

"You're the one who thought it would be a good idea to start a reality TV show to find one!"

"Oh?" Jake put one hand on his chin. "And which one of you two idiots came up with the bright idea to use *my* club as a middle school talent show stage?"

Piers and I just looked at each other and both leaned forward for the whiskey bottle at the same time.

The girl ended with a high-pitched scream, sending a squeal of feedback through the system. Piers winced, and Jake just shook his head sadly. I leaned forward and put my head in my hands. There was no way this was going to work. We'd listened to dozens and dozens of singers, and while there had been a few who were decent, the process of sifting through the horrible ones was taking longer than I liked. Worse yet, none of them had jumped out to me as star material.

"Thank you, Jenny," the announcer woman was saying. "That was Jenny Ray singing *Dance All Night*. And now…"

I was beginning to think that my dad was insane for letting me try to find the studio's next star. I was beginning to think Jake was right, that Piers and I were complete idiots to do this. I was beginning to think that I should disguise myself with a wig and start another band myself. At least I could carry a tune.

Just then, the next girl strode onto the stage. She was wearing six-inch gold heels and a gold sequin minidress that dipped down in front, all the way down to her navel. She bent over and waved to the crowd, showing off her cleavage.

"Ladies and gentlemen," the announcer said. "Sophia Leone singing *Crazy*."

"Wow," Jake said. His eyes widened.

"I like her," Piers said.

"She hasn't even opened her mouth yet!"

50

"So?" Piers shrugged. "I like her."

"What do you like about her?"

"I like how… jiggly she is."

"Ah, Christ."

It was true. She *was* jiggly. As she started to sing, she bounced across the stage, letting her tits work the crowd.

Her voice was fine. Good, even. But there was no heart to it, no soul. Every single girl who had come up on stage was singing some bullshit pop song, and I was sick of it. But both Piers and Jake were transfixed.

As we watched, she came over to our side of the stage and began to twerk. I shook my head as the crowd went wild.

"I can't believe this."

"Isn't she amazing?" Piers said, his mouth slightly open. "Definitely finalist material."

"Really?"

"I'd buy her album. Can we do nude cover art?"

"Too risque for Walmart," I said absently. "You gotta have mainstream appeal."

"Damn. She's terrific. Bloody terrific."

"She's okay." I turned to Jake. "Where's that singer your girlfriend was talking about?"

Jake looked at his phone. "I don't know if they're coming. Haven't heard anything from them."

"Whatever. I'm going to take a piss. We're shutting down soon, right?"

"Yeah. After this one, we'll put the house music back on and shut it down," Piers said. "We already have… nine girls on the roster."

"Nine?"

"This one makes nine."

Nine contestants, and I didn't remember a single one of them.

I was disappointed. I wanted a star, and I was getting singers who would be great after a shit-ton of auto-tune. Maybe it was enough for Piers, but it wasn't enough for me.

I hoped that some of the girls we picked had just been nervous, or trying to impress in the wrong way. Maybe they would open up once we got into the studio. But I wasn't going to hold my breath.

I hopped over the back of the couch and left Jake and Piers to listen to Miss Goldtitty sing the fifth chorus. The last shot of whiskey hit me as I stood up, but instead of comforting me, the alcohol just heightened my frustration. Nobody was any damn good, and how was I supposed to wring a star out of this material?

I was walking fast, my attention more on the bathroom sign leading to the hallway, when a girl in a red dress ran straight into me.

She shrieked, and almost fell over, but I caught her by the waist. Immediately my hands sent the signal up to my brain. Luscious curves that begged to be caressed. My dick stiffened in a half-beat, even through the whiskey haze.

I would have let her go right away, though, if she hadn't looked up at me with those eyes. They were a deep mahogany, but around the inner rim of her iris was a ring of gold. Her eyelashes were long, red-gold and lined with something shiny that made them pop. Staring into her eyes was like looking into a vault of treasure, all rubies and gold.

Her hair was gorgeous, too—I wouldn't have noticed if I hadn't been up close, but there were red-gold highlights in her auburn waves. *Huge* auburn waves. It looked like she had done herself up for a costume convention. Not quite the redhead I normally lusted after.

I realized after a second why she looked so worried: she was trying to sneak in through the contestant entrance. I might have fucked Jake's club up for the night, but I wasn't going to let this slide.

Oh, who was I kidding? I just wanted an excuse to talk to her.

"Hey sugar, where do you think you're going?"

I leaned forward, making sure she could hear me, and

inhaled her scent as I pressed my lips close to her ear. She smelled different from any girl I'd ever been with. No perfume, nothing over the top. Just a sweet smell that reminded me of picnics in Central Park. It was so strange, so incongruent with her appearance. She looked like a party girl, but she smelled like sunshine.

I don't know what I expected. Any other woman would have melted in my arms. And for a moment, I thought she would, too. But instead, she pushed me away with both hands.

"Um, excuse me," she said. She stepped to try and go around me, but I blocked her way.

"You're not excused yet," I said, smiling as I stood in front of the hallway entrance. "Unless you want to dance with me."

Irritation flashed on her face. A challenge… *interesting.*

"I don't dance," she said flatly. She strained to look past me into the club. I glanced down at her hands: no ring on her finger. She must be looking for a friend.

"If you don't dance, I don't know why you're here," I said. "This is a dance club, you know."

"I have a song to sing," she said, stamping her foot down, "and *you* are in my way."

I almost laughed in her face. So she was another contestant. I eyed her up and down again, a slow smile spreading on my face. I hadn't figured her for a singer, but maybe she would be lucky number ten. I wanted to have a bit of fun with her first, though.

"If you didn't have such beautiful eyes, I'd throw you out of this club in a heartbeat."

Her eyes widened at that, but then settled back into a hard gaze.

"Must be nice to be the gatekeeper."

"It is nice some nights. You run into the strangest people here. Or rather, they run into you."

She sighed, crossing her arms and biting her bottom lip impatiently. Christ, my dick almost jumped out of my pants at that. Such full, delicious lips. I wanted to nibble them, and then keep going, nibble her earlobe, nibble her nipples...

"I'm sorry I ran into you," she said, her words coming out clipped and fast. "It was an accident."

"Oh, I don't think it was an accident. I think you did it on purpose."

That got her attention.

"*What?!*"

"I think you wanted to get me all riled up. You wanted to get my dick hard."

Her eyes went as big as a couple of LPs, and she began to sputter. God, it was adorable. It was like she didn't know how hot she was. That kind of fake innocence was something most girls didn't know how to master, but she was pulling it off perfectly.

"I didn't... I never..."

"Well congratulations," I said, grinning into her beautiful wide eyes. "It worked."

CHAPTER EIGHT
Rachel

I was standing only twenty feet away from my goal, and I'd managed to run afoul of the one bouncer who—*God only knows why*—wanted to flirt with me. He stared down, his tattoos peeking out from the top of his black leather jacket. I swear he flexed his pecs to make them jump at my face. My adrenaline was thumping through my system, but even if I would ever have fallen for someone with eyes like that—*so dark, so desirous*—and a body out of a daydream—*jeez, were those muscles in his NECK?*—even if *was* attracted to him, which I *wasn't*, I was taken. I had a fiance. And I wasn't here to flirt.

One thing was clear, though: I wasn't going anywhere unless I could convince him to let me through.

"Look," I said, trying to be reasonable. "I'm already late—"

"You are late," he said. His voice sounded familiar, and I didn't know why. It was like honey running over gravel, smooth and low and *Lord, what was wrong with me right now?* "Maybe too late. Plus you haven't paid the price of admission yet."

"And that is?"

"A kiss."

I gaped up at him. His dark eyes twinkled, and I felt a thrilling shudder go through my body at the thought of stepping up on tiptoe to reach his lips with mine. Revulsion and desire warred in my body, but my rational side thankfully intervened. I shook the image away.

"Sorry, but that's not going to happen."

"You don't want to kiss me?"

"I'm not here to kiss! I'm here to *sing*!"

I could see the girl on stage finishing her song. Oh, I hoped there was still time left for me to perform.

"Come on. Just one kiss. I promise you'll enjoy it."

Holy cow! This guy's ego was off the charts. It threw me for a serious loop. Especially when he smiled, and my eyes were impossibly drawn to his lips. Stubble darkened his cheeks, making his smile pop. It made me think about what his kiss would actually be like and—no! What the hell was I even thinking? I shook the image from my head.

"I—I don't— How can you even promise that?" I sputtered.

He only grinned wider.

"Every girl I kiss enjoys it. I'm the best kisser in the city."

"Uh huh."

"It's true. I'm the best at a lot of things."

He winked, and a rush of anger swept through me. It wasn't fair that he was abusing his power like this. Even if it cost me the chance to perform, I couldn't stay quiet. I stepped forward with a burst of confidence.

"Do you harass every girl who comes into this club? *Huh?* Do you try to kiss all of them?"

"Only you."

"Yeah. Right."

"Nobody else is gorgeous enough to kiss. And you have eyes like sweet burled maple, *even* when you're rolling them at me like you are right now." He brushed a strand of my hair behind my ear, and for some reason a shiver went down my spine. "You look like an angel."

That stopped me cold. I had dealt with ranch hands and farmers, and I could hold my own with bantering in the fields. But I'd never had a guy throw such compliments at me before, not even Derrick. It was something I was completely unfamiliar with, and I didn't know how to ward it off.

"I...No... I..."

He reached out and lifted my chin, and I froze. His

fingers were warm and strong, and every part of my brain was screaming *RUN*, but my body wouldn't listen. The stage was behind him and *oh, Lord,* why was he touching my cheek with his fingertips like that?

"Please—stop…"

I had to struggle to get the words out, and he ignored them anyway. He turned sideways, leaning back against the wall, his arm barring the hall. I could maybe squeeze by him now if I went under his massive arm, but he wouldn't let me get through. I knew he wouldn't.

"Do you not know how gorgeous you are?"

"G—gorgeous?"

"Tell me you're teasing. Let me kiss you once, and I'll let you in."

I swallowed hard, trying to get my bearings. The girl on stage was done with her song, and the whole club erupted in cheers and shouts. I knew I could sing just as well as she could; maybe better, and they had loved her. I *needed* to get on that stage.

Over the speakers, the announcer was thanking everyone for coming out tonight to audition. I was losing my chance right before my eyes, all because of this guy.

Think fast, Rachel.

"Uh—Just one kiss?" I said, tilting my head and tossing my hair back in what I hoped was a flirtatious gesture. I had never been the flirtatious type, not that Derrick minded.

The bouncer grinned. He thought he had me.

"Just one," he said. "But you'll beg for more before I'm done with you."

God, this guy was arrogant.

"Well…" I said, drawing out the word as I turned. Then, my jaw dropped. "Oh my God!"

I plastered on a shocked expression, looking past him over his left shoulder. He turned to see what had happened, and his body swiveled away from the hallway entrance. Quickly, I ducked into the opening under his arm and burst through the hallway into the club. Before he could turn back to me, I had raced into the crowd of dancers, pushing my way through to the stage.

The announcer was sitting by a raised table in front of the stage. I burst through the crowd of dancers just as she was taking down the sign that said "Contest Entry."

"Wait!" I said. "I want to enter the contest!"

She looked down at me with lidded eyes. I didn't dare look back around; I knew the bouncer was looking for me.

"Sorry," she said. "I just got the call to close up."

"Please!" I said breathlessly. "Just one song. I drove all the way here from New Jersey, and—"

A hand closed down on my shoulder, but I didn't turn around.

"Please," I begged. But she was looking past me, towards the bouncer. I cringed. He had me. I knew it. But I couldn't give up so easily.

The bouncer let his hand unclamp from my shoulder and drift down my back. I shifted in my heels, biting my lip as his hand came to rest on my lower back. If I wasn't trying to get on stage, I'd turn around and smack his hand away. But I knew that was the quickest way to get thrown out of the club before I'd even had a chance to sing. And his hand…

Possessive. That's what it felt like. Like his hand was claiming me, taking charge. I'd never met anyone who commanded such power with a simple touch. For a horrible second, I imagined what it would be like to turn around, have him take me in his arms so possessively and kiss me, really kiss me like I was his.

I tore the thought away as quickly as it came. I was *not* that kind of girl. New York was bad for me, if it made me think those kinds of thoughts.

I gritted my teeth and turned to face the bouncer. He didn't look angry, weirdly enough. He looked… he looked *amused.*

"Mr. Terrance?" the woman asked. "Do we have time

for one more?"

Oh, God. My fate was in this guy's hands, and he was grinning down at me like he owned me. Why had I even bothered to run past him? I should have known it would end like this. I glanced around, trying to find Lacey in the crowd, but she was nowhere to be seen. I closed my eyes and took a deep breath, ready for him to throw out on my ass like I deserved.

But he didn't.

"I think we have time for one more," he said, giving me a sly smile. "Are you ready to sing?"

His voice was a flirt, and his dark features danced with delight as he teased me. I swallowed the lump in my throat.

"I'm always ready to sing," I said.

CHAPTER NINE
Clint

"Alright," I said. "Let her sing."

"Thank you," the girl said, relief washing the terror off of her face. She turned away from me toward the announcer, refusing to make eye contact. I let my hand drift down her back even lower, but she swatted my hand away from her ass without even looking behind her.

Who the hell was this girl? I wasn't expecting her to fall to my feet in gratitude, but she had managed to sneak past me after completely shutting down my advances. And now she was acting like she didn't even know who I was!

Maybe she didn't. The thought made me grin. She would definitely be a challenge. And if there was one thing I liked, it was a challenge.

"I just need you to fill out this disclaimer and pay the audition fee," the announcer was saying to her.

"Fee?"

The girl's confident demeanor slipped, and again she bit her lip. My erection hadn't gone away, and the sight of her biting that sweet soft lip made my cock throb even harder. Forget the audition. I wanted to drag this girl into one of the back rooms of Jake's club and fuck her silly. Just imagining her bent over a couch, her full round ass up in the air—

"It's a hundred dollars."

"What!"

The girl breathed out, her nostrils flaring. Her face was turning red, but I was too preoccupied with the red dress stretching tight over her sweet hips to care. I licked my lips. Yeah, Jake would have a couch somewhere in the back. I bet he even had private rooms...

"I didn't… I mean, I didn't know there was a fee to audition."

The announcer leaned forward and plucked the pen away from the girl.

"No, please! I can pay it after. I just don't have the money on me now. Look—"

"Sir?"

I refocused my attention, trying to ignore the hard throb in my groin as she turned, brushing against my front with her hip. Both women were looking at me expectantly. The announcer looked irritated as hell, and the girl looked like she was going to cry.

"What's the matter?" I asked.

"You know exactly what the matter is!"

"Can't pay the price of admission?" I grinned, enjoying her twist. But instead of pushing back with a feisty jab, like I expected, her face crumpled. It was like all the fight just went out of her at once. Her shoulders slumped, and she took a step past me.

I grabbed her by the elbow, stopping her. She put one hand up to cover her face, but I saw tears brimming in her eyes.

"Wait," I said, not knowing what I'd said that had set her off. She shook her head, looking away.

"I don't… I just don't…"

"Hey, look. Don't worry about it. Go on. You can sing."

She stared up at me, her tears receding.

"Are—are you sure?" she asked. She looked past me, at the announcer, as though for confirmation. I couldn't help but grin. She really *didn't* know who she was talking to.

"Let her sing, okay?" I said, waving her to the table. The announcer sighed and pushed the pen over the table again.

"Yes, sir."

"Thank you. Thank you," she whispered in a hushed tone.

"Impress me," I said, winking at her before turning away. I must be going soft. But there was something about this girl, a passion in her eyes and voice that I couldn't help but be intrigued by.

I'm here to sing!

Man, what a feisty one. I backed away from the table, heading toward the couch where Jake and Piers were laughing and drinking. I wondered whether I'd set us up for another round of awful karaoke. At the very least, I expected that she would be a lot more willing to flirt with me after she'd gotten to sing on stage.

I almost hoped that she was a terrible singer. Then I could take her home tonight, fuck her, and have it out of my system. Even if she was mediocre, that's probably what I would do, I resolved.

The house music cut off as the girl made her way onto the stage, and I heard a few dancers boo from the floor. I stopped at the end of the couch, still standing.

"Who's this girl?" Piers asked.

"I don't know," I said, leaning against the couch where they were sitting. "But she really wanted to sing."

"Oh, so she's your next fucktoy? Do you really have to put us through another three minutes of agony for that?" Jake asked with a laugh. But I didn't answer him.

I was looking at the girl on stage. I was hoping against hope that her audition would shine. I didn't know why, but of all the girls we'd seen, I thought she would be different. Special.

She was standing nervously in front of the microphone. Her shoulders squared and the speakers picked up her breath, fast and shallow. And then… something about her *changed*. Her face calmed, smoothed, and her hands rested softly at her side.

She began to sing. And man, it was different, alright.

Caritas habundat in omnia…

She was singing… opera? I glanced over at the couch. Piers gave a short laugh at first, like *What the hell are we*

63

listening to?

Her voice drew my attention back to the stage. It was deep and throaty, hitting the first note perfectly. One pitched operatic note melted into the next, a perfect waterfall of song reverberating through the club. There was no background music, and she didn't need any. Her voice was song enough. It rose in pointed arches of sound, turning the club into a cathedral.

The echoes of the chant drew more and more power as she went on, drawing syllables out into multiple notes in a fluid melismatic piece that was heaven to listen to.

All of the conversations around me fell silent, and even Jake and Piers shut up for a moment to listen. But they didn't know what they were listening to. I did.

And I couldn't believe what I was hearing.

This girl was a true contralto. The rarest of voices; only one percent of women fell into the range of singing, and even fewer could train their vocal cords to make the notes come out purely.

But she was singing these notes like she had written them, Latin and all.

I stared up at the girl on stage, not sure if this was someone playing a trick on me or not. My whole body tensed up, and I leaned forward, not wanting to miss a single word.

Piers yanked on my shirt.

"Hey."

"Shhh!" I said. God, I didn't want to listen to anything but her. She was glowing under the lights, and as I watched, she closed her eyes, lifting her head up.

"What the fuck is she singing?"

"Hildegard Von Bingen," I hissed.

"What?"

I looked down at Piers. Both he and Jake looked utterly confused. Then I looked around the club. Everyone had fallen silent, it seemed, because they didn't know how to react.

"This isn't dance music," Piers said. But I wasn't paying attention to him anymore. I walked down from the couch to the dance floor, where most of the dancers had cleared out or were standing around, unsure what to do.

The song ended. She looked down, her face shining with expectancy. The final notes trailed off into a silence as pure as it was damning.

Nobody clapped. I could see her blinking, trying to understand what had happened. Then a terrible realization, as she understood that nobody was applauding. Her face fell. I pushed my way through the dancers into the middle of the floor. I needed to catch her, to tell her that at least one person had appreciated her song.

She looked around the club in fright, as though trying to find someone who wasn't there, and her gaze locked onto mine. Tears filled her eyes, and before I could do anything, say anything, she spun and ran off stage.

The house music came up, blaring another mindless pop song. People started to talk and dance again. I shoved the dancers out of my way and vaulted onto the stage. I could hear Jake yelling at me as I chased her into the back of the club, where she had disappeared into the darkness.

CHAPTER TEN
Rachel

I finished my song to dead silence. I stared out numbly into the audience. They hated me. They hated my singing. I'd ruined the night.

My face burned; I could feel it going red, starting from my ears. It was what my mom called "lobster ears," and she always knew when I was telling a lie because I couldn't hide my shame.

Now I ran offstage, tripping every other step in my heels. Overhead, I could hear the woman speaking: "And that was our last open-mic contestant." The dance music roared up again, and I half-ran, half-stumbled off of the stage. There was an audio technician on the mixing board, and he didn't even meet my eyes as I came off the stage and into a back hallway.

I hoped that there was a back exit, because I didn't think I could go back through that club and out the front. Not with all those people watching me, hating me.

Tears spilled down my cheeks and I didn't bother wiping them away. There was an open door with a big red EXIT sign above it that opened out into the back alleyway.

I hurried, my steps going faster as I got closer to my escape. I couldn't wait to get home, to tear off this stupid dress, to wash off all my makeup. I was just a fake, anyway. A big fat fake.

Midnight was here, and I'd turned back into a pumpkin.

"Fake, fake, *fake*!" I muttered, hurtling towards the exit as fast as my heels could take me.

As I strode forward, only a few feet from the top step, another figure stepped into the doorframe.

"*Ah!*" I gasped.

I tried to stop, but all of the momentum in my body kept me flying forward. My heels slipped on the top step, and I went tumbling headlong into the last guy on earth I wanted to see again.

He caught me in his arms and set me back down gently on the step, not letting go. Then he stepped forward, one hand still on my waist, and I had no way out. As he stepped up onto the step, he towered over me. I backed up into the hallway of the club. His dark eyes twinkled as he looked down at me.

I felt his fingers on my waist through the dress, hard and insistent. I swallowed the lump in my throat. I'd failed. I'd failed miserably, and now he was going to lord it over me. I tensed up as his fingers slid over my hip.

"You're doing that on purpose," he said.

"What?"

"Running into me. You're doing it on purpose. Aren't you?"

"You wish!" Tears stung my eyes, and I wiped them away angrily so that he couldn't see. "Let me go, will you?"

"Where are you going?"

"I'm leaving."

"No, you're not."

I wasn't going out the back way, that was for sure. His huge frame blocked the doorway completely.

"I thought that bouncers were supposed to keep the unwanted riffraff out of the club, not lock them in."

"You're not riffraff. I'm not a bouncer. And you're certainly not unwanted."

His voice was dark and low. I shivered at the implication in his words, still suppressing my tears.

"Right," I said, summoning up all my powers of sarcasm. "All those people out there really wanted to hear a monastic chant from yours truly. Silent death glares are the new standing ovation, silly me."

He let me rant, that stupid arrogant perfect smile

spreading across his equally perfect face. At the end of my tirade, he leaned forward.

"You know what would make you feel better?" he asked.

"What?"

"A kiss."

I stared up at his face, frustration bubbling up inside of me. He didn't get it, did he? Tears burned at the back of my eyes, and I turned to go. Even going back through the club would be better than this.

"Hey." His hand turned me around. He was so strong. Fear mixed with something else as he pulled me back to him. I pressed my dress down; it had ridden up my thigh as I ran off the stage. I could feel his gaze burning into the tops of my thighs. "Hey, don't do that. You look great in a minidress."

"Ha. Right. I shouldn't have worn this stupid dress anyway." I was still torn between trying to push my way past him or retreating through the crowd of dancers who had hated my singing.

"It looks amazing on you. You look like Jessica Rabbit."

"Who's that?"

He chuckled, not answering me.

"Come on," he said, tugging me forward. "How about that kiss now that you've had your song?"

So that was why he'd let me make a fool out of myself? For a stupid kiss? Anger burst through my body. I shoved him away with both hands.

"No! I'm not going to kiss you!"

"Why not?"

"Why not?" I echoed dumbly.

"Yeah. Why not?" He grinned, like he was used to getting shoved away by girls. Probably he was. My anger grew.

"One," I said, holding up a finger. "I don't know you. At all."

"That's what makes it fun. You'll know me a lot better after you let me kiss you—"

"Two," I said, soldiering on, "I'm engaged."

"So you're *not* married. That's a good sign."

"Three…" I said, my mind searching for a third reason not to kiss this horrible, beautiful man, "Three…"

I couldn't think of anything. It was the last straw. I'd driven all the way out here from New Jersey for this contest, and I had done terrible. And now I couldn't even run away from my mistake. He had me stuck here.

I couldn't keep the tears back any more. They streamed down my face and I hiccupped back the sobs, pressing my hands to my face.

"Hey, wait. Don't cry. Why are you crying?"

His dark featured softened, confused. I couldn't believe it.

"Are you *serious*?" I cried out in between sobs.

"Of course I'm serious."

I waved with one tear-dampened hand toward the club.

"They—they all hated my song."

"Of course they did," he said, matter-of-factly.

"*Of course they did*?" I pressed back my sobs. He pulled a handkerchief from his leather jacket and handed it over to me. I only debated for a moment whether or not to take it, but I couldn't hold back all my tears with just my palms. I blew my nose noisily into the fabric and he rubbed me on the shoulder. I wanted to shove his hand away, but I could barely breathe, let alone defend myself against being comforted.

"Hey, don't listen to those idiots. They're philistines. But I liked your song."

"Y—you did?" I sniffed into the handkerchief.

"And I'm the only one who matters. Right?"

"Uh, well—um—" I frowned. His handkerchief was covered in gold eyeliner and black mascara. There was no way I could give this back to him.

"Do you know who I am?"

70

I wiped the last of the tears from my eyes and shook my head.

"The lady said your name was Mr. Terrance?"

"That's right."

He looked at me like I should have known who he was. I shook my head helplessly.

"Clint Terrance?"

The name rocketed through my head, and all of a sudden I realized who this man was. Oh my God. I was such an idiot.

"Clint *Terrance*? As in Terrance Records?"

"The one and only."

"You're the front man for *Talismen*," I said, my mouth agape.

"That's me. And I think you're perfect for this contest. I want you at the studio Monday."

He handed me a business card, and I took it dumbly.

"But—I—How did I not recognize you?"

"I must have blinded you with my charm."

He leaned forward and brushed away a rogue tear with his thumb. I swallowed. I could see his tattoos edging across his chest up past his collar.

"Here," he said. "Let me make it up to you."

He kissed me.

I don't know why, but my body reacted completely by instinct. His kindness had made me lower my guard, and for a brief moment I was too confused to pull away.

No, it wasn't just confusion. It was the shock of the sensations that came rushing through my body when he kissed me. His hand was on my back, and I could feel him kneading the muscles there, massaging me as he kissed me hard, his lips performing the same duty on my mouth.

I hadn't ever experienced a kiss like that before. When Derrick kissed me, it felt forced and slightly... disgusting? Maybe not that bad. But it wasn't a kiss, just wet lips pressed against wet lips.

But when Clint kissed me, it was what I imagined a kiss

to be—not the mechanics of lips and teeth and tongue. No, this was a caress that swelled my whole body. His body was pressed against mine, and I could feel him hard against me, his hands and lips taking control of my body, melting me from the inside out.

It was only an instant. One awful, wonderful instant. All of my senses were electrified, and time slowed down, but even as I knew that I had to pull away, my whole body strained to stay there, to stay in this embrace that possessed me completely.

Then I came to my senses and ripped myself away from the kiss. Clint stood there, grinning, as though he was waiting for me to ask him to kiss me again.

I slapped him across the face.

CHAPTER ELEVEN
Clint

"Whoa! Hey! What was that for?" I recoiled from the slap. The girl's expression had turned from passionate to fire-mad in an instant.

"For kissing me!"

"I've never had a girl slap me for giving her the best kiss of her life," I retorted. "Especially when she enjoyed it so much."

I reached to brush a stray hair from her cheek, but she dodged me and brushed it back herself.

"It wasn't—I didn't—"

She tried to protest, but her words tripped over themselves.

"You're so cute when you're flustered. Come on, one more kiss." I pulled her into my arms again and she twisted.

"No!"

"Feisty *and* cute. You know how to seduce a guy," I said.

"I'm not trying to seduce you!"

"You're not? That's a damn shame. So you're going to make me do all the hard work?"

"Wha—no!"

She turned away as I leaned down and my lips brushed her neck instead. A shiver went through her body even as she twisted in my arms.

"Stop!"

I paused.

"I can't tell if you're being serious," I said.

"Of course I'm serious!"

I tilted my head. Her face was flushed with desire, and I

had felt her heartbeat quicken with the kiss. It was obvious that she wanted me. Why was she playing so hard to get?

"Hmm," I said. "I still can't tell if you're serious. We should have a safe word."

"I am engaged!"

"That's not much of a sexy safe word. How about *rutabaga?*"

"No. What? No!"

"You don't like rutabagas?"

"No, I'm really engaged. To someone else."

"That's even more of a shame."

I held her at arm's length. Her hands were at my wrists, clutching them tightly. Small hands, they couldn't even wrap around my wrists. My eyes burned their way down her body, resting for a moment on her breasts, then her hips, then her legs. By the time I looked back up at her face, she was flushed red and hot all over.

"A damn shame."

"Only for you."

"And you too. You have no idea what you're missing."

Her red-gold irises went wide. I could tell what she was thinking—and if it had been any other girl, she would already be in my bed. But she seemed to have a thing about not cheating.

I guess that was good. Not good for me, but it made me even more intrigued. There weren't that many girls who would turn down Clint Terrance. This other guy must have been something.

She was licking her lip, and I stared as the small pink tip of her tongue wetted her lips. God, she had tasted delicious.

"What are you thinking?" I asked playfully.

"I'm thinking…"

"About me, I mean," I clarified, grinning. "I don't care what you're thinking about if it's not about me. And how much you want me."

Her face steeled. All of the desire I saw in her was

being carefully pushed away. I could see her distancing herself, even as I held her waist. Even as her body responded to my touch.

"I'm thinking that I don't want you. You would be very bad for me, Mr. Terrance."

"Don't call me that. Call me Clint."

"And," she continued, not bothering to respond to me, "I'm thinking that if you ever so much as *think* about kissing me again, I'll slap the silly out of you."

"Too late," I said. That brought another flush to her face. "And you can't slap all the silly out of me. That would take *way* too much force."

"Let me go. Seriously," she said.

I opened my hands instantly from around her waist. She stumbled back a couple of steps. I guessed she wasn't expecting me to let go. I smiled. What a challenge.

"Thank you," she said, smoothing out her dress.

"Of course," I said. "I'm not the kind of guy who wants a girl who doesn't want me." But what girl didn't want Clint Terrance?

"Thank you," she repeated, this time a bit more softly.

"See?" I said, arching one eyebrow and resting my elbow casually against the wall. "I'm not that bad for you."

She licked her lips again nervously, and my whole body tensed, aching to take her back into my arms.

"So does this mean…"

"Hmm?"

"Do you… I mean, did you still want me to come on Monday?"

"I always want you to come." I grinned at my joke. She kept setting them up, and I kept knocking them down. But she was completely oblivious to my double entendre. Her face was twisted with uncertainty.

"What does that mean?" she asked.

"I'm sorry. What are you talking about?"

"The singing competition."

"Oh, right." Damn. I'd forgotten all about that when

75

I'd gotten close enough to see her full lips up close and personal. A brief flash of guilt went through me. Was that why she'd let me kiss her?

Nah. I dismissed the thought instantly. This wasn't the kind of girl who would do that. Plus, she'd slapped me. And now she thought I was going to take back my offer.

She twisted my business card in her fingers.

"So? Am I still in the contest?" she asked.

"I don't know. Do you think you can stop throwing yourself into my arms all the time?"

She blushed furiously.

"I didn't—"

"Oh, I'm not complaining."

Before she could respond, I bent my head and kissed her again.

This time, I only had a whisper of a kiss. She yanked herself back immediately and slapped me again. I only grinned.

"What the hell!" she shouted. "I told you—"

"Totally worth it," I said. "Don't worry. I won't try it again."

"Wh—what…"

"See you Monday, beautiful!"

I smiled at her stunned expression and waved before heading back down the hall. I whistled as I walked. I'd found her. My star.

CHAPTER TWELVE
Rachel

"Eee! I'm so excited for you!" Steph squealed. Lacey was helping me get the remainder of my mascara off of my cheeks.

"Me too," I said. And I was. My stomach was twisting in knots, though. Not about the singing competition, but about Clint Terrance. The way he'd held me tightly in his strong hands made my senses awaken every time I thought about it. I felt completely guilty about the way I'd frozen. The way I'd let him kiss me, if only for a few seconds. I wasn't that kind of girl. I was a good girl. Wasn't I?

But both my body and mind were conspiring to betray me. I couldn't go more than a few minutes before my brain would spin out a reel of sexy daydreams involving the most arrogant jerk I'd ever met. I couldn't even stop myself from imagining Clint taking off my dress, or taking off his shirt, or kissing me again, or even worse. And my body would play right along, igniting all of my nerves.

Forget a cold shower. I needed an ice bath to calm down this awful, sudden desire.

"Did you get to meet Clint Terrance?" Steph asked, her chin cradled in her hands. My head snapped around, and Lacey clucked at me as the cotton ball she was holding went straight into my eye.

"Uh, yeah," I said.

"What was he like? Lacey said he was a big rock star."

I snorted.

"Well, honestly? He's a total jerk."

"Really?" Lacey asked.

"How is he a jerk?"

I wasn't sure how much to tell them, but I needed to

vent.

"For one thing, he flirted with me like crazy. Even after I told him I was engaged," I added quickly.

Lacey and Steph gave each other a glance.

"You *were* looking super sexy," Lacey said.

"What?! That is victim blaming!"

"I wish I was that kind of victim," Steph sighed.

"He tried to kiss me twice, even after I slapped him for trying the first time!"

"Sounds like you need a safe word."

"Yeah. *Rutabaga*," I muttered.

"What?"

"Nothing." I was done talking about Clint Terrance flirting with me. "Anyway, I told him in no uncertain terms that I was taken. So he can just go be an arrogant flirt to some other girls. I hope he stays far away from me."

Steph and Lacey eyed each other.

"What?"

"Nothing," Lacey said quickly. "What about the contest?"

"Oh, right," I said. "His assistant sent me an email with all of the information. It seems like a lot."

"A lot of what?"

"Time, for one. They said it could be for two weeks. I don't know if I can stay here for two whole weeks."

"Can't stand New York? Are you already longing for the dairy farm?" Lacey teased.

"I know how that is," Steph said reassuringly. "If I didn't have Andy around, I would miss my family too. Little brothers can be good for something, I guess."

"You can stay here as long as you want, you know," Lacey said.

"That's the other thing," I said. "They're going to put us up in an apartment near the studio for the whole contest, starting Monday."

"So it's like *The Real World: New York Music*?"

"Sure. Something like that." Apart from my mom's

soaps, I didn't know anything about TV. It was a luxury to sit down at the farm, let alone waste time watching reality shows.

My phone buzzed and I reached over to pick it up.

"Oh, it's Derrick!" My excitement turned to disappointment as I read his text.

Can't come to the party tonight. Have fun without me!

"Seriously?" Lacey asked, after I read it out loud. "Did you tell him how awesome it was going to be?"

"I told him," I said, trying to keep the disappointment out of my voice. I'd really been looking forward to spending some quality time with him.

"Too bad. *But*, I'm glad there will be another single lady with me at the party," Steph said, trying to cheer me up.

"Not single. Engaged." I flushed as my mind flashed back to Clint kissing me.

It hadn't been my fault. I'd told him no. And I'd slapped him, hadn't I? But I couldn't help shake the thought that I had done something wrong. I'd *liked* it.

"Hello? Rachel?"

I blinked. Lacey was staring at me.

"What?"

"I said, how's the wedding planning coming along?"

"Oh, that?"

"Yeah, that."

I swallowed and tried not to think about the way Clint's stubble had grazed my chin, about how his lips had felt so hot against mine. It was impossible to control my thoughts, but I clamped down on them hard and tried to bring up Derrick's face instead.

"We haven't chosen a date yet," I said.

"Haven't you been engaged for like, two years?"

"A little more than that," I said, pinching my lips together. "He wanted to get a firm position before we settle down, and he's still working on passing the test to get that promotion."

"Have you ever thought about anyone else?"

79

"Not really." I could feel my skin flush as the image of Clint Terrance popped into my mind. "I mean, no. He's perfect for me. Our families have known each other since we were kids, and he's always been a perfect gentleman."

"Perfect in every way, huh? Why'd he cancel tonight?"

"He had work. He's really busy," I apologized.

"I hope I can meet him sometime," Steph said.

"Me too," I said, staring down at my phone as though looking at the text could change the message somehow. "Me too."

Lacey's boyfriend had the most amazing apartment. There were chandeliers hanging off of the tall ceilings, the lights sparkling over shiny marble floors. And the artwork! I didn't know half as much about art as Lacey did, but I could tell that was one thing they had in common with each other. Every wall had a painting on it; every surface had a statue.

Steph plied me with bruchetta and wine, and soon we were giggling like a couple of fancy ladies in a royal palace. I couldn't believe that Lacey was dating a billionaire.

Things were going great. That is, until Clint Terrance walked through the door.

"Jake! Lucas!"

I froze next to Steph as I saw him walk in. He had a tight black shirt on that showed every single muscle in his chest and arms. I could see the top of his tattoo—just the top of it, a few lines of some design hidden below the collar. He had on black jeans and dark sunglasses, and he looked like a rock star should. That wasn't what made my breath catch in my throat.

No, it was the girls he had hanging off of his arms that did that.

Two redheads, tall and beautiful. Both of them were in slinky gowns, one green and one blue. They looked like accessories for him, and as he jumped down the steps toward Jake and Lucas, they trailed behind him.

"Did I miss anything?" he said, laughing. "Where's the orgy?"

He scanned the room, and when his eyes locked on mine, he stopped. His smile froze on his face as recognition dawned. My skin turned hot.

"You didn't say he would be here!" I hissed to Steph.

"Lacey really wanted you to come," she whispered back. "Don't worry. You'll be fine. I'll stick close by and punch him if he tries to kiss you again, okay?"

I nodded, fear clenching my chest. And something else—jealousy. It was utterly ridiculous. There was no way Clint Terrance was going to try to kiss me, not when he had brought two beautiful women along with him. They looked like supermodels who had just stepped off the catwalk.

Oh, no. Jake was bringing him over to introduce him to us.

"Everyone, this is Clint Terrance."

"*The* Clint Terrance?" Steph's brother asked, obviously impressed. Andy was gay, and I almost rolled my eyes. Clint didn't need to have another person gushing over him. He was arrogant enough.

"What Clint Terrance?" Steph asked, giving me a meaningful look as she pretended not to know who he was.

"The rock star—" Andy broke off as Clint shook his hand.

"That's right," Clint said. "I play guitar and sing for Talismen."

"You are the absolute *best*," Andy gushed, still holding onto Clint's hand.

"What band?" one of the other girls at the party asked. I'd already forgotten her name. One of Jake's friends, Lacey had said.

"*Talismen.*"

"I'm sorry. I've never heard of it," Steph said, tilting her head coyly.

"Then you'll have to let me tell you all about how amazing we are," Clint said.

I pinched my lips together and walked away to get a refill of something that wasn't wine. If I was going to make it through the night, I needed to be far away from Clint Terrance.

I watched Steph and Clint talking and laughing from my post over at the drink table. They seemed to be having fun, and the two redheads he'd brought hung back talking to each other. They didn't seem the least bit jealous.

Then why the hell did I feel that way?

I stayed away from Clint for the whole dinner. It was hard not to look at him, but I studiously avoided it. I looked at everything else—the asparagus garnish, the way the chandelier above the table twinkled, the cleavage of the two women on either side of Clint that seemed to become more and more exposed as the evening went on.

The one time I darted a glance at him, he was staring at me. I immediately blushed and covered my face with a napkin, pretending to wipe my lips. In the light, I could see his features much better than I had in the club. His eyes were still dark, dark as the night sky in the country, and twinkling with just as many stars. His eyebrows were two dark slashes on his brow, and when he laughed—oh, Lord, it was like music in the form of a man.

I tried to forget about how he'd kissed me, how he'd held my body against his, but it wasn't working. I clenched my jaw and focused on the food, pushing out the intrusive daydreams for the rest of the dinner.

Afterwards, though, I went to the bathroom. When I came out, he was leaning against the wall, as though he was waiting for me.

"Hey, Rachel," he said, smiling like we were old friends.

"Hi," I said nervously. My fingers smoothed down the folds of my dress.

"Why didn't you tell me you knew Jake?"

"I don't know Jake. I know Lacey," I said. I looked past him, but there was nobody else in the hallway. My heart thumped. I didn't know what I would do if he tried anything. I could scream. Yes, that's what I would do. I would scream.

"What is this dress?" he asked. He chuckled as he looked down on it, and irritation pricked my nerves. Good. I could be irritated. That was better than all of the other feelings that were currently trying to take me over.

"It's a dress," I said.

"I can see that. With flowers all over it."

"They're blackberry blossoms," I said flatly.

"I hope you have something else to wear on Monday." I bristled.

"My mother sewed this dress for me."

He held up his hands in mock surrender. His muscles flexed, and again I thought of how he'd put his hands on my waist, how his palms had held me—*no*. No thinking about that.

"I didn't mean anything by it," he said. "This is just... so totally different from how you were dressed on stage. I almost didn't recognize you."

"Sorry to disappoint. You seem to be dressed up exactly the same. Rock star chic, right?"

He tilted his head, his hair falling forward again. He hadn't shaved for the party, and the way he was looking at me made me feel like he was a predator, some wild thing that wanted to catch me. A brute.

"Would you prefer it if I dressed up in a suit and tie?" he asked. "Is that what you like?"

"It doesn't matter what I like."

"Of course it does."

"Why don't you ask your date what she likes?" I asked, pretending innocence. "I mean, I guess you have two dates, so you would have to ask both of them. To be fair."

I couldn't stop talking, even as Clint's face darkened. He didn't like being made fun of, I guess. But he was the one who had cornered me. I gestured in the air with one hand as I kept going.

"I hope they both agree on what you should wear. If not, maybe you could make them mudwrestle for it. Or—"

"I don't care what they think," Clint said, cutting me off. He encircled my wrist with his hand and brought it down from out of the air where I'd been gesturing. His touch on my skin sent an electric shock through my body, and my mouth went dry as his thumb pressed against the inside of my wrist. Could he tell my pulse was racing?

He leaned forward.

"I asked what you think."

His voice was as dark as his eyes, so low and throaty it sent shivers through my nerves. I wetted my lips. His fingers tensed around my wrist. I wanted to pull back, but my body wouldn't. It was frozen.

"I think you should wear whatever you want," I choked out. "Be—be yourself."

Clint's black eyes flashed down over my dress. No, not my dress. My body.

"What about you?" he asked.

"What about me?"

"Who are you, Rachel? Are you the girl next door? Or the lady in the red dress who came to sing for me."

I gulped. I didn't even begin to know how to answer that. Before I could even try to answer, though, one of the redheads poked her head around the hallway.

"It's time for dessert!" she called out. She didn't even look like she minded that Clint was talking to me, his hand around my wrist. His eyes, though, never left my face.

"We should head back to the party," I said.

"Sure," he said. "Whatever you want."

He let go of my wrist, his gaze still fixed on me. With a jerk, my body unfroze itself, and I walked past him, my breath held the whole time. As I walked down the hallways, I could still feel the force of his stare on my back and the shadow of his touch on the inside of my wrist.

CHAPTER THIRTEEN
Clint

Jake's party was fun, but I couldn't get over the fact that the girl in the flower print dairy dress was Rachel, the girl who had wowed me with her contralto vocals the night before. I kept looking over at her during the dinner, hoping to catch her eye. But she didn't look at me at all. And when I tried to talk to her alone, she seemed like she wanted to escape.

If it had been anyone else, I might have backed off. But there was something in her eyes that drew me irresistibly in. On the outside, she kept herself in control. Inside, though, I could tell there was a fierceness, a sensual passion that she couldn't quite hide. It made my blood run hot and desirous.

It was interesting to see her dressed down for the party. She didn't seem like she wanted to impress anyone at all. Her dress was plain and not form-fitting at all. I had to imagine the way her curves flowed under the fabric. Her hair hung down her back in a braid, the red-gold highlights like strands of gilt woven into her braid. I couldn't help but imagine tugging it back as I rode her, her luscious body under mine—

"Where are we going, Clint?"

My attention was brought abruptly back to reality by the girl on my left. The two redheads I brought were hanging off of my arms as we all walked out of Jake's apartment to the sidewalk.

"Yeah, Clint, where are we going?" Lucas asked with a grin.

"You'll see," I said. I snapped my finger, and a cab pulled up to the curb with a squeal. The redheads piled in, giggling and drunk.

"Downtown," I said to the cab, and tossed him a hundred dollar bill. Then I shut the car door and stepped back onto the curb. Before the girls knew what was happening, the cab had pulled away. I heard one of them shout, but the cabbie knew what I was about. He didn't stop, going around the corner with a screech of the tires.

"Did you just ditch those two girls?" Lucas said.

"Sorry. Did you want to go with them?"

He laughed.

"Nah. I'm good."

"Me too."

"So why'd you bring them? Keeping up that rock star image?"

"Yeah, I guess," I said. There was an itch under my skin, and I didn't know how to get rid of it. We started walking down the street, side by side. "You're a photographer, right? Why didn't you bring one of your models to the party?"

"Eh. Jake would have just stolen her away."

"He has that girlfriend now."

"Yeah. How weird is that?"

"Good, so I'm not crazy. I thought Jake was going to be a bachelor forever."

"Must be something about her."

"Yeah," I said. I hadn't ever known what that would be like—to find a girl and fall head over heels. It had never happened to me. But after meeting Rachel, I could almost imagine going crazy over a girl.

Almost.

We headed down the street, taking in the night sidewalk scene. I pulled out a joint and dug in my pockets for a lighter. Before I could find one, Lucas had a light out for me. We paused as I lit the joint. After a couple of puffs, I handed it over to him. We walked in silence for a block, letting the smoke drift up into the air between the skyscrapers.

"I like her friend, though," I said finally.

"Me too."

I turned my head sharply.

"Wait, who are you talking about?"

"Steph, of course," Lucas said.

I let out a breath that I didn't know I had been holding.

"The blonde one? She was kind of cute."

"You liked the other one? Rachel, right?"

"How'd you know?"

"You stared at her for basically the whole dinner, didn't you?"

"Was it that noticeable?" I laughed and took another hit off the joint. My brain was starting to smooth out, all of the thoughts in my brain calming down. "Don't tell anyone. My rock star image will be ruined."

"I met her before. Steph, I mean. She's a baker."

"Oh yeah?"

"I don't think she liked me coming to the party with another girl."

"Yeah? I don't think Rachel liked me coming to the party with two other girls."

That struck Lucas as impossibly funny. Maybe it was the weed, but he burst into uncontrollable giggles, leaning against a rosebush planter. Two older women passing by gave us a nasty look. I waved to them as they walked by us on the sidewalk.

"Good evening, ladies!" I said. Lucas burst out into another peal of giggles, and the women picked up their pace.

"Don't worry!" he shouted. "We're harmless!"

"You sound like a goddamn schoolgirl," I said, laughing as I passed him the joint. It was half finished. I felt good. My brain felt clear. I didn't even feel bad about the way Rachel had shut me down at the party.

"They're gonna call the cops on us," he said, hiccuping with laughter. "My reputation will be ruined."

"I think my pops would like it if I got thrown in jail

again," I said. "He thinks I'm getting soft."

"Aren't you?" Lucas wiped tears of laughter from his eyes.

"What's that supposed to mean?"

"You did send home those two redheads."

"So?"

"So, are you falling for that girl Rachel?"

"I've never fallen for a girl before," I said. The joint was almost done, and I tried not to burn my fingers as I took it back from Lucas.

"Me neither."

I looked over at him. He was trying to keep a serious expression on his face.

"This one, though," he said. "This one is different."

"How?"

"I don't know. She's the only girl who hasn't fallen all over herself to please me."

"That's so fucked up," I said, but it was the same with me. "Why do we want the kind of girl we can't have?"

"Be real, though. You can have any girl you want," Lucas said.

"So can you."

"Except for this one. Steph hates me."

"Yeah, well, Rachel's engaged."

"Fuckkkkkk." Lucas drew out the word for a solid five seconds before shaking his head. "We're really fucked, aren't we?"

"As my friend Piers would say, we're *proper fucked*."

"Cheers to that," Lucas said, looking completely uncheerful.

I took the last hit off the joint and ground it under my shoe on the sidewalk.

"Well, see you around," I said. I was itching to get back to the studio and write down the notes that had been humming around in my brain all night. "Try not to get caught up in that one girl."

"Yeah, you too," Lucas said.

We both knew we were lying, but I guess that was okay. It was impossible not to think about the one thing you couldn't have. And Rachel had made it clear: she was completely, one hundred percent off-limits.

CHAPTER FOURTEEN
Rachel

Monday rolled around, and I arrived bright and early at the address Clint had given me. . I was excited. I would be around a bunch of New York singers, in an awesome recording studio! So what if Clint Terrance thought I was a dowdy farm girl in the dress my mom had made? I was going to rock this.

I walked up to the studio, where a guy in a staff shirt looked up at me with heavy eyes from the chair he was sitting in. He looked hung over.

"I'm here for the singing contest... uh, thing."

"Everyone's up in the apartment," he said in a bored tone. "Where are your bags?"

"This—uh, this is my bag."

"Oh. Okay. Just take the elevator up to the twenty-second floor. The code is 3141." He thumbed the direction, turning back to his phone.

"Um. Okay." The twenty-second floor? A code?

"Did you need help with that bag?" he asked, obviously not wanting to help me.

"I'll be fine," I said, hefting it up over my shoulder. This wasn't as dramatic as I thought it was going to be. But that was before I opened the door. When I walked into the building, my jaw dropped.

The whole first floor was a music studio. Not just a music studio. That would be like calling a pair of Louboutins "just some high heels." This was the real deal. The whole floor was decorated in black and chrome. My kitten heels clicked on the black hardwood floors.

A few well-dressed men and women were lounging around with drinks in their hands, apparently not caring that it was nine o'clock in the morning. One man was smoking something that definitely wasn't a cigarette. Two women eased back onto a black leather couch at the side of the room, while a businessman stood in front of them, gesturing.

Then I saw the other side of the room.

"Oh, my God."

The room was huge, but it was split into two parts. I could see the recording side of the studio through a wall of plate glass. I walked over to it. Inside, cords ran from the most expensive amplifiers to the most expensive sound boards. I went over to the glass and peered through longingly.

"Hey!" A man walked over to me. He was older, with fierce dark eyes. He had an expensive jacket on and a gut that spilled over his too-tight suit pants. He was chewing on a toothpick. "What are you doing here?"

"I was—I was just looking. I'm here for the contest."

He looked me up and down. I felt completely self-conscious. I was wearing a simple blue dress with pockets in the front and blue kitten heels. It was a work dress, but I didn't have anything more elegant, except of course my red dress. And I was saving that for later.

"You're one of the contestants?" he asked in a disdainful voice.

"Yes," I said, trying hard not to be offended.

He laughed, a hard laugh, and switched the toothpick from one corner of his mouth to the other.

"I don't know what the fuck Clint is doing," he muttered.

"Excuse me?" I spoke up. If he was going to insult me, I wasn't just going to stand there and take it.

"Nothing," he said, waving me off with one hand. "Maybe it's a TV thing. They gotta have all types."

I flushed red as his eyes went down, examining my body again. Now, though, my adrenaline was up, and I wasn't going to let him walk all over me. That was the old

Rachel. In New York City, I had to be the new Rachel. The confident Rachel.

"I'm going to win this contest," I said boldly. "You'll see."

Now he really laughed, and he took his toothpick out of his mouth. Leaning forward, he stared into my eyes. They looked strangely familiar.

"We'll see about that, babe," he said.

"I'm a great singer," I insisted.

"Yeah? That and a dollar gets you a cuppa coffee," he said, obviously done with me. "Scoot along now."

Before I could reply, he had turned away to go back to the black couch where two younger women waited, sipping their drinks. I didn't know why his words shook me, but they did.

I shuffled into the elevator at the end of the studio. Instead of buttons for each floor, there was a number pad. I pushed the buttons for floor twenty-two. The elevator whooshed up with a metallic hum, speeding past all of the floors to reach the twenty-second level. There was no *ding*, and the elevator doors didn't open.

"Um. Hello?"

There was no response. I waited, but the doors still didn't open. I stepped back and looked down to see the number pad flashing "Enter Code."

Oh, right. The code. I thumbed in the number the staff guy had given me, and now the elevator doors opened up right into the apartment.

It was a gorgeous apartment. The kitchen was all black granite and stainless steel, and the huge living room had a glass fireplace against the back wall. There were two girls stretched out on the black leather couch. Both of them were texting furiously on their phones.

"Hi," I said, but it came out as a squeak. One of the girls looked up and eyed me in the same way the older man downstairs had eyed me. She was skinny and blonde and had perfectly straight, white teeth.

"Who are you?" she asked. The other girl didn't even look up from her phone.

"Uh, my name is Rachel," I said brightly.

"You're not here for the contest, are you?"

"The singing contest, yeah," I said.

She laughed, a short unkind laugh, flashing her perfect white smile, and went back to her phone. I bit my lip. Rose had told me that New Yorkers were rude sometimes, but this was beyond belief.

"Um, where should I put my stuff?"

She looked up, annoyed to be disturbed again.

"Down the hall. There's three rooms. Ten beds."

"Are they assigned, or—"

"Look, I don't know."

"Fine," I said, biting my tongue. I don't know what I had hoped for, but this wasn't it. I hauled my bag through the living room, not meeting the blonde girl's eyes as she watched me critically.

On the other side, a hallway stretched down fifty feet of black marble tile, with a red door at the end. I walked by an abstract chrome sculpture and peeked into the first door. It was all black and chrome, nothing on the white walls. Two girls lay on the beds on opposite sides of the room. One of them had headphones in, and her eyes were closed. The other one was reading Cosmo and snapping her gum. Neither one of them looked up at me.

Jeez. This was ridiculous. I took a deep breath and walked down the hall, checking each one. Every bed so far was taken, and I started counting the contestants. Six, seven, eight... How could I compete with all of these girls? A hollow feeling came through my chest as I realized just what I'd gotten myself into.

At the end of the hall, I ran into another blonde girl. I expected her to snap at me, but she only looked up innocently, fluttering her white-blonde eyelashes.

"Who are you?" she chirped.

"Uh, Rachel. Hi."

"Hi, I'm Taylor!" She sounded more excited than even I felt. I began to feel a little better about coming here.

"Nice to meet you, Taylor. Is—uh, is this the last room?" I pointed at the red door.

"Don't go in there!"

"What? Why?"

"See the door? It's an emergency exit only."

I looked more closely. Right at waist height was a small paper sign that said "Emergency Exit." It was taped over the door handle.

"That doesn't look too official," I said, raising one eyebrow.

"One of the girls opened it when she came in," the blonde girl whispered. "She said it was just a dark chute with a ladder. Like a trash chute."

"Huh."

"And there was a silent alarm, because some guy came in and yelled at her before she could even go in! Well, not that she was going to go in. It was dark. And who knows, if you slipped on the ladder you could fall twenty floors!"

"Wow," I said. "That doesn't seem like a very safe emergency exit."

My curiosity was piqued, but Taylor was already chattering away about something else.

"This is your room," she said, pointing in through the doorway. "There's two big rooms with four girls. The first room is me, I'm Taylor, and Jessica, and Vivian, and Jen. Then the other room is Second Jessica and Second Jen, only Second Jen said that she's First Jen—she's a bit snobby—and Teresa and... and..." She looked up, counting on her fingers. "And Annette! Right. Annette."

"What about this room?" I pointed to the only other doorway, next to the red door that was marked "Emergency Exit."

"That? That's the two-girl room. Sophia already claimed it. Then she said for nobody else to come in because she wanted a room to herself." Taylor shrugged.

"But there's no other beds, so I guess you have to go in."

I sighed.

"Great."

"Well, good luck!" Taylor said brightly. I wasn't sure if she was wishing me luck with the contest, or with my new roommate. It sounded like I needed luck with both.

I pushed open the door and peered in through the doorway.

There was an empty bed on one side of the room. Well, kind of empty. There was a pink suitcase spread out over it. The girl inside was sitting on the edge of the other bed, having a conversation with the air. Number nine, Sophia. I realized as I walked in that she had a phone earpiece in.

"No, it's fine," she said, staring at her fingernails. As I came in, she eyed me up and down. "Yeah, and I guess I have a roommate now."

I smiled tightly at her and she looked away.

"Okay. I'll talk to you later. Bye."

She plucked the earpiece out of her ear and picked up her phone from the bed.

"Hi," I said, after a brief pause. I held out my hand. She looked up from her phone and took my hand in hers gingerly, like she was going to catch a disease from me. Frumpiness syndrome, maybe. I stood there until she realized I wasn't going away anytime soon.

"So you're the last girl."

"Yeah," I said uncomfortably. "My name's Rachel."

"I knew I wasn't going to get my own room. Ugh."

"Um, what's your name?"

"I'm Sophia Leone." She ran the words together in a honeyed voice that I recognized. Then I remembered.

"You were the singer right before me," I said.

"Uh huh?"

"I didn't get to hear your whole song, but… but you sounded good," I finished lamely.

"Oh, wait." She frowned, pursing her lips as she looked at me again. She paused.

"Yeah?" I asked.

"Wait. Wait."

"*Waiting*," I said.

She snapped her fingers.

"You're the girl who sang that crazy chant thing! Oh. My. God. I can't *believe* you got in."

I breathed out through my teeth, my jaw clenching at the insult.

"We were all talking about you after you ran off stage. Did you fuck the host or something? Because holy shit, when you started singing! I was just like, I can't even."

She laughed, and I swallowed back the lump in my throat. The other girls were all talking about me? I felt tears stinging, and pushed them back. I wasn't going to cry, not in front of her.

"Thanks," I said blankly.

"Sorry, but it was just like, what the hell is this? You know?"

I didn't know. I guessed I would never know. I had thought that I would fit in with a group of singers, but apparently I was going to be the outcast here.

"So I guess this is my bed," I said, gesturing to the mattress that had her suitcase on it. "Could you... uh..."

"Oh. Yeah." She sighed, as though I was making a grand request. "One second. Is the attendant still out there?"

"Attendant?"

"The one who brought up my bags." She poked her head out into the hallway. "Hello! Attendant?"

I realized that she was going to wait for someone to help move her suitcase. With a shake of my head, I picked up her stuff and moved it over onto the couch between our beds.

"Oh, you don't have to do that!" she cried out, but she made no offer to help as I moved all of her bags over off of my bed. She plopped back down on the bed, texting on her phone as she talked.

"I can't believe they stuffed us in these little rooms. Who wants a roommate? Ugh."

Not me, I thought, but didn't say.

"I thought they were going to put us in a luxury apartment."

"This is pretty luxurious, isn't it?" I ventured.

"Ha! Maybe you would think so. What, did you come from a farm or something?"

I didn't say anything, my face growing hot.

"Oh my god. Did you seriously come from a *farm?*" She said it like it was a swear word. "Seriously?"

"Seriously."

"Ah! I can't *even!*"

She walked out of the room without a glance back, laughing to herself. The door slammed shut behind her.

"Yeah, I *can't even* either," I muttered.

I took out the few clothes that I had brought and put them in an empty drawer on my side of the room. Then I sat in the bedroom alone. At least I was here, I told myself. At least I had a shot. I had impressed Clint-freaking-Terrance. Even if it was just because he wanted to kiss me. And it wasn't just that. When he told me I was a good singer, I'd believed it. He wasn't just giving me compliments to get into my pants.

At least, I hoped that wasn't the case.

I pulled out my phone and dialed my parents. Weekends were always busy on the farm - usually that was when the trucks came to ship out the milk to the processing plant. The loading was backbreaking work, and I felt bad that I wasn't around to help. I expected Rose to pick up the phone, but it was my dad instead.

"Rachel! Sweetie, how are you?" He sounded a bit distracted. "How's New York treating you?"

"Great," I lied. "I sang on stage in this club, and I got into the contest."

"Oh, sweetie, that's wonderful."

"Yeah," I said, my mood picking up a bit as I heard his

familiar voice. "And we're staying in this awesome apartment in the same building as the recording studio. And I met the head of the studio, Clint Terrance. He's—"

"Hold on, one second." I heard a mumbling on the other end.

"Is that mom?" I asked. "Can I talk to her?"

"Sure. Charlene? Charlene? It's Rachel."

"Rachel?" I heard her say from far away. Then her voice came through clearly. "Hello?"

At the sound of her voice, homesickness flooded my body. I missed the farm. I missed being with her. Heck, I missed taking care of her. It was a lot of work, but at least I knew she was safe.

"Hi, mom. How are you doing?"

"Oh, there's no more blackberries. I thought I would make a pie today, but I couldn't find them."

I bit my lip. I tried to imagine her face in front of me, her gray hair flowing down her back. Her hands in her lap, knitting needles clacking away at a scarf that grew longer and longer and was never quite finished.

"When I get back, we'll make a pie together, okay, Mom?"

"Of course, sweetie. But I wanted to make a pie for Rose. She is such a smart little girl."

"Yeah?"

"She's showing me all of her college books. How wonderful is that?"

I swallowed the lump in my throat. She hadn't asked about my singing at all. I wondered if she remembered that was why I had left.

"I'll be back soon, Mom," I said. "As soon as my singing contest is done, okay?"

She didn't say anything.

"Mom?"

A pause. A whisper of something.

"Mom? Hello?"

"Hey, Rachel? You there?"

It was my dad.

"Is she alright?" I asked.

"Sure," he said, but I heard a waver in his voice. "Rose is doing as good job as she can, but we'll be glad to have you back. I—look, I have to go. You want to talk to Rose?"

"That's okay," I said, a bitter taste in my mouth. "I'll talk to her later. The competition is starting soon, I think. I have to get ready for that."

"Alright. Well, I love you, baby girl."

"I love you too. Can you tell Mom I love her?" I hadn't even gotten a chance to say it.

"Sure. Bye, sweetie."

"Bye."

The phone went dead in my hand. I stared down at it, and a tear dripped down my cheek. I wiped it away angrily.

How could I feel so sorry for myself? I was in New York, in a lavish apartment, with a chance to win a singing competition. I should be more than grateful for this opportunity. This was my dream come true.

Then why did I feel like I was falling headlong into a nightmare?

Before I could compose myself, the door burst open. A handsome man, tall with blue-green eyes, leaned into the room. He was wearing a dark gray suit and carrying a microphone in one hand.

"The last contestant! Up! Get up! Get your bum into the main room!" He spoke with a British accent, all manic energy. I followed him as he bounded out into the living room. Every single one of the other girls was already out there.

Did I miss something? How had they all known to come out of their rooms? Frustration pulsed through my body as all eyes turned to land on me.

To make things worse, there was a camera crew set up in the middle of the room. The camera swung around toward me, and my mouth dropped open. I was sure my eyes were red from crying, and I was wearing the plainest, most dowdy dress in the room.

"And here's our last contestant, coming into the group fashionably late!"

"It's the only thing that's fashionable about her," Sophia whispered, loud enough for me to hear. I flushed hot, my collar burning at my neck. I could feel the sweat beading on the back of my neck.

"Oh, I thought—sorry, I was on the phone—"

"Tell America your name," the British guy said.

"Rachel," I said, clearing my throat. "Rachel Ritter."

"Do you think you're going to win the recording contract, Rachel?"

Oh, God. Everybody was looking at me. A recording contract? Was that what we were competing for? I hadn't known that. I sputtered out a response into the microphone.

"I'm not—I'm not sure."

"You're not?"

"Well, I mean… I hope so!" I said, swallowing my nervousness and trying to sound optimistic. "It's a great opportunity."

"Who were you on the phone with?"

"My—uh, my parents," I blurted out.

"Your parents. How *cute*. Are you homesick?"

This man was even worse than Clint. He shoved the microphone in my face. The cameraman came closer, right behind the British host. Another man hovered close by with a big metal stick that had a black fuzzy thing on the end of it. It dangled just above the camera.

"A little, yes." I nodded, trying to regain my composure.

"Great! Let's hope that tonight's performance will cheer you up."

"We're performing tonight?"

The host raised one eyebrow and I wanted to smack myself in the face. What a stupid question. I'm sure everybody else knew what we were doing. I was the only one left out. I wanted to sink into the floor, sink all the way down all twenty-two stories, and skulk out of the studio.

"Of course! Your first competition. One of you lovely singers will win a cash prize of ten thousand dollars, and two of you will be sent home for good!" The cameraman spun around as the host gestured at the room. "Who will it be? Find out next—on *Sing and Win*!"

The host motioned at the camera crew, who lowered their equipment.

"Alright, great intros," the host said. "Break for five, and we'll get started again when Clint shows up. Late prick."

Now a murmur of excitement rose around the room.

"I know, I know, you all want to meet Clint Terrance." The host turned away from the living room and pulled out a flask from his suit jacket. He took a swig from it, ignoring the excited girls in the living room.

"What's your name?" I asked him politely. He frowned at me, like I was putting him on. I felt like a jerk for asking.

"Really? You've never watched my shows?" he asked.

I shook my head helplessly.

"*America's New Dance Star*?"

I shook my head again.

"*My Cheating Life? Secret Baby Bachelor?*"

"Sorry," I said. "I don't really watch TV."

He laughed, and then cut off suddenly.

"Wait, you're not joking?"

I shook my head yet again.

"Oh, dear Lord. You're perfect. Absolutely perfect."

With the British accent, I couldn't tell if he was being sarcastic or not. So I just smiled at him, hoping he wasn't teasing me.

"Want a sip?" he asked, offering me his flask. I raised my eyebrows, and he pulled the flask back. "Should have known. You'll need it by the end of the day, believe me."

He took another swig.

"Um, no thanks."

"I'm Piers Letucci," he said, and put his arm around me in a half-hug. I stood there awkwardly.

"I'm Rachel," I said.

"I know," he said, his breath alcoholic. "You just introduced yourself to America."

"Oh. Right." God, had I lost all of my brain cells today?

He let go of me and burped into his fist.

"Welcome to reality TV, Rachel," he said. "I need to take a wicked piss."

With that, he disappeared down the hall. I was left staring out into the living room, full of a bunch of girls whose names I didn't know, all of whom hated my guts. My heart sunk down to the bottom of my stomach.

I was lost, completely lost. This was what I'd longed for, what I'd dreamed about forever—a chance to be a real singer!

But now that I was here, I wanted nothing more than to go back home.

CHAPTER FIFTEEN
Clint

I was late, as usual. I tried to make it through the studio without anyone noticing me, but my dad was there already.

"Kid! Get over here!"

"Hey, Pops," I said, gritting through a smile.

"I met one of your contestants," he said.

"Oh, yeah?"

"What did you think of her, Kaylen?"

The young Asian woman in a silk sheath tilted her head, wrapping a strand of silky dark hair around one of her fingers.

"She was a bit… porky? And her dress, ugh. She looked like a hobo!" The girl tittered, her laugh grating over my nerves.

I knew without even asking that she was talking about Rachel. It made me even more irritated. I was sober and sleep-deprived, and I wasn't in the mood for any of this.

"Ha! A hobo!" My dad slapped his knee and put his arm around the girl. She leaned into his chest.

"And not even a Manhattan hobo," the girl continued. "Like, a North Bronx hobo."

"Nice. Thanks for the advance review of my singers," I said. "By the way, Pops, Sherry called about your date tonight."

My Pops glared at me. The Asian girl turned to him with an uncertain face.

"I told her you'd call her back as soon as you could," I said. "I'll text her now and let her know—"

"Get outta here, kid," my dad growled.

"Sure! See you later!" I said. I knew he would get back at me for doing that, but I didn't care. I was in a piss poor mood after being shut down completely by Rachel at Jake's dinner party. If I couldn't get the girl I wanted, I wasn't about to sit by while my pops paraded around another young bit of arm candy.

I stepped out of the elevator into my apartment's living room. Piers was nowhere to be seen, and I was immediately mobbed by the girls inside. The camera flashed red and the crewman swung his boom mike over our heads. Oh, Jesus. I hadn't even had a moment to prepare. I forced a fake grin.

"Hello, ladies!" I said, holding my hands out. They flocked around me in a cloud of odors: body lotion, shampoo, a half dozen perfumes. I held my breath and gave out hugs like autographs.

Then I saw Rachel at the other end of the room. She was wearing a simple blue dress and her hair was pulled back in a braid. She looked scared and alone.

A completely new feeling swept through me. I wanted more than anything to cross the room and take her in my arms, hold her, tell her it would be okay. I could see that she was overwhelmed by the whole thing. I normally wouldn't care about things like that. I don't know why this time was different. But I wanted…

I wanted to protect her.

"Clint, can I get an autograph?" one of the girls asked.

"I love your band!"

"You are the most talented guy *ever!*"

The girls were mobbing me, crowding closer. I felt a hand brush my ass.

It was a lot, sure, but I had been on stage for the past few years. I knew how to handle crowds, and I knew how to handle cameras. I spread my arms out to clear out a spot, stepping forward and twisting away from the groping. Normally I wouldn't have minded this attention. Normally. Why was I so completely out of tune with myself today?

"The one and only Clint Terrance!"

Piers was standing in the hallway. He came in and waved the girls back to their seats. I sighed, relieved. Then he leaned toward me, and I smelled whiskey on his breath. The relief washed away as quickly as it had come.

"Are you drunk?" I asked under my breath. "What is it, nine thirty?"

"I'm fine," he said, brushing off my concern. "I already recorded the intros."

"What do I do, then?"

"You do the first day exposition," he said. "Just explain how it's all going to work."

As we were talking, the girls were murmuring on the couches. Rachel was staring at me with a blank expression. Well, they all were staring at me, but I was looking at Rachel. Had I offended her that badly during the dinner party? I hoped she could forgive me.

What the hell was I talking about? *Forgive me?* I was Clint motherfucking Terrance. I didn't need anyone to forgive me. I shook myself back into performance mode. Shoulders square. Chin up.

"Okay, let's go," I said.

"We're already going. Just start talking," Piers said.

"You don't need to say *Action* or whatever?"

"We're always rolling."

"What does that mean?"

"It means get on with the bloody explanation."

"Fine," I said. I cracked my knuckles and put on a bright smile. I didn't look at Rachel. For whatever reason, the way she was looking at me made me feel more nervous than standing in front of a crowd of twenty thousand at Shea stadium. "Welcome, ladies!"

"Face the camera." Piers pointed at the crew.

I did what he said.

"Welcome, ladies! Let me explain—"

"No, talk to the girls. Just face the camera."

"Jesus Christ, Piers."

"It's fine. You're doing fine."

I gritted my teeth and started again.

"Welcome, ladies! Let me explain how all this is going to work. This week and next, we'll be pulling you out of this apartment—"

"—this gorgeous luxury penthouse apartment—" Piers chimed in.

"To compete against each other in different challenges."

My eye caught Rachel. She looked terrified. Again, the feeling came over me that I wanted to comfort her. I tore my eyes away.

"This evening we'll be doing a jazz singing challenge. And you'll all be singing... at Sardi's."

A gasp went around the room. I let the talk die down before continuing. At the very least, I knew how to work a crowd.

"That's right. And we'll have a surprise guest—someone from the industry—who'll be listening to all of you sing."

My eyes drifted again to Rachel. It was crazy—she was like a magnet drawing my attention. A very nervous magnet. She smoothed down the front of her dress.

The girl downstairs had been right. Her dress wasn't a hobo outfit, but it certainly wasn't anything to wear to a club. It was a plain dress that looked like it came out of the 1800s. Kind of like the one she'd worn to Jake's dinner party.

No wonder she was nervous.

"You'll have all day to prepare a jazz number to sing at the club," Piers was saying. "We'll have a live band, and—"

"But first," I said, interrupting him, "we have a special surprise for all of you!"

"A surprise?" Piers said, eyeing me sideways. "This is a surprise to me!"

"A shopping spree," I said, plucking the idea out of thin air. As soon as I said it, I knew it was a great idea.

Rachel looked visibly relieved. "If you're all going to Sardi's for dinner, you'll need to look your best. So get ready to go, and we'll meet downstairs in ten minutes!"

I clapped my hands, and the girls scattered to their rooms, murmuring excitedly. Rachel sat down on the now-empty couch, clasping her hands in her lap. I stepped toward her, but Piers caught my arm.

"Clint—"

"What is it?"

"What the hell are you doing?"

I thought at first that he knew about my attraction to Rachel, and my response caught in my throat.

"A *shopping spree*?" he continued, and my throat relaxed.

"Sure," I said. "I thought we could treat them to a shopping day."

"Are you going to be the one explaining this line item on the reimbursement form?"

"I'll pay for it personally," I said. "Don't worry."

Piers glanced over at Rachel, sitting primly on the couch. His gaze swept down over her dress, and all of a sudden I felt a stab of something so unfamiliar, I had to think twice before I could identify what it was: jealousy.

Stupid, I know. I was jealous of a guy looking at a girl who was engaged to another guy. I was insane.

"Is this because—"

"Because I'm the most generous guy in the world? Yes."

I thought Rachel smiled a little bit at that, but I wasn't sure. Piers leaned close to me, turning me away from the couch.

"Clint, if you want to get into someone's pants, wait until after two week is up, alright?"

"I don't know what you're talking about," I said, staring back at Piers with a look that said *Shut up already*. "I just want to go on a shopping trip."

"Alright," he said, dropping his hand away from my arm and eyeing me. "Does this mean I get to pick out a suit for you?"

"A suit?" I looked down at my leather jacket and jeans. "I don't need a suit."

"If you're going to Sardi's, you do."

I sighed. It was obvious that I wouldn't be able to talk with Rachel here. Not with Piers around. Not with the camera crew filming my every move.

"Fine. You can pick out a suit for me. That's pretty gay, you know?"

"I'm British," he said, by way of explanation.

"Does that make it more or less gay?"

"Who's this industry guest you have coming to Sardi's?" he asked, ignoring me.

"My pops," I said, gritting my teeth. "I just volunteered him."

CHAPTER SIXTEEN
Rachel

The whole time Clint was talking, I was able to get a good look at him. Not that I cared about looking at him. But I had no idea why he was so attracted to me. He was attractive, of course. Everybody knew that. The girls had all rushed up to touch him like he was a lucky charm, throwing compliments at him. He could have his pick of any one of them, and they were all beautiful. More beautiful than I was, anyway. Sophia had sidled up to his side and rested one hand on his shoulder.

I burned with a feeling I couldn't name. Or maybe I didn't want to name it.

Jealousy wasn't the right word. When you're jealous, that means you're scared of losing something you have. And I didn't have Clint. He wasn't mine, even if he had been hitting on me like crazy the past two times I'd seen him.

As I watched him explain the contest, I decided that he just wanted to be the center of attention. He was the kind of guy who needed to have every woman hanging off of his arm. He thrived on desire.

Well, he wasn't going to get it from me. Even if I couldn't help look at the top of his shirt, where he had left two buttons undone to draw attention to the top of his tattoo. What was it? I could only see the ends of some lines—they looked like dark scratches on his throat. When he looked at me, though, I looked away. I wasn't giving him one iota more attention.

Still, when he left, I let out my breath and realized that I had been tensing up in my whole body. I couldn't tense up like that. It would affect my singing. I took a few deep breaths, inhaling and exhaling. I couldn't get his face out of my mind, the feeling of his lips as he drew me to him—

No. No way. I needed to think about something else. *Anything* else.

While everybody else was touching up their makeup, I called Derrick to let him know when the contest was. He'd said that he was free tonight, and I needed as much support as I could get. Plus, if he came to see me, I was sure that my stupid brain would stop obsessing over Clint.

"What's up?" Derrick said.

"I love you too, honey," I said, teasing. I wanted to hear the love in his voice, to remind me of what was really important to me.

"Rach, I'm on break at work. I need to get back in," he said.

I immediately felt bad about calling him. Of course he had more important things to attend to.

"Sorry," I said. "But we just found out that we'll be singing tonight at Sardi's!"

"Mmm?"

He sounded so distracted. I hoped I hadn't taken him away at a bad time. He probably was thinking about a thousand other things.

"Um, do you think you can make it?" I asked.

"Where is it again?"

"Sardi's! Isn't that amazing? We have to sing a jazz song—"

"Right. Sure. Maybe. I'm pretty busy with studying for this test."

Of course. His test. I bit my lip, some of my excitement fading.

"I mean, you don't have to come. If you're too busy. I understand it's important."

"I'll try. But no promises."

"Okay. Thanks, Derrick."

"Sure thing."

"I love y—" I started to say, but he had already hung

up.

I stared at the phone for a second, then put it back in my purse. I wished—I didn't know what I wished. I thought that coming here to follow my singing dreams would make everything better, but I felt like it was all getting worse.

I started to dial my parents' house. Even if I could only talk to Rose, I'm sure she would be excited for me.

Before I could even finish punching in the number, though, all of the girls came stomping out of their rooms. I stood up to join them as they piled into the elevator together, talking and laughing. I wasn't going to be the last one downstairs, late again.

"Wait for me!" I cried, hanging up the phone.

"Sorry," Sophia said, standing in the center of the elevator and blocking my way in. She pressed a button. "You can take the next one."

My jaw dropped. There was plenty of room in the back, if any of them would bother to squeeze a little. It was a huge elevator—they had fit all nine of them inside, surely a tenth person would fit. But none of the girls met my eyes, except for Sophia, who was still staring me down.

"I—I—" I stammered stupidly, not knowing what to say to defend myself. I'd been made fun of sometimes when I was a kid, but I'd never been completely excluded like this. A pit opened up in my stomach.

"See you later!" Sophia said, waving goodbye like I was a baby. As the elevator doors closed in my face, I heard a smattering of giggles from inside.

My face burned. I stood there, hatred roiling my stomach like acid as I waited for the elevator. I punched in the code angrily, trying not to cry. I couldn't let them see that they had gotten to me.

I ran through the studio out to the front door. As I pushed open the door, I saw the backs of two black limos driving away, the camera crew driving in a black van behind them.

I took a few steps down the sidewalk, waving both arms wildly.

"Stop! Wait! Wait for me!"

I stopped after only a few steps. The cars were already gone, without me.

"Are you kidding me!?"

I said it aloud, my hands dropping helplessly to my sides.

They had left me standing there alone. And it wasn't a mistake, I knew it. I bet they had told the driver that everyone was in. It was like *Home Alone*, only instead of leaving Macaulay Culkin on accident, they had driven off on purpose.

"Dammit!" I screamed. It was the first time I could remember that I had said a swear word out loud. But this situation deserved it. I tried it out again. "Shit! Dammit!"

"My, my," a voice said from right behind me. "I thought you were a nice farm girl."

Clint was sitting in a fire-engine-red convertible. He must have been waiting to pull up to the curb next to me. My face turned as bright red as the car.

"They left me," I said, my shoulders slumping.

"Good," Clint said. "Hop in."

I stared at the passenger seat that he was patting. A car behind him honked, and I scrambled to open the door. But Clint only raised one middle finger, not even bothering to look at the driver behind him. I turned and waved an apology.

Clint roared away from the curb, sending me flying back into the leather seat. I hurried to click my seatbelt in as he careered around a corner, narrowly missing a hot dog cart.

"I told Piers he could go ahead with the limos," Clint said.

"Oh," I said. A strange warm feeling swept through me. "I thought you had left me behind."

"I would never do that," Clint said, grinning at me.

"Besides, I thought you might need a personal shopper."

"A personal shopper? You mean *you*?"

"The one and only," Clint said.

"Am I that bad a dresser?"

"You're ridiculously beautiful," Clint said. I turned away to hide my flushed cheeks. "It's a shame that you're hiding it all behind that thing."

"My mom made this for me!" I said, anger driving away any good feelings that I might have had for Clint picking me up.

"It's a perfect dress for family reunions. For New York, not so much."

"And you're going to pick out a dress for me?"

"That's right."

"I don't know if I trust your fashion advice," I said. "After all, a man who doesn't know how to pick out a suit…"

"I know how to pick out a suit," he said. "Believe me, I can wear a suit like nobody's business. I just prefer to dress more casually."

"Well, so do I." I crossed my arms.

"Not tonight," Clint said. "Not for this competition. I want you dressing up for every single contest."

"Will you be wearing a suit for every contest?"

He growled. He actually growled. I stared at him until he answered me.

"Fine."

"Fine?"

"Sure," he said, although he didn't seem to be very convinced. "I can do that."

"Good," I said, satisfied with myself.

"Who were you talking to on the phone before you left?" Clint asked.

"Before—you mean, in the apartment?"

"Yeah."

"How did you know I was on the phone?" I frowned. He had already left in the elevator before I called Derrick.

"The whole apartment is rigged up with cameras," Clint said. "You didn't notice?"

"No!" I cried out, flushing again. "You mean, you were taping my conversation?"

"Of course. Did you not read the waiver you signed? Don't pick your nose in the apartment unless you want it on TV."

"I don't pick my—"

"So who were you talking to?"

There was more in his voice than the words he was saying. He was acting like a jealous boyfriend. I breathed out, trying to contain my irritation.

"My fiance, actually."

"Oh? Is he coming tonight?" Clint tried to slip the question in casually, but I could see his fingers tighten around the wheel as we made another sharp curve.

"Maybe," I said. "If he's not too busy."

"Too busy? Too busy for you?"

"He's very important," I said.

Clint eyed me, raising one eyebrow. I cringed. Clint Terrance was probably the most important person in the NYC music scene. Compared to him...

No. That was not a road I wanted to go down. Clint Terrance was a jerk. An arrogant bastard. A playboy. I was not going to compare him to Derrick at all, and definitely not in a flattering way.

"How long have you been engaged?" he asked.

"About three years," I lied. Lacey had thought it had been two years, and I hadn't corrected her. In reality, it had been more like four. Four long years. I tried to think of the way Derrick had looked at me when he proposed. I couldn't even remember the words he had said.

Clint whistled long and low.

"Must be some kind of asshole," he said.

I snapped my head to the side. He was *not* insulting my fiancé like that!

"Excuse me?!"

"What kind of guy makes a girl like you wait so long? Shit or get off the pot."

"That's a lovely analogy," I said sarcastically. "You're *so* romantic."

"If I were you, I'd dump him."

"And if *I* were *you*, I'd be having a threesome with two redheads."

He slammed on his brakes at a yellow light, and the seatbelt caught me with a jerk. He turned to face me, leaning over the center console. I smelled his cologne. It was the same one that he'd worn at the audition, and I found myself remembering what it was like to be crushed against his chest, inhaling his scent—

I crossed my arms and shut the memory out of my mind.

"What are you doing?"

"If I ever ask a girl to marry me, I wouldn't wait that long."

"No, absolutely not," I agreed. "You'd be married and divorced before the Elvis impersonator could pronounce you man and wife."

The light turned green. He slapped both of his hands on the steering wheel but didn't press on the gas. His tongue was between his teeth, and again the thought of his kiss sent flames racing through my lower body. I clenched my jaw.

"The light is green," I said.

"So?"

"Oh, nothing. Just making an observation."

The car behind us honked. He didn't even bother to give them the middle finger. He put his arm over the back of my seat and leaned even closer. The vein at his temple pulsed. I couldn't stop staring at the top of his shirt collar, where his tattoo began. I wondered what was inked on his skin further down. I wondered...

"I bet you think I screwed both those redheads, don't you?"

117

"Of course not," I said, biting my lip. "I think you all played a rousing game of Yahtzee and then had a warm milk before going to sleep."

"As a matter of fact, I didn't even go home with them. With either one of them."

"How noble of you."

"Thank you."

"Why do you think I care?"

"Don't you?"

He stared into my eyes, and all of my courage left me. Because the fact of it was, I had cared. I didn't know why, but I'd felt horrible at the thought of him going home and jumping in bed with those two girls. His dark eyes searched mine for something, but he wasn't going to find it. I faced forward.

"Can we just go?" I asked meekly.

I thought he would throw it back in my face. I thought he would push farther. He seemed to be thinking about it. But instead, he let off of the brake and eased back into the flow of traffic.

After a minute of silence, he spoke.

"Look," he said. He stopped, struggling with his words. It was the first time I'd seen him look so uncomfortable. He seemed like the kind of guy to always keep his cool. "Look. I was just trying—I was trying to show you that I'm not the kind of guy who sleeps around. I mean, maybe I used to be. But I don't always."

"Why?"

"Why what?"

"Why do you even care what I think?" I asked. "Is it not enough to have nine out of ten girls fawning over you? You have to have all ten? Are you a perfectionist, or do you just have OCD, or what?"

"That's not—"

"I'm engaged," I said flatly. "I am not interested in you. Period. You have a million stupid fans, you don't need one more. Got it?"

"Got it," he said. His knuckles were white on the steering wheel and the pulse at his temple was jumping off the chart.

"Good," I said. "Then that's the end of it."

He didn't say anything, and I felt utterly unsatisfied, like I had cut him off from saying something. I pushed the thought away. There was nothing Clint Terrance could say to me that would make me want to throw myself at him like all those other girls.

Absolutely nothing.

CHAPTER SEVENTEEN
Clint

God, this girl was infuriating! Why did I care about her at all? She was completely stubborn and self-centered. She didn't want to be one of my *million* stupid fans? What did she know about my fans? I seethed silently, wishing that my cock would come to its senses and stop lusting after the one girl who was immune to my charms.

"Who are you texting?" I asked, to make conversation.

"My fiance."

"Oh."

"Maybe you'll get to meet him tonight. He's coming to see me perform."

"How nice."

"He is nice. Very nice."

"Yeah? I bet he's good for you." I couldn't help remarking.

"Yes. He's perfect for me."

I rolled my eyes at her tone. Why the hell was I so attracted to this girl?

We pulled in behind the limos, and Rachel got out of the car before I even had a chance to open the door for her. I couldn't be a gentleman even if I tried—she wouldn't let me!

And while it was nice to watch the way her ass swayed left and right as she walked away from me, I knew it would be a lot nicer in a new dress. I jumped out of the car and rushed to the door. We reached for the handle at the same time. My hand touched hers, and she pulled away like I'd burned her with my fingers.

"Wow, you're in a hurry. You must really like shopping," she said, stepping back with her hands on her hips.

"I only want to be a gentleman." I opened the door for her.

"Too bad."

"Too bad?"

"If all you want is to be a gentleman. Because you're failing. Miserably."

She brushed by me without even a thank you. I bit back the curse words on my tongue and followed her in.

She had stopped right in the middle of the doorway, and I ended up bumping right into her from behind. At the contact with her plump ass, my dick pulsed. But she wasn't paying any attention.

"What's the matter?"

I came to her side and saw that she had gone pale. I didn't know why until I looked into the store.

"None of this is going to fit me," Rachel whispered, so softly that I almost didn't hear.

It was one of the many designer shops on the block, but this one in particular was aimed towards petite girls. *Really* petite girls, if the mannequins lined up along the side of the room were any indication. I didn't know why Piers had decided to go into this shop rather than one with a better selection. It was silly, really.

All of the other girls were already storming the dressing room with arms full of dresses. The camera crew looked like they were setting up right next to the fitting room curtain. Hoping to get a peek inside, I realized. Ah, reality TV.

"Clint, you made it!" Piers came bounding over to us, eying Rachel with suspicion. "Why didn't she come in the limos with the other girls?"

Rachel's face, already pale, went ash-white. It was just then that one of the other contestants came over, wearing a long, slim white gown.

"What do you think?" the dark-haired girl asked, twirling around like she was on the end of a catwalk.

"You look incredible!" Piers said.

"Yeah," Rachel squeaked, in a small voice that sounded nothing like the singer I'd heard the night of auditions. "You look great."

"Thanks, *roomie!*" The girl put her hand on Rachel's shoulder.

"Such a beautiful dress," Rachel said. Her roommate pouted.

"You know, I don't know if this is a great store for you. I mean, there's really nothing—"

"You're right," I interrupted. "This is some seriously low-quality shit. Who decided to come in here, anyway?"

The girl narrowed her eyes at me, her lips pressed together in a thin line. She wasn't going to argue against me, I could tell. She was one of those girls who wanted to impress me at any cost. Good.

"I guess it's fine for most of these girls." I waved my hand nonchalantly. "Tell them each to pick something and I'll be back to pay for it later. It should be cheap enough."

Rachel bit her lip. I put a hand on her lower back. She twitched but didn't make a move away from me.

"You were right, Rachel," I said, leading her away from her venomous roommate and back toward the door. "I really like shopping, and I know a much better place down the block. Right next to the suit shop. See you all later!"

The dark-haired girl stood next to Piers, her mouth gaping open. I held back a grin as I led Rachel outside onto the sidewalk. She hadn't even resisted when I pulled her to come with me. Her skin felt smooth and warm under my hand, and I longed to run my fingers down further, to cup her gorgeous ass.

"It was too crowded in there, anyway," I said, filling the silence between us as we walked down the block. "Piers is a great guy, but he's not a great shopper."

Rachel only nodded, her face still pale.

"I hate those kinds of stores, all the dresses look the same. Now where we're going, I think we can find something really unique, something perfect for you."

"Stop, Clint."

"What?"

"I—I know what you're doing. I would never have found a dress in that shop."

"Well, obviously," I said, as we came up to the custom shop I'd looked up earlier. "You're a high-quality girl, you deserve high-quality clothes."

She laughed, and it was the most beautiful sound I'd ever heard. She gestured down at her dress.

"Right. High-quality."

"Rachel, I want to give you the best of everything."

Her laugh cut off, and her mouth twisted. I could see her bottom lip trembling. It must have been something I said that was wrong, but I didn't know what. I held open the door, and she went through without any protest.

This shop was smaller than the other one, more intimate. As we came in, the saleswoman appeared from in between two racks of dresses. She was an older woman, with hair that was dyed red.

"What can I help you find, dear?" she asked kindly.

"We're looking for a dress," Rachel said.

"The sexiest dress you can find," I added.

"What? No!"

"Absolutely," I said, grinning. "Make her look like a diva."

"I have a few things that I think would work for a rock star's girl," the saleswoman said, winking at me. I was surprised that someone her age recognized me—most of *Talismen*'s fans were younger. She was a perfect professional, though, and without another mention, she went to work picking out dresses.

"Come with me, dear," she said. She led Rachel to the back of the shop, pulling dress after dress from the racks. "Into the fitting room with you."

Rachel tried on a green dress first. I liked it, but it was too loose and flowy for a jazz singer.

"Something tighter," I said. "To show off her curves."

"I think this is tight enough," Rachel said. But the saleswoman nodded silently, and handed her a different gown. When she was in the fitting room, she came over to me.

"I believe the miss could use some new lingerie," she said, in a conspiratorial whisper. "Her bra isn't doing her figure any favors."

"You know best!" I said, embarrassed. The woman obviously thought we were a couple, and I wasn't going to tell her otherwise. When she disappeared into the fitting room with an armful of different colored bras and panties, I leaned back against the wall.

Rachel's head popped out from behind the curtain after only a few seconds.

"Did you do this?" she hissed.

"Do what?"

"Ask her to give me underwear!"

I walked over to her, and she tugged the curtain tight against her neck so that I couldn't peer in. She flushed pink around her neck as I looked down to where she clutched the fabric to her collarbone.

"Why? Are you naked?" I asked.

"No! Hush! This bra is hundreds of dollars! That's not part of the deal, is it? I can't afford this."

"If you need special new underwear for the dress, that's part of the outfit," I said.

"But—"

"Or you can go naked under the dress."

Her mouth dropped open.

"Your choice! I would personally love to see your nipples poking through—"

"Shut up!" she said, flushing redder and pulling the curtain shut. I grinned.

When she came out again, she was wearing a skin-tight blue dress that showed off her cleavage. She kept tugging up the collar, trying to hide her bosom.

The saleslady was right. The new bra pushed up her tits like *whoa*. I whistled a low note, and Rachel looked up at me.

"What?" she asked.

"That bra! I didn't realize you had such nice—"

"Stop it!" She crossed her arms over her chest.

"Stop what? I was just admiring your perfect cleav—"

"Shhhhhh!" She clenched her eyes shut, her face turning red with embarrassment. "What do you think about the dress?"

"I like it," I said. I tilted my head, examining her in the mirror. "But it's not quite right."

Rachel looked at herself, her hands stopping at places along her body. She frowned, sucking in her stomach and trying different poses.

"It's the color," I said finally.

"The color?"

"Do you have a dress in gold?" I asked the saleswoman.

"Gold?" Rachel echoed.

"Like your hair," I said.

"My hair isn't—"

"It's got those little gold strands," I said, squinting at her. I thought it would work, but I wasn't sure. I normally spent more time taking girls *out of* dresses than putting them *into* dresses.

"I think that would look wonderful," the saleswoman asked. "Let me see…" She started digging through a rack of dresses.

Rachel turned to the mirror. She combed her fingers through her hair, peering closer. Then she glanced over and caught my eye in the reflection. I smiled at her.

"What is it?" I asked.

"I just… I never really noticed… Nobody's ever noticed that about my hair before," she trailed off. She opened her mouth, as though she was going to say something else, but then the saleswoman pulled out a hanger with a gold dress.

"This one!" she cried out. She leapt into the fitting room and yanked the curtain shut between me and Rachel.

When she emerged, it was like looking at a photograph from the 1930s music scene. The gold dress sparkled, sliding over her body like a second skin. Rachel looked nervous as she came out.

"Turn around," I ordered.

I half-expected her to snap at me, but instead she twirled meekly in place. The dress curved over her tits, covering them while still showing off their shape. And her ass—

"Jesus," I whispered under my breath. I couldn't help staring at her.

"What do you think?" she asked.

What do I think? I think I want to shove you against the wall and slip between your creamy thighs. I think there's nothing stopping me from snapping my fingers and taking you now, right now, hard and fast on the floor or up against the mirror. I think you would fit perfectly around my cock.

My mouth was dry, and from the way Rachel was looking at me, she knew what was going on in my head. But I swallowed the desire, my cock throbbing under my jeans.

"Perfect," I said. It was all I said, but every thought of mine was contained in that word. Rachel ignored the throaty growl of my voice, turned instead to the mirror.

"Really? Don't I look like Vanna White? All these sequins!"

"You're a star. Dress like it."

The order came out too harsh. Rachel looked at me in the mirror, dumbstruck, and I had to pull myself together. Pull a smile onto my face. I was so hard, so fucking horny. How could she not know what she was doing to me?

"You have some shoes to match this dress?" I asked the saleswoman. She nodded and scurried off into the side of the shop. I came over to Rachel's side and put my arm around her. To my surprise, she didn't pull away.

"It's perfect," I said again. *You're perfect.*

"Thank you," she murmured, and her eyes glistened with emotion. I turned away. She looked gorgeous enough to eat, but she had another guy coming to watch her tonight. She was thinking of him, not me. And if I didn't control this stupid urge to pull her into my arms and kiss her, I was going to ruin the whole competition.

My dad's words rang in my ears. I needed a star for the studio, not another girl in my bed. No matter how beautiful she was.

CHAPTER EIGHTEEN
Rachel

When we got back to the shop, the other contestants stared at my gold dress. They were envious, I could tell. I thought I would be happier to see them envy me, but it felt false, hollow, like a victory I hadn't won myself.

Then Sophia walked behind me and coughed.

"Whore."

My whole body tensed up under the beautiful gold dress. I spun around to confront her, but she was already walking out the door, arm in arm with another one of the contestants. They whispered to each other and tittered, their laughter like beads on a fake pearl necklace scattering across the floor.

I looked back. Nobody would make eye contact with me. They avoided me the whole way out. I turned to Clint, hoping that he would give me a ride back.

"Oh, sorry," he said, keeping his distance from me as he stood next to Piers. "We're going suit shopping. But we'll meet you at Sardi's."

He smiled at me, a perfunctory smile that made me want to rip his head off. He had just been the nicest guy, helping me pick out a nice dress. And when he'd put his arm around me, I'd felt...

Safe.

But now it was like he was abandoning me, throwing me into the cage with a group of lions. I started to protest, but then bit back my words.

Stupid, stupid me. Of course he was leaving me. I had basically done everything I could to make sure that he wasn't going to hit on me again. He probably pitied me. The only girl who couldn't get along with all the others.

I couldn't let him see that I was so weak. Not after everything he had just done for me. I tacked on a fake, forced smile.

"Thanks for the dress!" I said. "I'll see you both at the competition!"

I nearly fell over my heels as I stumbled to the limo, yanking open the door just as Sophia was closing it behind her.

"One more coming in," I said, gritting my teeth and trying not to notice as the other girls rolled their eyes and shifted in their seats away from me. So I wasn't welcome. So what? I had spent most of my life alone, and I wasn't about to give up my dream now just because I didn't fit in. I leaned back in the limo seat and closed my eyes. My fingers stroked my dress where it stretched over my knees.

When he'd touched me—

I let the thought pass through my mind, the sensations reliving themselves on my skin. And then I let the thought waft away, banishing it from the forefront of my brain. No more daydreaming.

Usually, I was good at banishing daydreams. But it took me a few tries before I could get Clint's face out of my mind, the way his hand had clasped my back, so tight, so possessive. And the way he looked at me, like he was stripping me down bare. Not just out of my clothes, but past that. Past my skin, down to the marrow of my bones. He had a way of looking at me like I was already *his*.

I spent the rest of the day trying to distract myself from thinking about Clint. Fortunately, we had a lot to do before the first contest. That whole afternoon, we spent hours in a fancy spa getting our hair, nails, and makeup done. I was finally able to relax after we'd split up to get individual massages.

When it came time for the pedicures, I was sitting next to Taylor. Her hair was almost white, it was so blonde. We were both sipping green tea, which I think was supposed to make my skin look more youthful. Taylor sure didn't need it—she looked like a teenager.

"I think you sounded great in the audition," she said. "Don't even mind what those other girls think."

I looked at her, trying to figure out whether she was meaning to insult me or not. But she only flipped through a celebrity magazine, a neutral expression on her face.

"What…what did they say about me?" I asked.

"Oh, you know," she said, waving one hand in the air. "Stupid stuff. It's because they're jealous."

"Jealous?" I knew that riding with Clint hadn't been a good idea. But what else was I supposed to do, when they had abandoned me on the sidewalk?

"They know you're a better singer than they are."

"Really? I mean, I didn't hear any of the other auditions. Except Sophia."

"Well, that, and also that you're getting into Clint's pants."

"What?" My blood turned hot and I squirmed in my chair. The pedicurist held my toes more tightly.

"It's alright," Taylor said. "I know you have to do what you have to do in order to win."

"But I'm not—"

"If he likes you, then you might as well. Just be careful you don't get caught on camera."

"I am NOT getting into Clint's pants," I said firmly. "I want nothing to do with his pants. His pants are the farthest thing away from my mind right now."

"Sure," Taylor said, winking at me as the camera crew walked by. "*Suuuuuuure.*"

"It's true! I'm engaged!"

"Oh yeah? Then where's your ring?"

"He—we haven't gotten one yet. We don't have a lot of money."

The excuse sounded lame, even to me. I'd told Derrick that he could give me a ring pop and I would have been happy. But he had insisted on waiting until he got a promotion and a pay bump to afford a big diamond. Now,

I wished I had bought a small ring for myself, just to stifle this gossip.

"Look," Taylor said, leaning over conspiratorially to me. Her long blonde hair swung down, perfectly framing her face. "It's none of my beeswax, but I know Clint likes your type."

"My—my type?"

"Well, from what I read, he's all about redheads. Your hair has a little bit of red in it, kinda. And, you know, I never knew he was into fluffy chicks."

If my hair wasn't red, my face sure was. I didn't even know how to respond to Taylor's remark. She didn't even seem like she was *trying* to be mean to me. But everything she said made me feel more and more awful.

"This is a singing contest," I said finally. "That's more important than—"

"What, how you look? Not really. If you want to be a star, you have to look the part. Why do you think we're all here getting all done up?"

"Well… I thought… Because we're going to be on TV tonight?"

Taylor shook her head, clucking like I was the naive one. A nineteen year old who thought I was naive. Maybe I was.

"Anyway," she said. "I know I'm not Clint's type. But if Piers says anything to you about me, you'll let me know, right?"

"Piers?"

"He is SO hot! And I absolutely love British accents!" Taylor sighed.

"Isn't he like, twice as old as you?"

"Yeah. Why?"

"Oh. No reason," I said, cupping the teacup to my lips.

"Do you think he would fuck me?"

I had been taking a sip of tea, and I spit it back out in my cup in surprise.

"Uh…"

"I hope so. Did you see him when he hosted the first *Secret Bachelor Baby*?"

"I—um—I didn't know there was more than one."

"Oh, of course! There were like, five seasons!"

Taylor chattered on happily, and I let her talk, nodding in the right places. I couldn't get past what she had said about me trying to get into Clint's pants. How could they think that?

But I knew that it was partially my fault. That I hadn't pushed away from him fast enough. Of course, if everyone had been at the auditions, they would have seen him chasing after me. Some of them might have even seen him kiss me. I burned with shame.

"So if you ever get a chance to talk to Piers, let him know I'm up for anything," Taylor was saying to me.

"Uh huh," I said.

"I mean it," she said, a hungry glint in her eyes that scared me. "Absolutely *anything*."

At Sardi's, Clint was nowhere to be seen. I smothered the feeling of disappointment that threatened to bubble up in my throat. I had to focus on singing.

Piers moved us through the restaurant to the back, where they had set up a small stage in the middle of the room. We had a list of jazz standards that we could choose from. Most of the girls were grumbling about the selection, and I realized that I was going to do alright in this challenge. I knew almost all the songs, and a lot of them were in the perfect range for me.

"I don't know, like, any of these," Taylor said, scanning the list. To my surprise, she didn't sound that worried. "What should I sing?"

"What's your vocal range?" I asked.

"My what?"

"Like, do you sing really high? Or really low? Or somewhere in the—"

"Oh, yeah! Yeah, I sing super high!" She cleared her

throat, then started screeching the highest note she could. From the booths in the restaurant, I could see heads turning.

"Great!" I said, to get her to stop. "Perfect. Let's... uh, let's see what would work for you." I scanned the list for anything that might work. Despite what she thought, Taylor was definitely not going to be able to hit the top notes for a few of the songs. I marked a few songs that might work - *Honeysuckle Rose* was a good one, I thought, or maybe *Frankie and Johnny*— and crossed out others that definitely wouldn't work for her.

"Thanks," Taylor said, yanking the sheet from my hand. "I'll look these up on my phone." She beamed at me, and for a brief second I felt like I had found a friend. But then she turned away and started chatting with one of the Jens. I stayed back, not wanting to overstep and be excluded again.

"Alright, ladies," Piers said, clapping his hands together. "The band is coming soon, so we'll be starting as soon as they get here."

"Where's—uh—" I cut off my question, but it was already too late. A few of the girls shot me sidelong glances.

"Clint Terrance?" Piers finished my question for me. "He will be here soon. I hope. Along with the other judges."

"Who's first?" Sophia said.

"Are you volunteering? Excellent!" Piers said, making the room giggle nervously. Sophia brushed her hair back and smiled confidently.

"Of course I'll go first," she said. "Is the surprise industry guest here already?"

Right. I had forgotten that there would be someone from the music industry here tonight to listen to us. I hoped that I could impress him. I hoped—well, my dad had a saying for that that my mom didn't like: *Hope in one hand and crap in the other, and see which one fills up first.* But I couldn't help it. I was going to be singing in a genre I was familiar with, and nobody else seemed to have a clue what was going on.

"Our surprise industry guest will be arriving with—wait! There they are!"

Every one of us whirled around to see who it was. My eyes fell on Clint first, and before I knew it, my mouth had dropped open.

He was wearing a suit, and he looked *incredible*. His chest looked even broader with the crisp lines of his dark gray suit jacket, and every move of his gave a hint of the muscles underneath without showing it off too obviously. The edge of his tattoo peeked up from under the collar of his white button-down shirt. He caught my eye and I dropped my gaze quickly, but not quick enough. He smiled at me, and I knew he had seen me looking.

Then I saw who he was with, and my heart dropped like an oak tree falling, dead branches crumbling as it hit the ground.

The older man he was escorting in, the industry guest—it was the same man who had made fun of me in the studio. The one who'd looked me up and down and said I couldn't win. All of a sudden, my confidence evaporated. My mouth went dry.

"Allow me to introduce our surprise industry guest," Clint said. "The head of Terrance studios, my father Skull Terrance!"

Everybody burst into applause. Everybody but me. I couldn't move. I couldn't even think. All of a sudden my gold dress felt tight around my waist.

His dad?

Taylor elbowed my side with a sharp jab, and I realized that Clint and his father were staring at me. I brought my hands up, starting clapping a little too late, a little too loud. There was a buzzing in my ears.

I couldn't sing for Clint's dad. He already hated me. He already thought I was a loser. And what had he said when

I'd told him I was a good singer?

That and a dollar gets you a cuppa coffee.

It didn't matter that I knew every song on that list. It didn't matter that I was a great singer. He didn't care. He wasn't looking for someone with a good voice, he was looking for someone he could put on TV. And I realized then that I was less than an underdog in this race. The head of the studio had already written me off.

The British guy was talking now. Piers. Beside me, Taylor leaned forward and watched him intently as he spoke.

"The winner of tonight's singing contest will receive a gift certificate for a free dinner for two at Sardi's—thank you so much for your generosity, Sardi's—as well as immunity from being eliminated in the next challenge."

He paused as all the girls cheered for the prizes. I couldn't force myself to cheer. I knew I wasn't going to win.

"The two losing singers will have to say goodbye to everyone here. Let the best singer win!"

That wasn't going to happen, I thought bitterly. The winner will be whoever Skull Terrance wants to get into bed with. Tears pressed against the backs of my eyes, but I fought them back. I would do my best. That was all I could do.

As I walked to the back room to wait my turn, I felt a hand on my back. I spun around angrily, ready for an argument with Clint.

But it wasn't Clint.

"Derrick!" I said breathlessly. "You're here!"

CHAPTER NINETEEN
Clint

I shook my head as the girls argued with me, tugging on my new suit. Rachel was in the doorway of the back room, talking furtively with a guy. The camera crew seemed to be focusing on them, and I couldn't help but look back there. Who was that guy? Was that her fiancé? He looked like a weasel stuffed into a business suit.

"Clint!" A voice tore me back to my current predicament.

"Not everybody can sing *Frankie and Johnny!*" I said in exasperation.

"But that's the only one I know!"

"It's my favorite!"

"You can't let her sing it," one contestant whined. "She only picked it after I picked it!"

I hadn't realized it, but Lindsay Lohan had sung a version of *Frankie and Johnny* in a movie, and that was the only song anyone even recognized. How could I have been so daft?

"This is a mess," I said to Piers, prying myself away from the clamoring girls. "How could we have ended up like this?"

"Well," Piers said, "normally the contestants get a chance to practice before the contest. But someone wanted to do a shopping spree instead."

"You didn't tell me this could happen! You're the TV guy!"

"You're the music guy!"

"What are we going to do? Should we just let them sing what they want?"

Piers glared at me.

"Sure," he said. "Let them all get up on stage at *Sardi's* and twerk to electropop. We'll never be allowed into a five-star restaurant in Manhattan again. Great idea, Clint."

"Do you have a better one?"

"Of course. Let them all sing the same song if they want to."

"A dozen *Frankie and Johnny*s? Are you serious?"

"It's better than bad karaoke, which is what you're going to get otherwise."

"Okay, okay." I turned to the contestants. "Is there anyone here who isn't going to sing *Frankie and Johnny*?"

Two hands went up. It was a young blonde girl, and Rachel, from the back. Of course Rachel would know more than one song. And the guy she had been talking to was gone. I felt a little relieved, but not much.

"Okay. We'll put you in between the *Frankie and Johnny*s. To—uh—to spread them out a bit."

"Remember," Piers said, addressing the girls, "If you want to stand out in this contest, you might want to choose something different. Original. If you all want to sing the same song, though…"

"That's fine with me," a dark-haired girl said, crossing her arms. "I'll be the best one singing it anyway."

"You wish!" another girl cried.

"Ladies, ladies!" Piers said, quieting them down. He looked torn between wanting to incite a riot and not wanting to be kicked out of Sardi's forever. "Remember how this looks on TV."

That got them to shut up.

"The band is setting up out in the restaurant," Piers continued, scribbling something on a sheet. "Here's a list of singing order. Write down your song next to your name so I can announce it. We'll start with… Sophia."

The dark-haired girl strode forward, shouldering one of the other contestants out of the way. The other girls crowded around the sheet to see when they were singing.

"Alright, let's get started," Piers said, nudging me back

out with a whisper. "We should leave before they all start clawing each other's throats out. Nice suit, by the way."

"Thanks." I'd gone to a place my dad had recommended. While I could tell it looked good, I wasn't comfortable in such a starched up collar. I kept tugging on the fabric at my neck, trying to loosen my tie.

"You'd better go back to wearing something normal tomorrow, or you'll steal my spotlight on TV," Piers joked. "You're only supposed to be the co-host."

"Are you kidding? I wouldn't want to make you feel bad. Plus, chicks already like me more anyway. If I don't dress down, I'll be overwhelmed by all the girls."

"Did you see that guy in the back?" Piers asked.

"The one talking to Rachel?" I frowned. "Yeah, I saw him. Is that her fiancé?"

"Maybe, maybe not. He kissed her on the cheek, so maybe he's her brother."

I could tell Piers was trying to get a rise out of me, so I ignored it.

"Whatever." I slid into one of the booths, across from my dad. "Hey, Pops."

"Hey, kid."

"I think Clint already has a winner picked out," Piers said to my dad, winking hard. The camera crew gathered around our table.

"We'll see who sings the best," I said.

"Sure we will. Mr. Terrance—"

My dad lifted his hand.

"Mr. Terrance was my father," he said, oozing charm. His grin glinted gold off of a front tooth. "Call me Skull."

"Skull," Piers said, "What will you be looking for in our contestants tonight?"

"Not the inside," my dad said. "The outside. I want to see what they have to show off. I want to see that they can work a room, that they're star material."

"And if a contestant isn't star material?" Piers asked.

My dad smiled, took the toothpick out from between

his lips, and snapped it in half.

"Then they're done."

"Done, indeed! Well, it looks like our first singer is up!" Piers moved to the front of the stage, the camera crew following him.

"Ain't you gonna go host?" my dad asked me.

"Piers can handle this part," I said. "I'm the one working the girls behind the scenes."

"Ha! Working the girls! I bet you are!" My dad slapped the table. I smiled weakly.

"Don't worry. We'll find a new star. Piers is doing great."

"Just so long as you don't let him steal the spotlight," my dad said. His brows furrowed into a tight knot on his wrinkled forehead.

"It's fine. He's the TV guy."

"Yeah, I guess." My dad already had another toothpick in his mouth. I didn't know where he kept his stash of them. "Ya know, I always thought I could be good on TV."

"Maybe twenty years ago."

"Hey!"

I raised my hands in surrender. I didn't know what had gotten into me to say something like that.

"Sorry, Pops. Just saying, TV is for the young."

"I guess you're right. Not just the young, huh. The good-looking young!"

I nodded in mute agreement.

"I remember when you didn't have to look like anything to be a star," my dad continued. "Brian Wilson, the motherfucking Beach Boys. You remember how dumpy they looked? Those boys never stood up on a goddamn surfboard. They sounded good, that was all. It was the sound that mattered."

"Sure."

"You think Simon and Garfunkle would play anywhere today? What with that Jew nose, that fucking afro—"

140

"Pops—"

"I'm just sayin'. It's not like it used to be."

"Sure, Pops. Hey, here's the first girl."

My dad shut up, thankfully, and looked up at the stage. He let out a wolf whistle at the girl.

"Now that's a girl would look good on a screen," he said. "What's her name?"

"Sophia."

"Sophia. Damn, Sophia. Those titties—"

"Pops!"

The camera crew was crowding around our booth, taping our conversation.

"What? I'm just sayin', those are some nice titties."

It was the same thing Jake and Piers had said at the first audition, but hearing it come out of my dad's mouth made it worse, somehow. Jake and Piers weren't in the music business. My dad was supposed to care about more than just that.

Now that I thought about it, though, he hadn't cared about any more than that. He had never talked to me about music, only how to sell it. But hearing him say it out loud, especially now in front of all of the cameras—I felt embarrassed. I felt ashamed. I'd never felt anything but proud of my dad. It rubbed me the wrong way, like a pick screeching down a guitar string. I felt a vibration of shame shudder through me.

I didn't look at him for the next few songs. The jazz band was obviously irritated at having to play *Frankie and Johnny* seven times in a row. I would be irritated, if I was them. *Talismen* had been on tour for months, and playing the same tunes over and over again just wore on your nerves. I crossed my arms, then uncrossed them. Piers had told me not to look bored.

"And now, Rachel Ritter performing *Ain't Misbehavin'*!"

I saw her friends that I'd met at the party up near the stage, taking pictures from every angle they could. And then I saw the guy.

He was leaning against the wall, his cell phone out. I thought at first he was taking a video of her, and then he smirked and tapped his fingers across the screen. I realized he was texting. I don't know which made me feel more angry—that he was her boyfriend, or that he wouldn't even bother to tape her performance.

I turned my attention back to Rachel. Her gold dress shimmered in the spotlight, making her look perfectly at home. The gold rims of the drum kit, the shiny brass sax, and now her sequined dress, shining brightly even in the dim room.

Her hair was styled differently, cascading down one side in soft waves. The stylist who had done it had put some product in that sparkled and shone, setting off her red-gold highlights perfectly. And I was glad that she had let me buy her some nice underwear. You couldn't even see the line of her panties; it looked like she was naked under her dress.

Naked. God damn, I should not have thought about that. Immediately, my mind went off of a thousand wrong tangents and my cock began to twitch. I tried to cross my legs and couldn't, not in this booth. I knocked my knee into the tabletop, and my dad glared at me.

"Sorry," I said.

Rachel began to sing, and her voice trickled out like a waterfall just starting to make its way down the rocks. Like glacial ice melting, so pure, so sweet. I could drink her words.

No one to talk with, all by myself
No one to walk with, I'm happy on the shelf babe
Ain't misbehavin', savin' my love for you

It was the perfect song for her, but she was singing it to the wrong guy. Her face shone with love at her fiance, but he wasn't even looking back. He stood at the wall, his eyes not even moving from his screen. I wanted to go over

142

there and punch him in the face. He didn't deserve a girl who could sing like that, not if he couldn't appreciate this perfection. She was killing it, for God's sake! And he was still tapping away at his fucking smartphone. I ripped my eyes away from him, so angry I couldn't breathe.

I know for certain the one I love
I'm through with flirtin', you that I'm thinkin' of
Ain't misbehavin'
Oh savin' my love oh baby, love for you

Her lips were bright red, the only part of her not understated. It was the right choice—as she sang, the notes came out in a stream of pouts and puckers. The audience at Sardi's was loving it, I could tell. She was a natural jazz singer, and she was making love to the air with her song. Even the band perked up once they heard the emotion she was putting into it.

All that love... wasted.

I wanted her to be singing to me. I wanted her words to be meant for me. I wanted her to give me all of her love the way she was giving it now to all the people in the room. I wanted her to open up and sing like this for me, in the studio. I didn't just want her to be a star. I wanted her to be *my* star.

The last chorus ended, but as soon as the song stopped, her face retracted, like she was pulling back into herself. She gave a small half-wave, and there was a scattering of applause from the restaurant, which had previously been silent.

"She's great, isn't she?" I said breathlessly. My dad shrugged.

"Meh."

"The fuck do you mean? Did you hear that?"

"Yeah, sure, she can sing. But look at her."

Rachel was stepping down off the stage. Now that she wasn't singing, she was awkward, withdrawn. She stumbled on the last step and her friends caught her. They burst into laughter and traipsed out of the room together.

"She looks good to me," I insisted.

"Stop thinking with your dick."

"I'm not—"

"You think I can't tell? You need to wet your goddamn dick before you go making any dumb mistakes."

The cameras had swung back our way. It was like the cameraman could sense drama and get near it wherever it was happening.

"I won't make any mistakes," I hissed at my dad. I bit my tongue before I could get any madder.

The rest of the contest was completely mediocre. I let my attention drift over to where Rachel's boyfriend had been standing, but he wasn't there anymore. I wondered if he had gone into the back. Was she kissing him right now? I felt something boiling up in me that I never felt: jealousy. I was jealous of another man's girl. Me! Clint fucking Terrance! If it had been any other girl, I could have snapped my fingers and she would have left him so fast he wouldn't have kissed anything but air.

But not Rachel. Not after the song she sung tonight. I knew who that was meant for, and I knew it was a warning to me. So she was through with flirting. Well, I was through with that, too. It didn't stop me from wanting her to get what she was due. She had the best voice in the room, and I knew it.

After the last few performers did terrible renditions of *Frankie and Johnny*, I turned back to my dad with a new sense of confidence.

"So who do you think should be the winner?"

My dad raised his hands as though he was uncertain. But there was no doubt about it, at least not in my mind. And he knew I was pressing him because it was that obvious.

"You don't think Rachel was the best?"

"She's fine. This was her night, right?"

"She can do jazz."

"Sure, I'll give you that. She can do jazz. But there are a million jazz singers, and none of them are superstars."

"So you think she was the best tonight?" I pressed.

"Sure," he said. "Sure. Give her a win tonight. We'll see what happens in the long run."

"I'm not giving it to her. She *earned* the win," I insisted.

My dad looked at me like he was going to push back, but then he just shrugged.

"Whatever you want, kiddo," he said. "This is your game. Throw it away if you want, it's no skin off my nose."

"I'm not throwing it away. She's the best."

He threw his toothpick down on the table and stood up, brushing his suit. He looked natural in a navy pinstripe suit. Like a real businessman. Me, I felt like a poser in a suit, and he knew it.

"See you later, kiddo," he said. "Give her my congratulations."

CHAPTER TWENTY
Rachel

When I got off stage, Lacey and Steph were both gushing.

"You were a-mazing!" Lacey said.

"I don't think there's much better than a red velvet cupcake," Steph said, "but your song was like a red velvet cupcake with gold frosting. Where did you even get this dress?"

"The host picked it out for me. Shhh, the next person is on," I said, waving them back away from the stage. Behind me, I could hear one of the other contestants singing.

"Where's Derrick?" I asked, once we had moved away from the stage. I'd seen him watching me before I'd gone up on stage.

"I don't know where he went," Steph said. "He disappeared right before you finished singing."

"Rachel, are you sure… I mean, is he really the one?" Lacey asked.

"What? Why would you even ask that?" My smile dropped off of my face. "Where is he?"

"He was on his phone, like, the whole time," Lacey said. "And he barely said hi when I introduced him to Steph."

"He's busy," I said coldly. "He was probably trying to finish up some business stuff."

Lacey and Steph gave each other a look that sent a rush of anger coursing through me.

"Sorry I don't have a billionaire boyfriend like you," I said, the grumpiness coming into my voice. "My fiancé actually has to work for a living."

"Come on. That's not fair."

"Well, it's not fair for you to criticize my fiancé when he took time out of his busy schedule to come see me sing! For all you know, he had to go deal with an emergency."

"Right."

"I'm going to go find him," I said. "Thanks for coming out to support me."

"Oh, Rachel, you know we don't mean it like that," Steph said, but she didn't make a move to stop me as I strode away.

I couldn't believe them! They were supposed to be my friends. They were supposed to be supportive. Maybe they were just envious. After all, Derrick had already proposed to me. Neither Lacey nor Steph was engaged yet. Envy, that's all it was. It seemed like New York City was full of it.

I cast my eyes around the restaurant. Sardi's was set up in a confusing layout—you couldn't see anywhere around the booths, and all of the walls were covered in autographed pictures and mirrors that reflected other walls. Thick columns made it seem almost like a forest.

I went around one booth, and an older woman put her hand on my arm.

"Miss?"

"Yes?" I said.

"I think that song you sang was just darling. I hope you win the competition." She smiled, revealing a row of false teeth.

"Thank you!" I said, genuinely surprised. "I—I hope I win, too!"

"You will, I know it! None of the other girls could hold a candle to you!"

"Th—thank you!"

In a happy daze, I moved off to find Derrick. I had just turned the corner when I saw him standing by the bar. He had his phone up to his ear. I sidled up behind him, not wanting to disturb his conversation.

"Yeah," he was saying into the phone, "she just finished."

A burst of happiness shot through my heart. He was talking about me with someone! I couldn't wait to tell Steph and Lacey just how wrong they were about him.

But then he continued.

"Nah, she doesn't have a chance. Not compared to the other girls. They were all way hotter. I don't know how she got in the contest in the first place."

I stopped cold, my muscles freezing me in place. Derrick leaned on the bar, sipping at his martini.

"Yeah. It's silly. I just hope she figures out soon that she's never going to be a singer."

My tongue wasn't working. A thick lump stopped up my throat, and the air around me began to turn hot. It was stifling. I wanted to tap him on the shoulder, to tell him I was there, but I couldn't.

"No, no way. If she wins, I'll eat my—"

He turned around as he spoke, and his eyes locked onto me. What he saw in my face turned him pale.

"Hey, I gotta go," he said, and hung up. Smiling at me uncertainly, he put his arms out.

"Hey, baby!" he cried. "You did great!"

He went to hug me, and I swatted his arm away.

"Really?" I said.

"What?"

"I heard you," I said, my voice starting to tremble. "I heard everything."

"Aw, Rachel, don't be like that. I only meant—"

"*I don't have a chance? I'm never going to be a singer?*"

"Look, you weren't supposed to hear that."

"No, you weren't supposed to say that! You weren't supposed to ever think that?" My voice rose. "You're supposed to support me!"

Derrick shook his head, looking down at his watch.

"I really don't have time for this conversation right now."

"Excuse me?" I couldn't believe he was saying this. He was joking, wasn't he? All of the good feelings about my song disappeared. The one person I cared about impressing didn't think I was any good. My chest felt hollow.

Derrick put his hand on my arm and pulled me away from the bar, towards the exit. I stepped awkwardly, zombie-like, following him as though I was in a dream. Or a nightmare.

"Look, I thought… Listen. I only thought that this would be good for you. Every time I see you, your mind is far away. You're always daydreaming about singing, about being a star."

"And?"

He pulled me out the doorway, into the alley. Now that we were alone, away from everybody, I thought I would cry. But no tears came.

"It's obvious it's not going to happen. Look at those women. And look at you."

It was impossible, what I was hearing.

"Derrick. What exactly are you saying?"

"When we get married, you're going to be my wife. You won't have time to waste doing silly things like this."

Adrenaline flooded my system, and my hands balled into fists at my side.

"Why did you even come to get me, then? Why did you drive me up to New York?"

"I thought this would be a chance to get it out of your system."

He didn't want me to sing. Every moment he'd eyed me sideways while I hummed a tune, every time he'd told me that I should keep it down because he was studying.

"You hate my singing."

"Honey, I don't hate it. I just don't want you to be disappointed when nothing comes of it."

I was seething now.

"So you want me to lose this contest?"

He opened his mouth, then closed it. Then opened it again.

"Honey, I don't know what to say to that."

"Yes or no! It's an easy question! *Do you want me to lose this contest?*"

"Honey—"

"What kind of a jerk are you?"

He looked at me with a mix of fear and anger, like I was a rabid animal he had to ward off.

"I only thought—"

"About yourself. You want me to be your perfect wife. You want me to care for you, and that's it."

"Rachel, be realistic. You're a caretaker, aren't you? You're not a music star. I just want you to realize—"

"Oh, I've realized something, alright."

He let out a sigh of relief. He didn't even notice that there was steam coming out of my nostrils.

"I've realized that you're a no-good self-important asshole who doesn't care about me at all!"

He looked at me agog. I'd never said a swear word in front of him before. And I'd certainly never yelled one to his face.

"*Excuse me?*"

His phone rang and he looked at the screen.

"Don't," I said.

"I have to answer this—"

"Don't!"

I slapped it out of his hand. It clattered onto the asphalt and the battery shot out of the back.

"You bitch!" He stared at me with a look of such hatred that I didn't even feel guilty.

"If you cared one bit about my feelings, you wouldn't want me to throw my singing away. It's only time I feel good! It's the only time I feel alive! Singing is the one thing that I care about!"

"What about me? So you don't care about me?"

His face was twisted and ugly. I felt like I was seeing

him for the first time, for what he really was. And I didn't like what I saw.

"Derrick," I said slowly, "I don't think I've ever cared about you." I started to step away, but he blocked me with his arm. Suddenly I realized we were alone in the alley.

"Rachel, you don't know what you're saying."

"I know exactly what I'm saying." My voice was trembling. "You're an asshole, Derrick."

"You ungrateful little *bitch*!" His hand clamped on my shoulder, and I winced. "Do you know how many women would love to be in your position?"

"What, having a cold-hearted boyfriend who keeps putting off your wedding because he's too dumb to pass a stupid test?"

He slapped me. The sound rang out in the alley, and I put my hand up to my face in surprise. I deserved it, probably. I don't think anyone had ever called him dumb before.

Before I could even react, though, two hands grabbed Derrick from behind. I gasped as Clint spun and slammed Derrick up against the other wall of the alley.

"Don't touch her."

CHAPTER TWENTY-ONE
Clint

"Let me down!"

Derrick's feet were dangling a couple of inches from the ground. I had one hand gripped around his neck, the other arm barred across his chest. I couldn't believe what I had just seen. He had slapped her. The son of a bitch had actually raised a hand to her. He stared down at me angrily from where I was holding him up against the wall.

"You fucking bastard!" I smacked my hand across Derrick's face, hard. It made a satisfying sound, and blood ran down his lip. Anger turned to fear in his eyes.

"Oh, fuck," he moaned. "Put me down. Put me—"

"You like getting slapped? Huh? You like that?"

I slapped him again, harder. His head knocked back against the wall, and his face went dizzy. Blood splattered from his face onto my jacket.

"And now you ruined my suit. I just got this fucking suit!" I slapped him again.

"Clint, stop!" Rachel said, tugging at my jacket.

"First this cocksucker needs to apologize."

"Clint, it's okay," she said, her voice tremulous. "Please, don't hurt him."

"It's not okay, Rachel," I said. I was trying to stay calm, but I could hear my heartbeat pumping in my ears. No. I had to be calm. Even now, when I wanted to rip this guy's head off of his goddamn neck.

"I can't—I can't breathe."

"Clint, please!"

His face was turning purple. Fuck. If I went too far, I could easily kill this asshole. The image of him raising a hand to Rachel made me shake him hard, but I bit back my anger. I let him down so that he could stand on his feet and, still holding him by the collar, shoved him around to face Rachel.

"Apologize."

"I'm—I'm sorry."

"More." My fingers tightened, and he made a choking noise.

"I'm sorry... I'm sorry for saying you shouldn't be a singer."

"And?" I shook him and he flopped in my hand like a little rag doll.

"And I'm sorry for slapping you." He spat the words. Hatred burned in his eyes. The little fucker.

I tossed him backward. He hit the wall with a crack to the forehead and stumbled, regaining his feet. His hand pressed against his split eyebrow. Did I do that? Fucker deserved it.

I stepped between him and Rachel, and he straightened out his suit, trying to look dignified.

"It's okay," Rachel said.

"It's not okay," I started to say, but Derrick beat me to it.

"You stupid cunt," Derrick hissed. "It's not okay. It's *over!*"

Rachel's mouth dropped open. He spun and left the alley, pushing his way through the pedestrians on the sidewalk. I brushed my hands off.

"Did—did that just happen?" Her voice was soft, scared.

"I couldn't believe it either," I said. "Asshole."

"He broke up with me," she said. She sounded dazed. "My fiancé broke up with me."

"You're better off without him."

"I don't... I can't..."

I turned to her and tried to put my arm around her, but she skittered back like a scared animal. Her face was dead white.

"Hey, Rachel, it was the right thing to do. If you want—"

"Leave me alone."

"Rachel—"

"Leave me alone!"

She ran back into Sardi's, her gold dress fluttering at her ankles. I sighed and looked down at my bloody hands.

"I can't believe he ruined my fucking suit," I said, to nobody in particular.

"Let's hear it for our singers tonight!" Piers said, standing in the middle of the stage. He caught a glimpse of me, then did a double take.

"Clint?"

My dad stared at me as I climbed up the stage, blood smeared on my hands. I tried not to show how pissed I was. Rachel was standing in the back of the crowd of girls. Her face was still white, and I could see that she had tried to wipe off her tears, smudging her mascara.

"What the hell happened to you?" Piers whispered.

"Nothing," I said. My dad didn't say a word. He'd seen me get in enough fights to understand what I'd done.

"Did the cameras get it?"

I gave Piers an *Are you kidding me?* look and didn't answer. He cleared his throat and turned back to the restaurant. I glanced over at Rachel, who was looking everywhere but at me.

"Yes, well, it's time to announce the winner of tonight's contest! And to tell us who sung the best tonight, here's Skull Terrance, multi-platinum record exec from Terrance Studios!"

He handed the microphone over to my dad. I glared at him as he took the mike. Was he really going to choose that Sophia girl because she had nice tits? If he did, I was going to kill him.

"Thanks, Piers," he said, dropping into his natural charm. When he was on stage, he was always *on*. "It was a hard decision to make, but after a lot of deliberation…"

He paused to keep the audience in suspense. I wondered if Piers had told him how to announce the winner. Chances are, though, he just knew. If anyone was born to perform, it was my dad.

"The winner is…"

I looked over at Rachel, who was staring down at the ground.

"Rachel Ritter, singing *Ain't Misbehavin'*?"

Her face snapped up, and I could see her bottom lip twitching. She didn't look happy at all, or excited. Just in shock. She stepped forward, and my dad shook her hand.

"Rachel, you'll win a certificate for two to dine here at the exquisite, famous Sardi's," Piers said.

She took the envelope from him and shook his hand too, then stood there awkwardly. All of the grace and beauty that she had projected when she was singing had disappeared. If I didn't know any better, I would have thought she had lost.

"And you'll also win immunity for the next challenge."

Rachel was staring at her shoes. I could tell Piers had no idea what to do. He must have thought that she would be happy at winning, and her reaction was totally unexpected. I saw a tear drip from her face to the floor.

"Congratulations, Rachel!"

She lifted her head up, her mascara running down to her cheek. It took all my willpower not to cross over the stage and take her in my arms right now. That asshole had no right to make her so miserable.

"She's so happy she's crying!" Piers said. "Congratulations!"

"Th-thank you," she said.

Rachel wiped the tears off of her cheeks and smiled through the hurt. I ached for her. This should have been her moment to shine, and it had been ruined.

"And now, the bad news. Two singers will be kicked out of our penthouse apartment. Who are they, Skull?"

My dad took the mike.

"The bottom two performers were... Kayden Radley and Taylor Oliver."

Rachel's head snapped up, her face looking even more stricken. The two girls who had lost were already crying, hugging the other contestants, and saying goodbye. The cameramen shoved their way in through the crowd to get close ups.

"We'll see you ladies back at the apartment!" Piers said. The girls shuffled off stage as he herded them out like sheep through the door. I saw Rachel's dress flashing gold, and then she was gone with the others.

"Okay," Piers said, all business. "I'll do the one-on-one interviews right now with the two losers, and we'll get Rachel back at the apartment. What is *up* with that girl? She looked like someone had just run over her cat!"

"Her fiancé broke up with her," I snapped.

"Are you serious? Tonight?"

I nodded.

"Did the cameramen get it on tape?"

"Piers—"

"Alright, alright. That would have been great TV, though, right? I'll make sure to ask her about it in the interview."

"Don't do that."

"Clint, I don't know if you were paying attention, but this contest was a wreck. How many minutes of bloody *Frankie and Johnny* can we use for this episode? We'll need lots of filler, and that means drama."

"I don't think—"

"That's right, Clint. Don't think. Leave the TV to me. And what in the bloody hell happened to your suit? Tell me that's cocktail sauce on your lapel. Who gets into a fist fight at fucking Sardi's? You bloody Americans."

I bit my tongue. Adrenaline was still flowing through me from the fight.

"I'll get cleaned up," I said.

157

"Do that. Meet you in a half hour or so," Piers said. He went out to talk to the two girls who had lost, and the camera crew followed him.

My dad was standing in the doorway when I finished packing up.

"Thanks for judging tonight," I said. I hadn't been able to find anybody else on such short notice, and Piers had insisted my dad would be the best "industry guest" to come judge the competition.

"Sure thing. You got an interesting set of candidates."

"Yeah."

"That girl, Rachel—"

"She's a good singer, huh?" I raised my eyebrows, wanting to see his reaction. But what he said shocked me.

"You make sure she doesn't win."

I was struck dumb for a second.

"She doesn't win? You said she was the best singer tonight!"

"She sings fine. But she won't be a star. Not in our studio."

"What? Why not?"

"She's not the right fit."

Confusion and anger swirled in my mind. And the adrenaline that had been winding down suddenly reared its head back up.

"How can you say that?"

"You saw her after she won. There was nothing there. No presence. She doesn't look like a star."

"But Pops, she had just—"

"No excuses." He punched a finger into my chest. "You're a star or you ain't. And she ain't. Keep her around for another few days. Fuck her if you need to get your dick wet. But she will. Not. Win."

His face went dark and ugly, and for a moment I saw him as others must have seen him—nothing more than a brute force that always managed to get his way.

"This isn't your contest, Pops," I said as he turned

away.

"It's my studio," he called back over his shoulder. "Don't forget that, kid."

CHAPTER TWENTY-TWO
Rachel

I'd won the first contest. My head spun with the news. Even that guy, Clint's dad, he'd chosen me as the winner! I wanted to celebrate, but then the other part of the night came rushing into my head, and any thought of celebration turned to tears.

Derrick had left me.

After four years of being engaged, he had just trashed me. I couldn't believe that he was so cold about it. And to top it off, *he* was the one who had insulted *me*! I should have been the one to break up with him!

But I couldn't cry. The cameramen were in the back of the limo with us, and I wasn't going to air my personal life on TV. No, I stared down into my lap, my fingers stroking the gold fabric of my dress. I wasn't going to cry. I wasn't going to cry.

"I can't believe you did that."

I looked up, tears stinging behind my eyes, to see Sophia staring at me. The other girls in the limo carefully avoided my gaze.

"Did what?"

"Threw Taylor under the bus like that."

I had no idea what she was talking about.

"I didn't—what did I do to Taylor?"

"Well, it was your suggestion for the song she sang," Sophia said. She clicked her fingernails on the window idly. "Are you trying to tell me you didn't sabotage her?"

"Of course I didn't sabotage her! It was a good song for her to sing!" I cried.

"Obviously not, if the judges voted her out."

"It was perfect for her range," I insisted.

"Yeah? Then why did she get kicked out of the competition for it?"

"I—I don't know! I thought she did fine! I don't think she should have been kicked out."

"So you think the judge was wrong?" one of the other girls chimed in. I couldn't remember if she was one of the Jens or one of the Jessicas.

"No. I mean, yes. I liked how she sang," I said helplessly. "I wish she hadn't lost."

"So which one of us do you think should have lost instead?" Sophia asked.

I looked around. Every set of eyes seemed to sear into my face with hatred. And the camera was pointed straight at me.

"N-nobody. I didn't mean that."

"So you were lying?"

"No!"

"Which one of us would you have kicked out instead?"

"I don't know," I said miserably, looking down at my lap.

"Do you think you should have lost instead?" Jen or Jessica asked.

"No!"

The limo pulled to a stop in front of the studio building, and I reached for the door, relieved to be able to escape. Tears were burning my eyes, and I was struggling to keep from bursting out into a sobbing jag.

Sophia got the door first.

"You're the most stuck up bitch here," she sneered. "And nobody here is going to listen to you, or let you throw them under the bus like you did to Taylor."

"I didn't—I didn't—"

"You think you're all that, but you're nothing. You're never going to win."

If it had been any other day, I could have come up with a better response to her insults. But my brain was whirling desperately, and I only wanted to get me away.

"Leave me alone, okay! Just leave me alone!"

I swatted her hand away from the car door and ripped it open, stumbling out onto the sidewalk. I heard the girls behind me murmuring to each other.

I almost wished that I hadn't won. I went into the studio, where there was another camera crew waiting. An attendant stood in front of the elevators and motioned me toward the studio instead.

"Drinks in the studio to celebrate," he said. "Clint Terrance will be here shortly, and—"

"I've had enough for tonight."

I shoved my way past the attendant and punched in the code for the elevator. He gaped at me, as though nobody had refused such an invitation before. But I was in no mood to party with a bunch of girls who hated my guts. As I rode up the elevator, the whole night came flooding back to me, and I burst into hard sobs.

"Stupid, stupid, stupid!" I cried, punching the wall of the elevator so hard that my fist was sore. How could I have let myself get sucked into a relationship with such a jerk? Derrick had never done anything like that to me before.

Looking back, though, I started thinking about all of the times he'd been dismissive with me. All the times he'd promised to call and never did, because he had too much to study. All the times he'd put me down, and I'd told myself he hadn't meant it.

He had meant it. He'd meant every word. And I had yelled at Lacey and Steph for telling me the truth about him. How blind could I have been? How stupid? I'd pushed away the only two real friends I had in New York City, and now I was alone. Completely alone.

I stumbled into the apartment crying, and went to the kitchen. I tore off a paper towel and blew my nose loudly into it, then burst into a fresh set of tears. I leaned forward on the kitchen counter. It was black granite, so sterile. My kitchen back home was all wood and wallpaper, familiar and cozy. There was nothing here that could comfort me. Everything was black and white and silver and empty, God, so empty! How could anyone live in a place like this?

I poured myself a glass of water with a trembling hand and forced myself to drink it in between sobs. I wiped my eyes, and the mascara smudged black on the back of my hand. God, I must look like a mess. If anyone saw me right now—

I looked up. There was a camera on the wall pointing straight into the kitchen. Then I remembered: there were cameras everywhere in here. I covered my face in my hands, still sobbing. I didn't want them to have my meltdown on tape. Where could I go that was safe?

I stumbled into the living room just as I heard the elevator ping behind me.

Oh, no. I couldn't face anyone right now, especially not Sophia and the cameraman in tow. I would rather throw myself out a window than have to deal with her again. I rushed out of the living room down into the hallway. My heels clicked on the black tile.

Get away. Get away. The thought echoed through my brain. I looked up to see a camera pointing down the hallway straight at me. I stifled a scream and threw my middle finger up at the camera, ducking my head. They couldn't very well put that on TV, could they? Even if they could, I didn't care anymore. I just wanted to get out of there.

I darted into the bedroom, but there was no lock on the door. Shit. I couldn't even hide out in here. I could hear the elevator doors opening.

I panicked. There was no way I could stay in here. I didn't want anyone to see me crying. I didn't want the cameras on me now. I just wanted to be alone!

Backing out into the hallway, the red door caught my eye. But no. It would set off an alarm.

"Where is she?" I heard someone saying.

There was nowhere else to go. I grabbed the door

handle, crinkling the paper, and pulled open the red door.

It was completely dark. The light from the hallway showed me a ladder with silver rungs just a few feet into the door. And just as Taylor had described, there was a hole in the floor—a shaft that could very well lead down twenty stories. I reached forward and gripped the ladder rung. I could hear people coming through the living room. I only had a few seconds to decide.

Well, even the possibility of plunging to my death seemed better than dealing with a bunch of mean girls.

I took a deep breath and pulled the door shut behind me. It was totally black, and for a moment I thought that I might already be falling down, I was so disoriented. My heel slipped on the ladder and I gasped, gripping my fingers tightly around the rung.

I found my footing again. Outside in the hallway, I could hear the bedroom door opening.

"Where'd she go?"

The voices were right on the other side of the door. I couldn't just stand here on the ladder. If they opened the door, they would find me right there, mascara-stained and clutching to a silver ladder in the darkness. And that would be even more stupid.

I started to climb.

Although I was scared at first, I kept pulling myself up, just like I was climbing up into the barn loft back home. As I moved slowly up the dark shaft, I could see something above me. There was a bit of light coming through the top of wherever the ladder was going. I didn't really care where that was. I just needed to get *away*.

The ladder ended at an opening. I scrambled through breathlessly, and stood up. What I saw in front of me made me shrink back so that I almost fell back into the shaft. I caught myself on the edge, and pressed against the wall with my hand to steady my feet.

I was looking down onto New York City. But it wasn't an opening like I'd thought at first. What was in front of me was a huge glass globe, like a fishbowl hanging out over the street.

I leaned forward, not wanting to fall either forward or back. I wasn't sure how thick the glass was, or if it would support my weight. Standing on this platform, with darkness behind me, I felt like I was teetering on the edge of a dangerous precipice.

The view from up here, though, was *beautiful*.

With the glass globe acting as a window, I could see out across all of Manhattan. All of my nervousness was replaced by a sense of utter awe. The lights sparkled from down on the street, red and orange and green. Cars crept through the city grid in lines of red and white light, and the people swarmed down the sidewalk like ants.

I crouched down and sat at the edge of the globe. Carefully, I unlaced my strappy heels and set them beside me. When I hung my feet over the edge, my toes could barely touch the glass bottom. It was slightly curved, and I let my feet slide across the cool glass. Between my legs, I could see a line of taxis stopping and going in front of the building. It was incredible.

Looking down onto the whole of New York City, I felt completely insignificant. Who was I to think about becoming a singer, when there were so many other people out there? So many people more talented than me, more beautiful than me.

The sorrow that I'd stamped down to the bottom of my heart came drifting back up. I was nobody. Derrick was right.

I was sinking down nicely into a bath of self-pity, when I was startled out of my wits.

"Enjoying the view?"

I shrieked at the voice coming from behind me. Instinct made me flinch forward into the glass bowl, and my feet slipped out from under me. I twisted around, catching myself on the edge of the platform. I clutched at the ledge desperately with both hands, and to my great relief the glass globe didn't break under my feet.

"Clint!" I gasped.

He climbed up into the gap, his white grin gleaming from out of the darkness. I would have clambered back up, but he was taking up all the space at the edge of the platform. I let a little more weight rest on my feet. The glass held up.

"Hey there," Clint said. He knelt down and put his face close to mine. "You weren't supposed to come up here."

"It said emergency exit," I said, still hanging off of the edge of the platform. "I thought that with my fiancé dumping me and a camera crew chasing me around… that qualified as an emergency."

"You know, if someone had a good pair of binoculars down on the sidewalk, they could look up your skirt," he said, peering over my shoulder down to the street.

"Really?" I huffed. "Now I know why it took you so long to find me. You were down there spying up on me."

"I would never do that."

"No?"

"I much prefer a closer view."

He kicked off his shoes and took off his socks. Before I could say another word, he jumped over my head and landed in the middle of the glass globe with a dull thud. I shrieked.

"What are you doing?!?"

"Nothing. Enjoying the view." He grinned at me. "Isn't that what you were doing?"

"Won't this—isn't this glass going to break with all this weight on it?"

"It's not glass," he said, coming forward to me. "It's double thickness pyrex. Bulletproof."

"Pyrex?"

"It's like… half-glass, half-plastic."

"Plastic?""

"Very sturdy plastic."

"That's… that's nice." My heart was still pounding.

"Come on."

He pried my hands off of the ledge. I yelped as I slid down the soft curve of glass-or pyrex, I guess—trying not to fall over. I could swear I heard the globe creak under our feet, but he didn't seem worried at all.

"Clint—"

"Shhh," he said. "You're fine."

That wasn't why I had protested, but now that I was standing in the middle of what seemed like thin air, I wasn't going to argue with him. For all I knew, he was a suicidal maniac who wanted to go out with a bang.

"Look," he said. He put his hands on my hips and guided me forward to the far side of the globe. The glass curved up in front of me, and it felt like I was stepping forward into the void. Below my feet, the lights of New York glittered and gleamed.

Even though the view was incredible, my attention was drawn elsewhere—to the twin spots on each side of my hips, where his hands were touching me. His touch turned into a caress, sending all kinds of warning signals racing through my body.

I was frozen, frozen still as his hands caressed my hips under the dress. Not because I was aghast at the way he touched me with such impunity—I was, of course—but I was frozen because of the sudden realization that love was a sensation.

I could feel love as his hands clasped my waist. His fingertips murmured love, love as they drew along the backs of my arms and down to the place on my wrists where my heartbeat was throbbing hard. It was all in my mind, I knew it, but that was what I felt as he touched me, and I couldn't shake the feeling.

"Don't," I said weakly.

"Lean forward."

I leaned forward and put my hands against the glass to brace myself. It was like I was flying above the city. Clint's hands held me firmly, and I wasn't scared anymore of falling. I was scared of something else.

I was scared of losing my heart twice in one night.

We stayed like that for a while. I don't know how long. A minute, maybe more. Clint's chest rose and fell against my back, and his fingers held me in his grasp. When he pulled me back up, I felt like I had been holding my breath underwater for a lifetime.

"Rachel."

"Please don't." I didn't know what he was going to say, but I knew I couldn't handle the emotions inside me right at that moment.

"I gotta say this."

"Clint, please—"

"That guy doesn't deserve you. He never deserved you."

I took a deep breath, trying to calm myself.

"Maybe. He's right, though."

"What? What is he right about?"

I blinked back tears. There was such kindness in his voice. Kindness, and anger. I was angry at Derrick, too, but he sounded like he was on the verge of fury. I shook my head.

"I'm not ready for this," I said, swallowing the lump in my throat. "I'm—I'm never going to be a singer."

"How can you say that?"

"It's true."

"You're wrong." He said it so firmly that for a moment, I almost believed him. "You just won the first challenge. And what do you mean, you're never going to be a singer? You already are a singer!"

I couldn't argue with him right then. The doubt had already torn through me, had already worn me down. I wasn't able to do what these other girls were doing. I wasn't going to win. It didn't matter how much I tried. I was too far behind, and I was never going to catch up. I realized that I hadn't been talking, just shaking my head softly.

"Rachel. Look at me. Look at me."

I could feel my bottom lip trembling as I looked up. Clint's face was dark with anger, but his voice almost broke my heart with how compassionate he sounded.

"Don't ever say that again. You're one of the best singers I've ever heard. And I have no reason to lie to you about that."

I couldn't answer him. I didn't know what I could say without breaking down into tears.

"The glass is too cold for bare feet," he said. "It's freezing. We should get you up off of this."

Something inside of my tore just then. It was how he spoke, how he treated me like a child—not in a condescending way, but in a caring way. He knew that I needed it. And I hadn't been a child for a long, long time.

Derrick had expected me to love him because he promised to take care of me. Clint's touch said something entirely different: he loved me, and so he wanted to take care of me. There were no strings attached to his gifts.

As he pulled me back up onto the platform, he drew me into his arms. All of my resistance had crumbled. I was lonely, scared and needing comfort. I was lost, and he had found me.

At the same time, I felt like we were on the verge of something dangerous for both of us, something more fragile than even a floor made out of glass. And if I touched it, it could shatter.

"Clint—"

I didn't know what I was going to say, and it didn't matter. I wavered, but the floodgates had already cracked open, and a rush of desire swept through my body.

He kissed me, and I let him.

CHAPTER TWENTY-THREE
Clint

I could feel her arching into me, and my whole body hardened at her touch. I gripped her hips, pulling her deeper into the kiss. If this was going to be my one chance to kiss her, I was going to make the most of it.

"Clint—"

Her voice was delicious, but I didn't want to let her talk me out of anything. I needed this.

I forced my leg between her two thighs, making her put her weight down on a place I knew would drive her crazy. Her bare feet slid up against my skin, under my pant leg. I could feel her tiny toes exploring my ankles, sliding across my feet. It was like she wanted every part of her body up against mine, and I wasn't complaining.

I needed this as much as she did.

My lips tore the breath away from her mouth, and I kissed her with a hunger I didn't know I had inside of me. Her body was exquisite, all soft curves and luscious skin. Every moment that passed made me ache for more.

I pushed her against the wall, holding her so that she wouldn't slide away. She moaned, a deep throaty moan that made my cock jump against her thigh.

"Christ, Rachel," I whispered.

My hands cupped her thick ass, her curves filling my hands, overflowing my fingers. I gripped her hard, kneading her muscles. She moaned again, her lips parting slightly.

I took the opportunity to kiss her harder. I was drinking her in, her soft lips submitting to mine. When I finally pulled back, she gulped for air, her hand fluttering to her chest.

"I've wanted to do that to you from the moment I met you," I said. "Every time I saw you speak, bite that pretty plump lip of yours. Every time you opened your mouth to sing. I've wanted to eat you alive from the beginning."

Her bottom lip trembled, and she looked up at me from under mascara-stained eyelids. She was a tragic Greek heroine. She belonged on stage. Every part of her was perfect, worthy of admiration. She looked like a goddess.

Then the light dimmed in her eyes. She refocused, her gaze drifting down to my collar. There was still blood there, I knew. I hadn't had time to change before she'd set off the alarm and I'd found her on the security cameras, exploring this part of my apartment. She swallowed and pushed me away slightly. Despite the ache in my groin, I didn't press her as she eased back from my body.

"Clint—"

I reached out to touch her cheek, to turn her face back to me. She caught my hand with hers.

"Please don't. We have to stop."

"Stop? I haven't even started yet."

She was already shaking her head.

"We can't do this. We shouldn't be doing this."

"Why not?"

She tilted her head at me with such sass that I almost laughed. If she wasn't rejecting me, I would have laughed.

"You know why not."

"I'm a perfect guy for a rebound fling. Everybody says so."

It was a joke I'd used before, but this time saying it sent a shock of pain through my system. I didn't just want to be Rachel's rebound fling. I wanted something more.

"I'm a contestant in your studio. We can't—even if I'm single. It's not right. It's not fair."

I laughed, then stopped once she looked up at me with hurt in her eyes.

"Sorry, Rachel. It's just—the whole music industry isn't fair. Every studio is rotten from the inside out. With bribery, with sexual favors…"

"With nepotism?"

She meant my dad.

"Yeah, that too. You know how many singers get a contract deal based solely on merit? It's as rare as a platinum record."

Her lips pressed together firmly. I went to kiss them again, but she put a finger to my lips. I kissed her finger instead. That only got a hint of a smile from her.

"I'm not one of those people," she said. "I'm not going to give you—give you sexual favors for a singing contract—"

"But you're already the most talented contestant here," I protested.

"Clint, come on—"

"By a huge margin!"

"And you're not just saying that so you can kiss me again?"

"No! I mean, yes, I want to kiss you again. But no, that's not why I'm saying it. I'm saying it because you're incredibly talented. Rachel, I feel like I met you at exactly the wrong time. This competition—this isn't the way to do things."

"Then why did you do it?"

That froze me up for a moment. I'd forgotten how I'd landed in the middle of this mess.

"Uh, can I blame Piers?"

She laughed a little.

"It sounded like a good idea at the time. Really, it did. My dad was pushing me to get a new star for the studio, so that I could quit the music stuff—"

"You mean, quit your band?"

Rachel's eyebrows furrowed together, like dark gold bands in a Celtic knot.

"Well, yeah. To take over the studio. I wouldn't have time to be in *Talismen.*"

"Do you want to quit doing music?"

173

I opened my mouth to answer her, then realized I had no answer. To be honest, I hadn't really thought about it much. My dad had always expected me to take over the studios, and I had followed along. My whole life had been centered around doing what he thought was best. Now, though, I had to stop and think if that was what I wanted.

Of course I wanted it, though. Didn't I?

"Well, I mean… I wouldn't stop playing for good," I said, hedging.

"But you wouldn't have time to do music if you were heading up the whole business."

"I don't know… look, I haven't really thought about it that much."

Rachel crossed her arms in front of her.

"It seems to me like you ought to think about it. Because if you don't like doing this just to pick one singer, what makes you think you're going to like running the whole studio?"

"I—I don't know. Hey, you realize that if you talk me out of this, you're talking yourself out of a singing contract too, right?"

"I guess I'm not as selfish as you."

"I never thought you were."

That got a smile out of her. She dropped her arms, and I went to kiss her. She blocked me with one hand on my chest.

"But for now," she said teasingly, "I'm still a contestant on your show. You have to play fair."

"I never play fair."

She didn't know what to say to that. I thought it was the right time to change the subject, to convince her that the contest didn't matter. After all, she was already up here. I might as well show her the cool stuff.

"You know, I don't normally come out here to stand on the globe."

"No?"

"That's not the best way to see out from up here."

"It isn't?"

"Plus you get footprints on the glass. It's better when you're floating."

"How could you—"

I reached above her head and pressed a button. The control screen flickered on and I keyed in the passcode. Above us in the darkness, the metal gears started whirling. Rachel's eyes widened, and I grinned.

"Let me show you something."

CHAPTER TWENTY-FOUR
Rachel

My whole body was shivering, but not from the cold. As much as I hesitated, as much as I pushed Clint away, his kiss had turned me inside out. I couldn't help but want him to take me in his arms again, and I knew I didn't have much resistance left.

There was no fairness to it, but my mind kept comparing Clint to Derrick. Derrick had never given me more than a perfunctory kiss on the lips, or a chaste peck on the cheek. He'd never touched my body like Clint had, like he wanted to caress every inch of my flesh. I had been his girlfriend for years, but I'd never known what desire truly felt like.

And now, it was tearing me apart.

Clint Terrance, of all guys. The guy who held my future in his hand and treated it like it was no big deal. This asshole, who acted like he already possessed me body and soul. How could I be so attracted to the one guy who was so bad for me?

My eyes drifted up his arm as he touched the screen on the wall. I wanted his fingertips to touch me like that, pressing me in the spot where I ached. I wanted his lips to move all over my skin. I wanted him to kiss me again like he'd kissed me minutes ago. I was trembling for it, my tendons vibrating with desire.

His muscles flexed under his shirt as he brought his arm down. He smiled, a broad smile that knew what real pleasure was.

I was startled when a mechanism dropped down from the darkness above us. It was a long metal beam that clicked down until it was just over our heads. Then the beam extended out like a ladder, out into the glass globe we had just been in.

Clint reached up and opened up a latch on the side of the beam. He winked at me as he tugged out—

"A sash?"

It was a long red sash, and as I watched, he pulled it out until it was long enough to pool at our feet. Then he clipped it back up around to the other side of the beam, so that it formed a loop of fabric.

"Voila!" he said. "A swing."

I laughed. It did look like a swing. I grabbed ahold of one side of the sash and tugged. The fabric held tight, fastened up in the top of the beam.

"Here, let me help you up."

I moved to the middle of the platform, careful not to knock Clint back off into the dark shaft behind us. He reached through and put his hands on my waist, just like he'd done before. Again, my body sent shocks of desire through my nerves. My face went hot, and I was glad he was behind me so that he couldn't see the blush spreading up my collarbone.

"Grab onto the sides," he said. I reached up and gripped the sash, as high as I could.

"Okay, now on the count of three," he said. "One. Two. Three—"

I jumped a little bit, and he lifted me up easily, settling me into the middle of the fabric swing. I kicked my bare feet and laughed.

"Ready?" he asked.

"Ready for what?"

"For this!"

He pushed me, and I gasped as the whole swing went rushing out into the glass globe. It was like a zipline, and the swing ran out ten feet before it caught at the end of the beam. I screamed as I swung out even further into the open air inside the globe, and then I reached the top of the arc and swung back, clutching the sash for dear life.

My scream turned into nervous laughter as the swing settled down. I twisted my head around to see all of Manhattan. Now, suspended in the air in the middle of the globe, I could barely notice the curvature of the glass. It was like I was floating in midair.

It was almost scarier than standing on the bottom of the globe—here, it looked like there was nothing to support me but the red sash under my butt.

"Oh my God, Clint! You could have warned me!"

"Where would have been the fun in that?"

I heard the same sliding metallic sound, and turned just in time to see Clint zipping down the beam, holding onto a handful of red sashes. Rather than tying them up into a swing, he was hanging on with just his arms. He was heading straight towards me, and I shrieked. But he leaned to one side, and when he reached the end of the beam, he swung out harmlessly past my side. He grinned as he arced forward, almost touching the glass before swinging back.

"You look like like Tarzan," I said. "If Tarzan was a billionaire rock star."

"AWWWWOHooooOOHHHHH!" he shouted, in a fair imitation of a Tarzan yell. The sound echoed loudly off of the glass walls of the globe.

He stopped himself from swinging back by grabbing one side of my swing. I gasped as I swung around in a circle. I looked up. Apparently the mechanism was more complex than I'd thought. I could turn in any direction, it seemed.

"What is this?" I asked, peering up at the beam which was holding the sashes up.

"It's my playground. And workout space."

"You work out here?"

In response, Clint grabbed a hold of two sashes and held himself upright, arms outstretched, right in front of me. Every muscle in his arms was flexed. His chest looked like it was about to pop out of his buttoned shirt.

I burst out laughing.

"What is this, Cirque du Soleil?"

"Maybe. Maybe I just like to pretend to be Spiderman."

He swung his legs up over his head, twisting the sash easily around his leg, and ended up upside down, his face inches from mine. It was strange, to see him so agile. On the ground, he looked like a linebacker. Like—

Like a bouncer. Here, though, he had the grace of an acrobat.

"Upside-down kiss," he said.

"Is that an order?"

"What, are you going to disobey Spiderman?"

I giggled, but when he reached out and pulled me close, I didn't protest.

His upside-down kiss was soft, probing. My nose bumped against his stubbled chin and I smiled into the kiss. In the warmth of his lips, the press of his hand on the back of my head, I forgot where I was. I forgot everything except the sweet, perfect sensation of desiring and being desired.

I could have stayed like that forever, but Clint pulled away suddenly. I let out a soft noise, somewhere between a whimper and a yelp.

"How was that, Mary Jane?"

"Perfect, Spiderman."

He swung back around so that he was right-side up.

"Are you ready for more?"

"More?"

I thought he meant another kiss, and I leaned forward, but he only grinned and put an arm around me. Before I knew what was going on, his fingers had lifted up my dress to my waist and he had resettled me on the edge of the sash swing.

"What—what are you doing?"

"You know what I'm doing."

My heart began to thump harder. I was a virgin. There was no way I was going to have sex on a swing hanging over the streets of Manhattan. I wouldn't know what I was doing in a normal bed, for God's sake! This—this was insane.

I started to protest, but my words disappeared into another kiss. Before, his kiss had been soft and sweet. Now, though, he was hard, insistent. His tongue forced its way past my lips, sending hot streaks of desire through my body. I felt myself go wet as he leaned into me, taking my breath along with it.

"Clint—wait—"

"Tonight is your night, Rachel," he said, his mouth against my ear. "You deserve everything."

"I don't—I don't—"

"Hush. No more talking, unless it's screaming my name."

I quivered as his hands moved over me, cupping my breasts. He kissed my neck, his tongue tracing small spiraling circles down to my collarbone. Every particle inside of me strained with desire. I moaned as his mouth opened over my skin, his teeth lightly biting my shoulder.

"Clint—"

"Much better." I could feel him smiling against my skin. Then he loosened his grip on the sash and slid down. I didn't know what he was doing until his arm was pushing my legs apart. My dress was bunched up at my waist, and he lowered his head to my panties.

"Oh, God—"

"You can call me that if you want to," Clint said, winking. "But we haven't even started yet."

I couldn't speak. His head was between my thighs, his breath already hot against my sensitive skin. My blood pounded in my ears, drowning out all other sound. His fingers brushed against the front of my panties, sending lightning bolts of electric pleasure through my nerves. I arched back, my hands clutching the sash on both sides of me.

"Hold on tight," he said, and then his fingers pulled down my panties and his tongue was inside of me.

Oh, my God.

I had never known that I could feel something like this. His tongue was alternately hard and soft, thrusting into me where I was already dripping wet and aching for it. His thumb stroked me around the outside, spreading my juices.

Even in my wildest dreams, I hadn't imagined that I could feel this *good.* I'd touched myself, but I hadn't known how to do it. And now Clint was stroking me, sending my body into shocks of pure ecstasy, like he had known my body for years. I closed my eyes, leaning back and letting the sensations overtake me.

"You have the most gorgeous pussy," he whispered. His breath was hot against my throbbing skin. "Such a beautiful tight pussy. I can't wait to fuck you."

I couldn't respond with anything but a moan. I knew even then that I needed more, I wanted more. I wanted him to fuck me, yes, even though I had heard that it would hurt and I was scared, the fear was nothing compared to this. The ache inside of me was unbearable.

His thumb was brushing the front of me, slow wet strokes of his thumbpad against me that made me arch into his touch.

Had it been cold out here? Right now, I was burning up inside, burning with hot desire that kept building and building with every slow stroke of his thumb. His tongue slid over me outside, pressing down, then letting go.

The swing I was sitting on began to rock. He used the momentum, following the slow rhythm and letting his tongue slip in, then out. In, then out, and all the while his thumb touching me where I needed it, pressing hard but not quite hard enough. It was torture, wonderful torture. I wanted it to last forever, and I wanted to fall over the edge now. I had never needed to climax so desperately.

Rocking back and forth, back and forth. I fell into the rhythm, my hips starting to push in when he met me with his mouth.

His arm gripped me tightly, a good thing—as the

pressure inside me built and built, I thought that I might slip off the swing completely. In the air like this, I was lost in the feeling that I was flying. We were both flying, flying too high, and the need in my body was too much for me to take. Like Icarus, I would burn up in this fire and fall to the ground.

"Please—" I breathed.

"You want to come?"

"*Mmmm!*"

The stroke, the slow, awful, beautiful stroke of his thumb.

"You have to tell me if you want to come."

I whimpered as he eased up the pressure. He looked up at me, tossing his dark hair back. His lips glistened with my wetness. I thought I should be embarrassed, but it only made me want to kiss him, to pull him back in, to let him take me in whatever way he wanted.

"Do you want to come?"

"Yes—" I breathed. "Please, oh God, *please*—"

The smile he gave me made me gasp, but then he plunged his head back between my thighs and the air in the globe was gone, all of it gone. His mouth was on me, sucking hard, his tongue thrusting deep, and I screamed as the suction increased, my body rocking hard into his mouth.

"*Oh God, my God,*" I screamed hoarsely. I was there, I was right there—

"*Ohhhhh,*" he moaned, and the low vibration of his lips sent me over the edge. I shattered, my body rippling with the orgasm. His arm held me tight as I bucked against his lips, his mouth pressing hard, never once letting go.

"Yes! *YES!*"

The spasms of my orgasm kept going and going as his tongue swirled around my most sensitive part. Jagged breaths of air ripped through my throat as I came and came.

"*Ohhhhhh!*"

Small strokes. His mouth lifting from between my legs. His breath, warm against my wet skin.

"We're going to have to get you new panties," he said, grinning.

"Oh my god," I gasped. "Oh. My. God. Oh my—"

"I take it that was a good one."

"I can't—I can't—" I slumped against the side of the sash, my eyes fluttering shut.

"That was just a start," he said. His hand moved down over my slick skin. His fingers slid into me slowly. "Now that you're relaxed, we can—"

He stopped talking suddenly. I could feel his fingers probing, and I moaned, rocking my hips forward onto his hand.

"Mmmmm, yeah—"

"Rachel?"

His fingers withdrew, and I smiled down at him from under heavy eyelids. I was in a happy daze.

"Mmmhmm?"

"Rachel look at me."

His expression was hard, almost scary. All of the good feelings running through me froze, and my muscles tensed back up. I didn't know what was wrong, but I knew something was wrong. When he spoke, though, with anger in his voice, my blood turned to ice.

"Rachel, are you a *virgin*?"

CHAPTER TWENTY-FIVE
Clint

I'd made a huge mistake.

This wasn't how it was supposed to be. I was supposed to fuck her once, fuck her hard, get her out of my system. That was how it was going to work. She would get over her asshole fiancé, and I would get over this stupid crush that I had.

But this changed everything.

"You're a virgin?" I repeated. She hadn't answered me the first time.

"Y-yes."

I almost slipped out of the sash. Trying to hide my disbelief, I blinked hard and then climbed back up. Reaching up, I pulled the swing back in, sliding us both back to the platform. She stayed sitting in the swing as I dropped to my feet.

"Let me help you out of there," I said. I lifted her down to the platform. She didn't say anything as I brusquely pulled up her soaking wet panties and smoothed down her dress. The gold gown stuck in spots where her skin was still hot and damp with sweat.

I tapped the button to retract the sliding rod. It clicked back slowly, the sashes rolling back up into the rod as it went.

God, how could I have been so stupid?

"Clint?"

I turned to see Rachel biting her lip, a nervous look on her face. Christ, my cock was so hard, and watching her bite her lip like that made a thousand images flicker through my brain. Her perfect pouty lips sucking me off, my hands tugging on her red-gold hair—

"Yeah?" I said, desire making my voice hoarse.

"What just happened?"

"Right now, you mean? I gave you an orgasm."

She looked even more confused.

"But you—you stopped—"

My whole body was fighting with my mind. I wanted her. Christ, I wanted to slam her up against the wall and fuck her hard. But my stupid fucking brain wouldn't let me. It told me that I would be ruining something forever.

I didn't know why she let me get this far. Whatever she thought I was, I wasn't that guy.

"Rachel, I can't take your virginity. You're not—you're not that kind of girl."

"What kind of girl?"

"The kind of girl that I would fuck."

"I'm not good enough for you?"

Her eyes brimmed with tears. Oh, God, I didn't want this. I'd seen her crying already too much this evening. I thought that I would make things better, but I had gone and fucked things up even worse for her.

"That's not—Jesus, Rachel, that's not what I'm saying."

"Then what are you saying?"

Her voice trembled, and I could see her arms prickling with goosebumps. I took off my suit jacket and wrapped it around her.

"Look. I don't—I'm not the right guy for you."

"That isn't what you were saying a few minutes ago."

"Well, I realized something." *That I don't deserve you.* But I knew she would never believe that. I was a rock star, wasn't I? I was rich as a Texas oil investor. I was Clint motherfucking Terrance. Any girl in the world would be lucky to have me. Right?

She didn't realize that I was nothing but poison. I would take her and ruin her in the process. She was perfect, and I would tarnish that, permanently. But how could I convince her? I couldn't.

"What?"

"You were right," I said, coming up with the words as I spoke. I had to find an excuse for her. "About the competition. It wouldn't be fair."

Her shoulders dropped, and I wanted to take her in my arms. I wanted to feel her gorgeous body soft and pliant against mine.

No. That way was trouble. Big fucking trouble.

Because I knew that if I gave in now, if I let myself take what she was offering... I couldn't stop. There was something about her that I wanted to have for myself, forever.

Forever? Did I just think that?

Yeah, maybe. Maybe forever. At the very least, I wasn't going to be sated by one night of fooling around. When I kissed those lips, I realized that I wanted more from her than I'd ever wanted from a girl before. Not just a quick fuck. Not just a hot and heavy make-out session.

I wanted her to be *mine*.

And I couldn't have that. So I had to back out now. I wasn't going to start this, I wasn't going to take her virginity, when my desire was overflowing like this. Because she was right in a sense. If she was mine, the competition wouldn't be fair.

It wasn't fair anyway—she was such a fucking amazing singer—but it really wouldn't be fair if she was my girl. I wouldn't be able to fight for her to win if I knew that someone else could point at us and say that it was because I was fucking her. She deserved the contract. She deserved to win. And I wasn't going to get in the way of that.

"Okay," she said.

I realized that I'd been holding my breath for her response. I let it go, a long whoosh of air. It felt like I was letting go of the best thing that had ever happened to me. But I wasn't going to be selfish. Not tonight.

Not with her.

"You're right. I'm not good enough for you."

"Rachel, I'm not—"

She nodded.

"I'm a virgin. Fine. I don't know what the hell I'm doing. You probably think I'm a terrible kisser, even!"

"Rachel, no—"

"No, whatever. It's fine. I understand. And it's not fair. It's not fair for you to lead me on like this."

"I wasn't trying—"

"To mess with me? Sure, I'll believe that in a million years. I may be innocent, Clint, but I'm not naive."

She looked up at me, her eyes wet with angry tears, her hair mussed up, her lips red from where I'd kissed her hard. And it took all my strength not to kiss her again. I turned around before I could change my mind.

"We should get back to the apartment," I said.

CHAPTER TWENTY-SIX
Rachel

God, that asshole! I couldn't believe I'd fallen for another jerk. I rationalized it by telling myself that it was because of Derrick. I'd been in a vulnerable spot, and Clint had taken advantage of that. No way would I have fallen into his arms so easily.

I tossed and turned all night, playing and replaying the conversation between us. I couldn't stop thinking about how his tongue had sent me screaming into a climax that eclipsed anything I'd ever imagined. I didn't know feelings like that were possible. And then… then he'd pulled back completely.

What had I done wrong?

Nothing, I told myself. Take him at his word. It wouldn't be fair for the competition if you were sleeping together.

Then why had he come up to me? Why had he kissed me, touched me, made me orgasm? Why, if he was just going to leave me and say it was over. I tortured myself with thinking of other ways it could have turned out, but in the end there was nothing I could do.

The next day the camera crew arrived early in the morning, and I was so tired I could barely get out of bed. I dressed normally, a blue dress with cream stockings to keep warm. Practical and utterly unsexy, but I wasn't going to wear any of the dresses Clint had picked out for me.

Sophia was up an hour before I was, hogging the bathroom to put on a metric ton of makeup.

While she finished, I checked my messages. Ten more voicemails from Derrick. The first two were apologies for insulting me. He never apologized for slapping me on the voicemails, and I was beginning to think he didn't want any proof of that recorded anywhere. Then the next voicemail was angrier. Then even angrier. He was upset that I hadn't called him back. He was upset that I was acting irrationally. He was upset that I'd broken up with him.

"*You* broke up with *me*, moron," I mumbled, before erasing the rest of the messages. It was nerve-wracking to realize that I was never going to marry the man I'd always thought I would marry. But it was more nerve-wracking to think about ever seeing him again face-to-face. After what he'd done, I could never forgive him.

"Sophia!" I cried out, banging on the door a bit more aggressively than maybe I should have. "Will you hurry up!"

"Beauty takes time," she said, opening the bathroom door at last. She eyed me up and down. "So you'll only need what, five minutes?"

She sauntered past me as I bit my tongue and shoved myself into the bathroom to splash cold water on my face and brush out my hair. When we finally all got out to the room, I felt like the only frumpy one there. Everyone else looked like they'd gotten a *great* night's sleep.

"Good morning, ladies!"

Despite myself, my heart leapt at the sound of Clint's voice. He smiled at me warmly and patted me on the shoulder. I smiled back uncertainly.

"Sleep well last night?" he said.

I started to frown. He'd crawled down through some secret exit and left me to fend for myself in the apartment full of clawed tigresses. Taylor had been the only semi-nice girl in this competition, and she was gone. Now I was alone, defending myself against a wall of hostility.

But I wasn't going to give him the satisfaction of knowing that.

"Fine," I said brightly. "Just fine and dandy!"

"Are you okay?" he asked, his tone hushed. The camera

crew slipped behind him into the apartment.

"I'm great!" I said. "Now that I have immunity for this next challenge, I can't wait to show off what I can really do!"

"Rachel, why are you acting like this?"

"Me? Why are *you* acting like this?" I tittered and slapped him on the arm, only semi-playfully. "I just can't *wait* to see what the next contest is!"

"Did I hear someone ask about the next contest?"

It was Piers, the co-host. He came over and stood next to Clint. I stepped away as they addressed the room.

"Today's singing contest is going to be a little different," Piers said. "We won't be entertaining the high class of society like we did last night. Right, Clint?"

"Uh, right."

"In fact, we'll be entertaining the low class! In height, that is! Today you'll all be singing songs at a *children's* hospital!"

They went on and explained the finer points of the contest, but I was too busy seething at Clint to pay much attention. When they stopped rolling, all of the girls flocked around the hosts. I guess they were trying to ingratiate themselves before the competition. I sat back on the couch and waited for the stupidity to end.

Sophia was all over Clint. She leaned toward him, shaking her long hair behind her. He'd said that I wasn't the kind of girl he fucked. Well, Sophia sure looked like that kind of girl. Her boobs looked like they were about to pop out of the front of her too-tight dress.

Good luck to her. I hoped her boobs popped right out while she was singing a Disney song at the kids' hospital.

"Feeling a little green around the gills?"

I hadn't seen Piers coming up behind me. He jumped over the back of the couch and linked his hands loosely over his knees.

"Green?" I asked.

"Jealousy is a wild creature," the co-host said.

"I'm not jealous. Who would be jealous of someone who uses a vacuum sealer to get into her dress every morning?"

Piers laughed.

"Look," he said. "It's natural that the hosts get up close and personal with the contestants."

"Oh. So that—" I said, pointing to Sophia, who was stroking Clint's arm, "—that's a natural occurrence?"

"A couple of bachelors thrown into a studio full of hopeful young women? Of course." Piers leaned closer to me. "There are bound to be attractions."

"Obsessions?"

"Furtive glances."

"Footsie games under the table?"

"Secret trysts."

"What the hell is a secret tryst, anyway?" I asked grumpily, crossing my arms.

"It's where you try on a new lover. That's why it's a secret."

"Right."

Was that what Clint had tried to do with me? He said something I couldn't hear from across the room, and Sophia let out a peal of laughter that scattered in the air like pearls dropped onto the floor. I sighed. Piers gave me a meaningful look.

"I'm *not* jealous," I said.

"Of course you aren't. That's why you're staring at Clint like you want to shove his head through the wall."

"I couldn't do that even if I wanted to," I said.

"No?"

"No. His head is already stuck way, *way* too far up his ass."

Piers laughed loudly, loud enough to get the attention of the other side of the room. Clint looked over and frowned when he saw Piers putting his arm around my shoulder. I tensed up.

"What are you doing?" I asked the British host.

"You know exactly what I'm doing, love," Piers said. He ducked his head and gave me a quick kiss on the cheek. "We can't let you be the only jealous one around here."

"I'm not—"

"Time to get going!" Clint stood up in the middle of the room. His booming voice commanded everyone's attention. "Let's head out to the hospital!"

"See?" Piers said to me, winking. "Now let's go rock out with some toddlers!"

At the kids' hospital, I tried to stay away from Clint. But I couldn't ignore him when he came over to "introduce me" to the cutest little kid.

"And this is Rachel," he said, tugging a little girl by the hand. "Rachel was the winner of the first contest. Rachel, this is Charlotte."

"Like in *Charlotte's Web*!" I exclaimed, kneeling down in front of her. She nodded shyly. She couldn't have been much more than four or five years old.

"Have you read that book?"

She nodded again. I could tell she was too nervous to say anything.

"I live on a farm, you know," I said. "Just like in *Charlotte's Web*."

"You do?" she asked in a soft, curious voice.

"Yup. We have lots of cows, and some chickens, and cats too. What's your favorite animal?"

"Cats!" she said, her face lighting up. I could tell I was onto something.

"Do you have a cat?"

"Yeah!" She held up her hand with two fingers.

"Two cats? What are their names?"

She started talking rapidly about her cats, who were named —I think—Bo Peep and Sister Cat. One was orange and one was gray, and they were both princesses. The story devolved from there, something about a magic castle and them protecting a king who ended up being a stuffed alligator. After five minutes of breathless storytelling, she pointed across the room at another girl who had just walked into the playroom.

"—and that's my best friend!" she cried out, not stopping to pause between sentences. "Claire! Claire!"

She went racing over to the other side of the room, leaving me and Clint alone.

"Wow," I said, standing back up. "And here I thought I was her best friend."

"Don't feel bad," Clint said. "Girls are always so fickle."

"Is that how you feel about all girls?"

"Kinda. It's not the first time I've been left high and dry by a cute girl." He shrugged.

"If I remember correctly, you were the one leaving me high and dry. Last night." I stared at him pointedly.

"I think you're remembering incorrectly."

"Am I?"

"You weren't dry at all when I left you last night. You were very, very wet—"

"Inappropriate!" I said, holding up my hand to stop him from speaking. "Totally inappropriate. We're in a kids' hospital, Clint. Keep it G-rated."

"Right, right," Clint said. He pursed his lips, as though trying to figure out something to say that wasn't on the wrong side of pornographic.

"It's alright," I said. "You don't have to talk. Honestly, it's better if you don't."

"You don't like me talking?"

"You look so smart in a suit," I said. "It's terrible when you open your mouth and spoil the impression."

"Ouch. That hurts."

"It shouldn't. *Sticks and stones may break my bones, but words will never hurt me.*"

"*If you don't have anything nice to say, don't say anything at all,*" he quoted right back.

"Touché. In that case, I'm going to go over to the

other side of the room to make conversation."

"What, with Piers?"

I saw a flash of jealousy in his eyes. It shocked me that such a little thing would have gotten under his skin.

"Maybe," I said, enjoying the way he pretended to care. "He's definitely the brains of this operation, isn't he?"

"He only sounds smart because he has a British accent. He's actually dumber than I am once you get to know him."

"Dumber than you? I didn't think that was possible."

"Is that really all you're looking for in a man? Intelligent conversation?"

"Lame, right? I know." I rolled my eyes. "After all, how could a big brain be more attractive than a big di—"

"Inappropriate!" Clint shushed me with one finger. "Tsk. Tsk. Rachel, how could you?"

"That's what comes from hanging around with the wrong crowd," I said, and coughed. "Excuse me. I have to go drink something, or I'll be rasping out the worst rendition of the little mermaid theme song you've ever heard."

"Voice a little hoarse from last night?" he whispered. "Understandable. You *were* screaming pretty loudly when I licked that gorgeous pussy of yours."

I gaped at him, unable to come up with a proper response to something so incredibly... inappropriate!

"And when you came, you looked just. Like. That."

I snapped my mouth shut so fast my teeth clacked together. Before I could come up with a retort, Clint was already in the middle of the room, clapping his hands in the air.

"Alright, people, let's get started!"

CHAPTER TWENTY-SEVEN
Clint

Rachel sang beautifully to the crowd of kids, although I could definitely tell her voice was a little raspy. It gave her a sultry edge that wasn't really appropriate for Disney music, but I was glad to know that she had it in her. I only wished I'd made her come before the jazz contest.

"What do you think?" I asked Piers.

"About what?" He seemed utterly preoccupied with his phone while the singing was going on.

"About who should win this contest."

"Oh!" he said. "I set it up so that the kids would be voting."

"The kids?" I stared at him. "You're kidding me."

"Ha, that's a good one. Kid-ding."

"I'm serious! Piers, we can't let the kids decide a singing contest!"

"Why not?"

"Because they'll pick the girl who looks most like a princess. Or they'll just vote for their favorite song! Or—or—"

"Clint, calm down."

"My studio is on the line here, and you're telling me that you want a bunch of toddlers to decide my fate! How the hell am I supposed to calm down?"

A couple heads turned, and Piers shushed me.

"No obscenities here, please," he said. "There are kids around."

"This isn't—you can't—"

"Oh, shush. Your favorite girl has immunity, right? So who cares?"

"Rachel's not my favorite."

"Right. And I'm a bloody Yankee."

"She's not!"

Again, heads turned. I tried to breathe calmly.

"Clint, look. It doesn't matter one bit to me. Sounds like you've already chosen the winner."

"I didn't say that."

"But you meant it," he persisted.

"Piers—"

"And hey, that's great. She wouldn't be my pick, but then again, I'm in TV, not music."

"She's not—I haven't—"

"It's fine."

"It is?"

"Sure!" Piers shrugged nonchalantly. "This is more for show, anyway. We'll make it look like she's struggling, maybe have her lose a couple contests in a row, then edit it up so that she has a comeback by the end."

I frowned.

"You can do that?"

"We do it all the time. Seriously, Clint, you're too stressed on this. Whoever you want to win, we can fix it so that they win. Like today. So what if Rachel loses? She has immunity. And once she's the underdog, she'll have more people rooting for her. Got it?"

I didn't get it, but I nodded anyway. Piers obviously had this TV thing down to a science. He knew what he was doing.

Except Rachel didn't lose. She won. When the votes were tallied up, she had won by a long shot.

"Today's winner... Rachel Ritter!"

All of the other girls had sour looks on their faces.

"Clint, how much did she win as a cash prize?" Piers asked, passing the mike my way. I took it, then hesitated.

"Instead of a cash prize," I said, "the winner today gets three hours of recording time in Terrance Studios! You'll be able to keep a professional recording of your songs, and the record will be played on a city-wide broadcast!"

I didn't mention that the broadcast would be a late-night college radio show by a friend who owed me a favor. It sounded good. And like Piers said, it was TV. You didn't have to tell the whole truth.

"Congratulations!" I said. Rachel was beaming, and I took the opportunity to give her a big hug in the middle of the crowd of cheering kids.

"You and me in the studio," I whispered in her ear. "We'll record tonight."

"Tonight?"

She looked astonished. I wanted to drop down right there and bury myself between her thighs again. What was I thinking?

I knew what I was thinking. Piers was right. This wasn't a real contest. It didn't have to be fair. This was *my* show.

And I was going to take what I wanted.

By the time we left the hospital, it was already evening. The rest of the girls were heading out with Piers to a fancy dinner.

"Be careful," Piers whispered to me before getting in the limo.

"What's that supposed to mean?"

"You know. Use protection."

I scowled at him.

"What are you, my dad?"

"Give me a break. Your dad wouldn't give you a condom. He's give you a bag of coke to share with the passel of groupies in your tour bus."

"Shhh!" I looked back at Rachel, who was waiting on the sidewalk, checking her phone. She had an irritated look on her face.

"Oh, are you going to pretend like you're a gentleman with her?"

"I'm not going to pretend anything. We're going to record a song."

"Are you coming out for drinks later with the rest of

the girls? I invited your buddies Jake and Lucas along."

"No, thanks. I'll probably be tired."

"Tired?!"

"From recording."

"Oh, sure. Tiring stuff, listening to music and pressing buttons."

"Like you would know anything about music."

"Do you want my advice?"

"No."

"I'm going to tell you anyway. Do what you obviously want to do. Sleep with this bird."

"Chick," I corrected.

"Sleep with this chick. Then get your head out of the clouds and get your ass back to Reality."

"I'm not delusional, Piers."

"No, I mean *Reality*. The new club on Fourth Street. That's where we're going drinking."

"Oh."

He clapped me on the shoulder so hard I winced.

"Ta-ta, motherfucker." He ducked into the limo, and I heard a crowd of cheering high-pitched voices stream out of the open door. Then he closed it, winking at me.

First my dad, then Piers. It seemed like everyone wanted me to sleep with Rachel once and throw her away. And I would have done it, too. I'd done it to a million girls before her. Hot girls were disposable.

But when I turned to her and saw her face dropping, I knew that I couldn't treat her like cheap trash. There was something about her that made me hesitate. I wanted to reach out and touch her, but an instinct inside me told me that I wasn't going to be able to detach myself so easily.

I didn't want to get too attached. What if I already was?

"So, are we going to do this, or what?"

Rachel stood with her hands on her hips. She was dressed plainly, the girl next door. But I knew what she had hidden under that dress. I smiled at her, and her cheeks pinkened up like she could read my mind.

"Sure," I said. "Let's do this."

The studio was supposed to be empty—nobody had signed up to record tonight. When we got there, though, I heard a light snore coming from the back couch. I found my dad stretching out across the black leather.

"Wake up, Pops," I said. If it had been any other girl, I would have just draped a blanket over his head and let him sleep. But I wasn't sure what was going to happen between me and Rachel tonight. I hoped that it would be more than just a recording, and I wasn't exactly okay with having my dad in the room when that happened. Even if he was sleeping.

"Hey! Wake up!"

"Hrrrmmm," he mumbled in his sleep.

I leaned down closer and shook him by the shoulder. He smelled awful, like whiskey and sour sweat.

"Pops! Get up!"

He started up, almost knocking foreheads with me. I fell backwards on my ass trying to avoid him.

"What? What?" he asked, swiveling his head around quickly. His pupils were dilated and he rubbed his upper lip, sniffing hard.

Shit. He was on a binge. I noticed the traces of white powder that I had missed before, on top of a stack of sheet music. And there was a bag of it on the couch. It had fallen out of his pocket when he sat up.

"You gotta get outta here," I said. I took the bag of coke and stuffed it into his front suit pocket. "You gotta clear out. We're recording."

I waved at Rachel to get into the recording section of the studio, but my dad caught her eye as she came close.

"Who's this?" he asked, squinting.

I could see her eyes narrow as she looked at him.

"Rachel," she said.

"Rachel. What's she doing here?"

"She's recording, Pops."

"In my studio?"

He looked at me like I was nuts.

"Yeah," I said. "She won the contest today."

"Ha! What contest? The dick sucking contest?"

Rachel flinched back.

"It's alright," I told her. "Go ahead inside."

"What contest?" my dad insisted.

"The one at the hospital today. She sang—"

"I don't care what she sung. And I don't care whose dick she sucked to get another win."

Rachel looked horrified. I was torn between wanting to defend her and just wanting my dad gone.

"Pops, you're not serious. Come on."

"Not serious?" He sniffed again. "Oh, I'm serious. That immunity thing was a cheap trick. Keep her around longer. A few more sloppy ones, huh?" he slurred.

God, I had to get him out of there.

"Pops, you gotta go."

To my surprise, he stood up without any other resistance.

"Sure. Sure. I'll leave you be. Where's Sugar? Sugar!"

To my surprise, a pile of clothes on the armchair in the corner began to move. A redhead shook off the coats that had been on top of her. She looked younger than Rachel.

"What's up?" she said, coughing. "Are we doing another round?"

"Not here, Sugar. We gotta go. Little Jersey Girl here is *recording*." His words dripped sarcasm.

"Come on," I said lamely. They shuffled out the door, the redhead hanging off of my dad's shoulder. I locked the studio door behind them so that nobody would come in. I scanned the rest of the chairs, making sure there weren't any other groupies hiding out inside.

Rachel was standing inside next to the piano, facing away from the door. She sang an arpeggio of notes, from low to high and back down again, accompanying herself on the piano chord by rising chord. I paused by the door

202

to listen to her.

God, her voice was beautiful. Her range was a low contralto's, the bass tones purring along like the engine of a Porsche. Her tone was like pepper and honey, a beautiful whisper on top of the thick smooth notes. And her reaches for the high notes... they weren't bad. She needed to loosen up a bit in her chest, open up that range.

It was her shoulders. I could tell that she was kind of hunching over as she played the piano. Yeah, definitely. That was what it was.

I came up behind her and put my hands on both her shoulders to pull them back slightly. I thought I used a soft touch, but her fingers splayed a discordant chord on the piano as she spun around.

"What are you doing!?" she cried. I realized her eyes were rimmed red, the irises shining brighter than before.

I raised my hands up, as startled as she was.

"Hey! Sorry I startled you."

"That's not what I asked. What. Are. You. Doing."

"I was pulling your shoulders back," I said.

"Why?"

"Because your chest is closed up. You don't have any abdomen separation. It's making you strain for the high notes."

She stared at me, agog. There was a silence between us that stretched out and out until I couldn't even remember how many beats had passed.

"Are you okay?" I asked.

"Sure. I'm fine," she snapped. "I'm just great. How are you?"

Her eyebrows drew together, slanted red-gold like an angry autumn whirlwind on her forehead. Her eyes still glistened.

"Hey! What's the matter with you?"

"What's the matter with me? Are you serious?"

I held out my hands, unsure what she was talking about.

"You bring me here, and your dad insults me right to my face, and you don't even say a word about it."

"What?" Indigence rose in my throat. "I told him to stop."

"Oh, sure. *Hey, Pops, please could you not call Rachel a dicksucker? Only if you want to, though.* You're a real knight in shining armor, aren't you? You think you're a hero?"

"I threw him out, didn't I?"

"You told him to leave, sure. So I should thank you that you didn't let him stick around to call me a whore again?"

"What did you expect me to do?"

"I don't know. After what you did with Derrick I thought maybe you cared about me enough to stick up for me. But not when it's your dad throwing names at me, huh?"

I rubbed my eyes. This wasn't going how I thought it was going to go.

"I'm sorry," I said.

"Yeah. You are."

"Look. I'm not—he's a dick, okay? He's always a dick. That's just how he is."

"Charming."

"Hey! I'm telling you he's an asshole."

"The apple doesn't fall far from the tree."

"Oh, come on. What does that even—"

"You stood there and just let him slander me!" Her nostrils flared, and she looked so damn cute I wanted to kiss her. I think she would have done more than just slap me if I tried, though.

"I didn't—"

"You let him call me a whore!"

I took a deep breath in and out.

"Yes. Okay. I shouldn't have done that. But look. He wasn't sober, okay? He's coked up like crazy right now."

It took Rachel a few seconds to understand what I had said. The realization dawned like a blood-red sunrise in her eyes.

"He's on *drugs*?!"

"Well, sure. That's why—"

"And you just let him go wandering out into the street with some random girl? While he's on *cocaine*?!"

I was confused at her anger. She was acting like it was some horrible crime, but that was how it had always gone with me and my Pops. It was like Rachel was coming at this from another planet.

I'd fucked up. Now I needed to show her that I was on her side. I reached for her arm, but she jerked away from me.

"Don't touch me."

"Rachel, come on."

"No. Absolutely not."

"Okay, can we just record? I just want to record." Maybe once she was singing, I'd be able to get her back into the mood.

"No!"

"No?"

"You are going to go out and find your dad and make sure he's okay."

"He's fine. The recording—"

"We can record some other time. Or never, if you're expecting a sloppy whatever from me. I'm not that kind of girl."

Her cheeks were flushed with anger.

"I never said you were."

"Oh, no, that's right. Your dad did. You just stood there and let him." She gathered up her purse and slammed the piano lid shut. I barely made it out with my fingers intact.

"Rachel—"

"Go find your father."

She strode out of the studio, toward the elevator. I debated following her for only a second. There were cameras up in there. And as much as I wanted her, I knew

I needed to let her calm down before going after her again.

Great. I had a half dozen hot girls staying above my studio in my penthouse apartment, and I was sleeping alone tonight. But there was only one girl I wanted in my bed, and it was the one girl who didn't want me.

"Thanks a lot, Pops," I said to myself, and I slumped down on the leather couch.

CHAPTER TWENTY-EIGHT
Rachel

Clint picked me up and placed me on the sash swing, his hands cupping my ass slightly. He stroked the outside of my thighs, lowering himself between my knees. The coil inside me tightened, and I felt my thighs grow wetter and wetter as he leaned forward to lick me. I wasn't wearing any panties. I didn't know where they had gone. Had I left them in the studio?

He smiled sweetly up at me.

"I love you, Rachel," he said. Then he plunged his stiff fingers deep into me, and I started to moan—

"Ahhh!"

I jerked awake in my bed.

On the other side of the room, Sophia rolled over with a sleepy mumble. She was wearing earplugs and a sleep mask, and I hoped she hadn't heard the involuntary noise coming from my throat. I picked up my phone and checked the time.

Two in the morning.

I'd already woken up twice from these dreams. It seemed like I couldn't stop remembering the way Clint had touched me, the sensation of his lips on my most sensitive flesh. And whenever I started to moan his name, I woke myself up.

Because I couldn't want him. He was an insensitive asshole. He didn't care about me.

"And I don't care about him," I said to the ceiling. I repeated it over and over in my mind, until the sky started to turn light gray outside the window.

I was bleary and weak. I didn't want to eat any breakfast, especially not with Sophia making comments about how many eggs I was eating. Stupid. They were all stupid. I just had to ignore them and focus on my music.

Today, though, Piers came in and announced that we were taking a break from competitions. Clint said that he had some important studio work to do, so we were all going to be treated to a spa day.

All of the other girls yelped with excitement. I was frustrated. I'd wanted to work on my singing. But I supposed I was overly stressed out. Maybe a spa day was what I needed to relax and get me to sleep at night.

As we were getting into the limo, though, I got a call from an unknown number. My heart fluttered. What if something had happened to my mom? Or my dad? Was it a hospital calling? The police?

"Hello?"

"Hey, Rachel. Don't get in that limo."

"Clint?"

I turned back on the sidewalk, squinting into the studio window.

"Come on back inside."

"Why?"

"I'll tell you when you're in here."

I looked at the limo. Then back at the studio. Then back at the limo.

"Come on." His voice pleaded with me over the phone. "Are you gonna make me beg? I will. I'll get down on my knees and—"

"You don't have to do that," I said, hanging up.

I went to shut the limo door.

"Bye guys," I said. "Have fun."

"Awww, are you not coming with us?" Sophia asked, with an exaggerated pout.

"Yeah. I don't feel well."

"Do you think you might throw up?" Jen asked, leaning forward with a faux concerned expression on her face.

"I don't know," I said flatly.

"Because you should maybe think about it. You could

stand to lose a few pounds."

The rest of the girls erupted into peals of mean laughter.

"Well, I hope you can stand to lose this competition," I spat back. "Because that fake-ass vibrato you sing sounds like you're strangling a ferret with both hands."

I slammed the limo door shut with a huff. New York was turning me mean. This competition was turning me downright nasty. And now I had to deal with an arrogant rock star who couldn't take no for an answer.

I walked into the studio to see Clint with a huge shit-eating grin on his face.

"I have a surprise for you," he said.

"Let me guess: it's eight inches long and rhymes with *rock*?"

He raised his eyebrows in shock. I guess I was changing even more than I thought.

"You have a filthy mind, Rachel."

"Only around you," I muttered. He grinned.

"Not to mention, it's much more than—well, you'll see. Anyway, no. Not that. It's a surprise visitor for you."

I didn't know what I was expecting when he opened the recording room door. But I definitely didn't expect my twin sister.

"Rose?" My mouth fell open and stayed that way.

"Rachel!" Rose ran over from the doorway and wrapped her arms around me. Clint looked way too excited to watch us hug, but worry was already ballooning up in my chest. "Surprise!"

"What are you doing here?" I asked, detaching myself from the hug.

"What am I doing here? That's a nice way to greet your sister. I wanted to talk to you, okay?"

"You could have called me on the phone."

Rose looked sideways at me.

"I thought I'd come and see how you were doing in the competition," she said. Was she hiding something? It felt like there was something wrong with how she was looking at me. But right now I cared more about the fact that she had left the farm.

"What about mom? Who's taking care of her?"

"She's fine. There's a neighbor who's coming over to watch her—"

"Mrs. Patterson?" The worry blossomed into a full-on panic attack. I could feel the air closing in, like my throat muscles tightening before I'd stretched my vocal cords.

"Yeah, her."

"She's not—she doesn't know how to take care of mom," I blurted out. "She sleeps half the day, and she can barely remember to take her own medication, and—"

"Rachel, it's *fine*."

Rose patted my shoulder like I was a little kid throwing a tantrum. Normally I would have backed down, but not today. I slapped her hand off of me.

"Are you fucking kidding me? Don't tell me it's fine. You have no right to abandon her like that!"

Rose looked aghast. I'd never raised my voice to her before. But she had never messed up so badly before. I was totally livid, and I wasn't going to hide it. This was serious. But Rose didn't see it that way.

"I'm not abandoning her—"

"You left her there! With an eighty year old caretaker who can't take care of herself!"

"Look, it's just for a few days. I'll be back there Friday."

"No. No way." I shook my head. "I'll go back there if you're not going."

"Wait! You can't leave!" Clint interrupted.

"Who are you, my parole officer?"

"But what about the competition?" he asked. For the first time since I'd met him, I saw a look of real worry in his eyes. It should have given me some satisfaction to know he wanted me here, but at that moment, I couldn't care less.

"Screw the competition," I said, looking pointedly at Rose. "This is more important. Rose, I can't believe you would leave mom without asking me."

"Derrick was supposed to take over anyway!" Rose said. "And then he called and told me you broke up with him."

Shit. That was right. I'd forgotten all about that. I wondered if that was one of the voicemails I hadn't listened to. But it still didn't excuse the fact that she'd left our mom essentially alone.

"So you just decided to leave?"

"Why on earth did you break up with him, anyway?"

"Is that why you're here? To talk with me about my ex-fiancé? Because that's none of your business."

"I don't know why you're acting like this!" Rose exclaimed. "This is so not like you, Rachel."

"What, you want me to just roll over and tell you that it's fine for you to abandon Mom? It's not fine! It's absolutely not fine! You've spent your whole life doing whatever you want to do. Getting whatever you want. And when I need one thing from you, you let me down."

Rose didn't say anything, but her face fell and her lip trembled. I turned and headed to the hallway.

"Where are you going?" Clint asked.

"To get my stuff. I'm going back home."

"Rachel, no!"

I turned around. Rose's face was starting to crumple up.

"Please, Rachel. I didn't mean—I thought she would be okay with Mrs. Patterson. I'll go back. I'll go back today. Alright?"

I'd never seen her like this. Her skin was white, a serious expression making her look even paler.

"I'm sorry. Okay? Please?"

I paused for a second.

"What about your exams?"

"I'll get an extension. My teachers love me. I'm sure

they'll let me take the tests in another week."

I let out a shaky sigh.

"Alright. You'll go back today? On what train?"

"I'll have my driver take her there right now," Clint interjected. I looked over at him, remembering that he had been standing there, witnessing the whole messy argument.

"Fine," I said. I was still worried, but less so. "Rose—"

"No, you're right. I'll go now. Good luck with the singing contest, Rach. I hope you win."

"Thanks," I said softly. I reached for her and gave her a hug. To my surprise, she was trembling.

"Rose, are you okay?"

"Yeah, yeah. It's nothing. I'll talk to you later, alright?" She waved to Clint and smiled, and just like that, it was like we hadn't even argued. "Nice meeting you!"

"You too!"

I didn't understand her. I never understood Rose. Why had she come here, now of all times? To talk with me? That didn't make any sense. And to leave mom…

I pulled my arms around myself and tried to keep everything in. I needed to pull myself together, now more than ever. I had left my mom for this competition, and it wasn't going to be for nothing.

CHAPTER TWENTY-NINE
Clint

Rachel was shaking, and when I drew her into my arms, she didn't even push me away. Her shape fitted perfectly against my chest, her soft hair cascading down her back. I couldn't help but draw my fingers through her hair tenderly. Soft, soft like silk spun with red-gold threads through the chestnut auburn.

She was breathing shallowly, and I felt her heartbeat pulse quick and hard. I pressed a kiss on top of her head, and she instantly pulled away.

"You didn't tell me about your mom," I said.

She wiped at her eyes. I could tell she was trying not to cry.

"Why would you want to know?" she asked.

"Because I want to know everything about you."

She laughed, a short quick mirthless laugh.

"You don't. Believe me."

"I do. Why didn't you tell me you had a sister who went to school here? I thought you would be glad to see her."

Her face tensed up. I could tell that it was the wrong thing to ask.

"Yeah, I should definitely have told you about my smarter, prettier twin sister."

Whoa. Yeah, some tension there.

"She's not prettier than you," I said carefully. "And I'm guessing she's not nearly as good a singer."

But Rachel wasn't even listening to me. She shook her head, looking off into space.

"I should call my dad," she said. "I should make sure Mom is okay. I shouldn't have let Rose take over in the first place. I've always been the one looking after her. Maybe I should go anyway."

She bit her lip, and although it was just as sexy as ever, I felt bad for how much she was worrying. I put my hands on her shoulders, rubbing them softly.

"Rachel, please don't think about leaving the contest. Your mom will be fine."

"She has Alzheimer's," Rachel choked out. "It's been bad. Getting worse. I don't know. Maybe I should go back to the farm."

"Your sister has it all under control—"

"Right. Because she's perfect."

"What? Hey, I didn't say that."

"But you were thinking it. That's what everyone thinks. Beautiful perfect Rose." Rachel's face twisted in pain. She was still a million miles away, off in her thoughts.

So I did the only thing I could do. Cupping her face in my hands, I locked eyes with her, pulling her away from her negative thoughts.

"Rachel. You have to stop this."

"Stop what?" The tears were there, pressing to get out. All the worry and anxiety she had locked up in her was swirling just under the surface, covering up the beautiful confidence I loved in her.

"I don't care about any other girl, alright? Not your sister, not any of the other contestants. I don't want them. I want you to stay here in New York because I want *you*."

That stopped her cold.

"But... but... I—I thought we agreed—"

I kissed her. I didn't know what else to do, and her lips were looking so goddamn perfect that I couldn't resist them any longer. I wanted to take her away from all of her worries, and this was the best way I knew how.

At first she tensed up, but as I deepened the kiss, she began to kiss me back. My cock grew hard in my pants, and I drew her against my body, showing her how much I wanted her.

She let out a small noise that caught in her throat, a little whimper of desire that made the blood rage in my veins. Fuck. I shouldn't have started this again, but now that I had, I knew I couldn't stop.

I needed her. I needed to be inside her, to possess her completely. I wanted her wrapped around me, clutching me the way she was now, only naked and damp with sweat. I wanted her entirely, her mind and her body and her sweet, sweet voice that at that moment was moaning softly against my lips.

But as much as I wanted it, I was going to take my time. The last time, she had been good and wet, but I needed even more than that. I needed her to be aching for it, begging me for it. I wanted to make her first time great, and that meant going slowly.

So I moved my hands down her body, slowly, thoroughly. I caressed her shoulders, kneading the tense muscles there until she melted into my hands.

"Clint—" she whispered. My name caught on her lips in a hiss as I kissed her neck. She smelled gorgeous, like a real girl, a delicate lilac scent on top of her natural richness. I licked the skin right below her ear and reveled in the hoarse breath that she took.

"Let me do this for you," I said.

"Yes."

It was only one word, but it was everything. I cupped my hands under her ass and lifted her. Her legs wound around me as I carried her over to the recording studio door. I paused at the leather couch outside, but no. God knows what had been done there at the countless studio parties.

As I wavered, I heard Rachel's voice in my ear.

"Inside," she whispered, so soft I could barely make out the words. "The piano."

My cock jumped, and she must have felt it because her eyes went wide, her eyelashes fluttering red-gold over the irises.

I carried her inside and sat down at the piano bench, turning her around on my lap so that she was facing the keys. I continued to kiss her neck, pulling the zipper down on the back of her dress.

"The door—" she said, eyeing the studio through the glass plate.

"It's locked from the inside," I assured her. "Everybody's gone today."

"Wait," she said. "Clint—"

"Yeah?"

"What is this?"

"What do you want it to be?"

She shook her head.

"I—I don't know. I can't give my heart away to anyone else right now. It's too soon after what happened with Derrick. I just—I can't—"

"You don't have to. If you want it to be nothing, then it's nothing." The words choked in my throat, but I forced them out. "It's just for fun. Just for now."

It was the exact opposite of what I normally told girls. I would lie to groupies, lead them on, make them thing that there was something where there was nothing. It was all a lie, and I tossed them away without any thought.

Now, though, I was lying in a different direction. I could never tell Rachel this, but I wanted more than just one night. Even now, I could tell that I wouldn't be satisfied with a night with her *just for fun*.

I didn't want to scare her away, though. And I was pretty sure that once I had her to myself, she would want more than that. I would make her scream and shake over and over, and she would be hooked.

I hoped.

She looked like she was weighing the decision.

"If you don't want anything serious, I completely understand," I said.

"You don't mind?"

"Of course not."

She swallowed, the pearly skin at her throat tightening. I bent my head and kissed it.

"Okay," she said, her voice loosening with desire. "Okay."

CHAPTER THIRTY
Rachel

Clint pulled me up onto his lap on the piano bench. I was facing the keys when he started kissing my back.

"Why don't you play me something?" he asked, in between kisses.

I stared down at the keys. My mind wasn't working coherently, but I put my hands on the piano. I'd learned to play at a neighbor's house, and while I knew a few songs by heart, right now I could only remember one. The one about the thorn bird, the one I'd figured out myself note by note.

I started to play the melody with one hand, humming along. As it came back to me, I added in the harmony with my left hand, playing soft chords. Then Clint licked me from collarbone to ear, his tongue pressing hard on my skin.

"Oh—" I cried softly. "Oh my God, that feels good."

"Keep playing."

His lips were hot on my skin, and his hands were all over me, caressing me through my dress, cupping and squeezing. He unzipped the back slowly, all the way down to my panties, his fingertips drifting over my naked skin. I shivered a bit as he pulled my dress off of my shoulders.

"Cold?" he asked.

"A little bit."

His lips were on my skin, and I could feel him grinning. He nipped my shoulder with his teeth.

"Well, let's fix that."

Before I could turn to see him, his hand slipped under the skirt of my dress. He held me firmly with one arm as his other hand applied pressure to me through my panties.

I almost burst into flames right then and there. The ache that shot through my body was so familiar and yet so strange— to feel someone else's hand touch me where only I had ever touched before.

And all the while he was kissing the back of my neck, sucking softly at the skin at the top of my spine. I shivered, but this time it wasn't because of the cold. He unhooked my bra and slipped one hand underneath, cupping and squeezing my breasts. I was torn between leaning back into his kisses and leaning forward into his touch. Every part of me felt exquisitely tender, aching.

Then he took my nipple between his thumb and finger and pinched it gently. My heart leapt in my chest and a hoarse noise came from my throat. It was pain, yes, but a delicious, throbbing pain that left pleasure in its wake. He rolled my nipple again, gently, then harder, and I moaned with delight.

"Yes—" I whispered. "Yes, yes, please Clint. Yes—"

"Looks like we found a spot for you," he said. "I'll remember that."

I had no doubt he would. His hands were exploring my body, taking notes on my reactions, testing with pressure and firmness every inch of my skin. I felt utterly naked, even though my dress was still mostly on. He explored me, probed me, until I was bare and open to him.

Then his fingers were between my thighs, suddenly, impossibly there. They began to lift up and pressing back down on my hot flesh, his hand fierce and strong. I was instantly wet, only this time I didn't feel ashamed at all. When he lifted his hand away, cupping me only slightly, I couldn't stand to feel the ache that he had left.

"Ohhh—" I moaned. My hands flew down between my thighs and I searched for satisfaction. He only gripped my wrist and clucked against my back with his tongue.

"You stopped playing," he said. There was a teasing lilt in his voice. "You have to keep playing."

"Oh, God," I said, but I put my hands back on the

keys.

"Play."

I played. I played the notes as he played me, and he slipped his hand further between my thighs, past my panties. I moaned as he slid his hand into my wetness, sawing slowly across my swollen flesh.

"Ohhhhh." I arched my back into his chest as lightning bolts of ecstasy shot through me. He released the pressure and I whimpered, my fingers slipping, playing a wrong note.

"Play."

I kept going, stumbling my way through the song, desire twisting my body inside itself. His fingers were so thick, so hard, and as he began to probe against my entrance, I cried out.

"Please!" I cried. "Please. Oh, please, don't stop. Don't stop."

He lifted my hands from the piano and kissed them, finger by finger. At my thumb he stopped and suckled me, his tongue moving over my thumbpad. The same sensation echoed further down, and I forgot to breathe. When he finally lifted his head from my hands, I was shaking with desire.

"You've been very good. It's time to reward you."

I felt his erection twitching beneath me, and I turned slightly, unsure of what I should do.

"Not yet," he said, and I knew he was smiling.

"No?" I ached so badly. I wanted him inside of me. I could feel how big he was and I was scared, yes, but I wanted him more than I was afraid of him. I had never wanted anything so much.

He shifted underneath me, picking up my weight with his strong hands. I inhaled sharply. Was this it? Was he going to take me right here? My heartbeat picked up, fear and adrenaline and hot want surging through my body.

Instead of that, though, he slid sideways and lay me down on the piano bench. He took his jacket off and tucked it under my head. It was a sweet gesture that I immediately forgot when he took my nipple in his mouth and sucked hard.

"AHHH!" I cried, my knees rising up instinctively. He pushed my legs back down with one hand and opened his lips, his tongue caressing my bruised nipple.

"Trust me," he growled, and the strange thing about it was, I did.

I trusted him even as his hand plunged back down, wet and hot between my legs. I lifted my hips and gave him access. I turned my body into his mouth as he suckled my breast, his lips hard and insistent, running from one nipple to the other in a series of kisses across my chest.

My bra was shoved up and aside, and my skirt was hitched up to my hips, and still I trusted him, some deep instinct inside my body wanting to give myself up to the feeling that was already coiling up tight and needy in my core.

My nipples were swollen and sore when I felt him easing up. Then his fingers pushed into my wet slit and I gasped at the intrusion. I tightened around him and felt resistance, the unfamiliar sensation of being *full*.

Was this how it was? I couldn't believe how unbelievably thick his fingers were. They stretched me, his thumb circling my opening. Electric lightning pulsed through me with every stroke. My legs jerked limply.

"Ohh—" I moaned, feeling myself open up.

Then his thumb pressed firmly against my clit, and his fingers thrust inward as he sucked my nipple. Everything exploded into white bolts of pleasure. I bucked up against his hand as the orgasm hit me with such ferocity that I thought I would break into pieces, a string wound so tightly I'd snapped into two.

The wave of pleasure was at its crest when he began sucking my nipple in pulses, matching the pulses with his thumb between my thighs. His other hand came up and rolled my free nipple, pinching with the same rhythm.

Another wave hit, coming from inside a part of me I hadn't even expected. Fiery pleasure shot through my breasts as I writhed on the bench, helpless to do anything but succumb to the orgasms that were rippling through my body.

I felt my body tighten around his fingers involuntarily. I flushed red but I needed it, needed to pull him deeper into me. There was no restraint anymore, no preserving my dignity. I was nothing but flesh and nerve, and he teased me out to the breaking point and let me ride him.

He was playing me.

The thought came through my mind in a brief spasm, and then every thought was erased again as a third, smaller orgasm shuddered through my body. He was licking my nipple now, his tongue softer against the bruised and swollen flesh. His fingers eased out, circling shallowly around my slit.

The air in the room was blistering, and I rasped as the orgasm subsided. My hands clenched his arms and let go, exhausted by even that minimal effort. I was so far gone, I didn't know if I could ever pull myself together again. I was his, his completely, and he could do with me what he wanted.

"Clint—" I whispered hoarsely. I closed my eyes but that only made the world feel more dizzy around me. "Clint."

"I'm here."

I hadn't known what I wanted from him, but that was enough. I turned onto my side, curling up and breathing small gasps of air. My heart roared in my ears as he stroked my sweat-dampened hair back. He bent down and kissed my cheek.

"I hope you're ready for this," he said. "Because I can't stand another second more. I need to be inside of you."

His hand moved toward his belt buckle as my heart swelled in my chest. Then my eyes flickered up to the studio window, catching movement behind the glass.

"Clint—" I said. "Wait."

"You want another one, baby?" he asked, chuckling softly and reaching again towards my panties. "Well, I guess—"

"No. I mean, wait!"

The door to the recording studio opened up and I scrambled to sit up, pulling my dress up over my shoulders to cover my chest.

It was Clint's dad. He laughed, an ugly laugh that turned into a sneer as he looked at my flushed face, my disheveled hair. Clint didn't say a word, only helped me to pull down the hem of my skirt. All the while, his dad was staring at us, that ugly look on his face.

"Good," he said finally. "I hope you got that piece of pussy out of your system."

Clint's eyes darkened, but he still didn't say anything. His hands pulled back from my body, leaving my skin cold with sweat. I felt utterly alone, abandoned. My heart sank.

"I'll be in my office," his dad said, turning away. "Come talk to me when you're done."

CHAPTER THIRTY-ONE
Clint

I pressed my knuckles to my lips as my dad left. My fingers smelled like Rachel.

God, Rachel. She shouldn't have had to witness that. I turned to her, but she was already zipping up her dress.

"Let me help—" I said.

"You've done enough." Her voice was abruptly cold. She struggled to clip her bra behind her, but her fingers fumbled at the strap. After only a couple of seconds, her face crumpled and she wilted down on the piano bench, her hands covering her eyes. I realized that she was crying a moment too late.

Crying?

"Hey! Hey, don't do that. Rachel, please."

"Please? Please what?" I could barely hear the words between her sobs.

I reached around her and gave her a hug, quickly redoing the bra clasp and zipping up the back of her dress.

"Please don't be so upset. It's okay."

"It's not okay!" she cried, snapping her head up. "How can you say it's okay?"

"Hey, everybody has someone walk in on them sometime. It's no big deal."

"It's not that!"

My mind reeled.

"What is it, then?"

"Seriously? You just let you dad treat me like I'm nothing, and I'm supposed to accept that it's no big deal? That's not okay, Clint!"

"He didn't—he was teasing me more than he was teasing you," I said, trying to deflect some of her anger.

"A piece of pussy? Is that what I am?"

Oh, God.

"Rachel, no. Of course not."

"Then you should have said something!"

She stared at me with such anger, I was completely at a loss. None of the other girls I'd ever slept with had any issues with my dad making fun of them. At least, they hadn't said anything.

It struck me then that maybe all of them had wanted to say something. But I was Clint Terrance, and my dad was Skull Terrance, and none of the girls I'd ever been with would have stood up to either of us. I thought back to all of the stupid things my dad had said. Sure, some of them were sexist. He was kind of...

Well, okay. He was kind of a jerk. So was I, by letting him do whatever he wanted. Say whatever he wanted. None of the other girls had mattered to me. But now, when it mattered, I was doing the same thing. Maybe I should go after him about it. The thought of it struck fear into me, but if that's what it took to make things okay with Rachel...

A smack on my shoulder sent my thoughts flying away.

"Say something!"

"I don't—I don't know what to say. You're right. Of course you're right. I just never looked at it like that until now."

"Really?"

"Really. Honest to God."

Her eyes were still flickering up to the studio window.

"Hey, let's get out of here," I said. "Let's go somewhere we can talk in private."

"Where's that?" Rachel asked. "I thought there were cameras all up in the apartment."

"Go back up to the globe."

"Uh, I don't think so." Her eyes narrowed suspiciously.

"Not for that!" I raised my hands. "I think tonight has been quite enough."

I didn't. I didn't think I'd ever get enough of Rachel. My groin protested. But I wanted her to trust me. I didn't even know why I wanted it so much, but it was stronger even than my desire to pin her down to a bed and bury myself in her up to the balls. And that desire was pretty strong.

"For what, then?"

"Just to talk. Okay?" I didn't give her a second chance to protest. "I'll meet you up there in ten minutes."

"What about your dad?"

I glanced toward his office door. A twinge of guilt floated through me, but then I shoved it away. I bent down and kissed the top of her head, caressing her soft hair.

"He can wait."

I climbed the ladder up to the globe very carefully, balancing a tray on one hand and climbing the rungs with the other. When I reached the platform, I was glad to slide the tray over before swinging myself up.

"Teatime is served," I announced.

She laughed. It was a soft, tentative laugh, but it was better than her crying. She picked up a mug from the tray and inhaled, her eyes fluttering shut.

"How did you know I liked chai tea?"

"Oh, I'm psychic," I said, pulling myself over to sit next to her. Our feet swung out over the platform into the big glass globe. I picked up my own mug. "Also, I heard you ordering one when we were out at Sardi's."

"Oh. Right. Thanks for noticing."

Her lip quivered a bit as she put the cup down.

"What's the matter?" I asked.

"I just—you notice things. It's nice."

"Of course I notice things. I notice everything."

"Everything?"

"Sure. Like the tea you drink, or the fact that you picked out all of your olives from your pasta dinner, or

227

that you tried every kind of cupcake at Jake's dinner party except red velvet."

She was laughing.

"It's true. Steph loves it, but I think red velvet cake looks so gruesome."

"Like how your underwear is riding up a little bit on your gorgeous ass right now," I continued. "Or how sometimes when you laugh, there's a little bit of sad sneaking out."

She stopped laughing, then, and looked up at me, her eyes looking me over carefully. It seemed like she was re-evaluating me. I wasn't the asshole she thought I was, at least I hoped.

"What are you thinking?" I asked.

She sipped her tea again, then looked out the globe. It was overcast, but the sun was burning brightly behind the clouds. The whole sky seemed to glow softly, a light gray glow infiltrating the entire city. The mirrored windows of the buildings reflected each other.

"You were right," she said finally. "About Derrick. He was a total ass."

I nodded serenely.

"Soon you'll realize I'm always right," I said, sipping my tea in utter seriousness.

That cracked her up a little.

"You believe me, right? I've never been wrong."

"Never? Not even once?"

I pretended to think.

"Maybe… maybe once, when I ordered a pumpkin curry at my favorite Thai restaurant. That was a mistake. But apart from that, I've never been wrong. Believe me."

"Sure, I believe you."

"Good. Then I'll have you know that you're incredibly talented and beautiful. And since I'm always right about everything—"

"Oh, hush."

"Really. I'm serious. You're the best singer I've heard

in a long time."

"Stop it." She shifted in her seat uncomfortably, gripping her tea with both hands like it was her only piece of armor.

I tried another tack.

"What do you want to do with your life?"

She laughed, a short unhappy laugh. Then she shook her head.

"What does it matter?"

"I'm interested."

"It really doesn't matter. I have to take care of my mom and help my dad run the farm."

"But what do *you* want to do?"

She stared down at her tea. I was beginning to think that she'd forgotten my question when she answered it.

"I want to be a singer, of course." Her voice was so soft I could barely hear it, even in the silence of the globe.

"Do you think you can do it?"

She looked at me like I was laying a trap for her. Then she shrugged.

"I don't know. I really don't."

It was the wrong answer. Maybe I shouldn't have prodded her further, but I wanted to know more.

"You can't get ahead in this business unless you believe in yourself, Rachel."

"Yeah? Is that why you're such a hot shot? Nobody thinks they're as great as you think you are."

"Very funny."

She shook her head, laughing softly, and that little bit of sadness came creeping into her laugh.

"I don't know what it is. I can't believe in myself like those girls do."

"I think I know what it is."

"Oh, yeah?"

"Do you think you deserve to win this contest?"

She raised her eyebrows.

"Come on. What does that even mean?"

229

"Exactly what I said. Do you think you're the best singer out of all of them?"

"At singing? Maybe. But there's so much else…"

"No. There's nothing else. Not as far as I'm concerned."

"What do you think?"

"Me? I think you could be the best. I think you're holding back, though."

She nodded, and I think she understood what I meant. Her singing was pitch perfect, but sometimes I felt like she wasn't fully there. She would draw back, not letting her emotions come through. And that's all singing was—taking emotions and putting them into words and melodies. Sending them out into the audience so that everyone would come along, feeling the same things you felt when you wrote the song.

Rachel hadn't gotten there yet. Once she did, she would be a star. But I didn't know if she could ever come out of her shell far enough to do that.

And I didn't know if I was the one who could bring her out of it.

"What about your mom?" Rachel asked suddenly.

"My mom?"

"I saw your dad with a woman down in the studio—"

"Sherry, maybe. Or one of his "dates". Either way, definitely not my mom."

"Where is your mom?"

I stopped for a moment and set down my teacup. It was nearly empty, and the last little bit of tea sloshed cold and bitter at the bottom of the cup.

"I don't know," I said honestly.

"You don't know where she is? How do you visit her?"

"I don't."

"Why not?" Rachel turned to me in blank surprise, like she couldn't imagine ever not visiting her mother.

Because she's a bitch who left us.

I wasn't going to say that. Hell, I didn't know anything

about my mom. Only what my dad had told me.

"She left when I was seven," I said, shifting uncomfortably. The floor had turned hard under my ass. "I barely remember her face."

"What do you remember?" Rachel's voice was soft.

"I remember…" I closed my eyes and tried to think. "I remember her voice."

"What did it sound like?"

"She used to sing to me. Lullabies, to put me to bed. I was too old for lullabies, I remember thinking. Did your mom ever sing you lullabies?"

Rachel nodded, a bit sadly.

"But your mom left you both? Why?" she asked.

"I don't know," I said, feeling uncomfortable that I'd never bothered to find out. "I really have no idea."

We sat in silence for a while, finishing the tea. Rachel didn't mention my mom again, and I didn't mention hers. It was too hard of a subject for either of us to handle. The sun had broken through the clouds, and it was starting to turn golden on the sides of the skyscrapers.

"I'm going to go back down to the apartment and practice for tomorrow's contest," Rachel said finally.

"Alright," I said, helping her to her feet. "Wait. Kiss for good luck."

I pressed my lips to hers, softly, tenderly, but she pulled back after just a couple of seconds.

"Clint, I— I thought we were nothing."

"Sure. But this is the best kind of nothing."

She bit her lip. I reached up and caressed it with my thumb, and she stopped biting.

"Can you promise me something?" she asked.

"Sure."

"Stay away from me for the rest of the competition, okay? Can we wait until this is all over?"

"I'll try."

"Good."

"But only if you give me a good enough reason. Why?"

231

She breathed in deeply.

"I want this win to be my own."

"You don't think that I would rig the contest, do you?" I would have, I totally would have, but as luck would have it, I didn't need to. Rachel was taking care of winning on her own. All I had to do was give her a bit of support and confidence.

"No, I don't think that. But others will. And I want this to be all mine."

"You're not as innocent as you look," I said, caressing her chin.

She pressed her lips together and kissed the palm of my hand, bringing it down between her two hands.

"I've had to grow up fast."

I thought about what she'd had to deal with. Taking care of her mom. Living in the shadow of her sister. God knows what else.

"I'll see you at the end of the competition, then?" I asked. It was only one more week. I wasn't sure I could make it, but I'd try.

"Sure," she said, a bit of a teasing note coming into her voice. "If you can handle waiting that long."

"We'll see."

"Thank you for the tea. And for talking."

I wanted to kiss her again, once more, but she was already climbing down the ladder, disappearing down into the darkness.

CHAPTER THIRTY-TWO
Rachel

The next two days went by in a blur. Clint stayed away from me, like I'd asked him to.

I hated it.

I hadn't realized how alone I was, and without Clint's attention, I was downright isolated. Piers flirted with me a bit, but then he flirted with every contestant. I didn't know if I could handle another day surrounded by girls who hated my guts. I didn't know if I could handle another *minute*. Sophia had managed to scrape by in every contest, and she was making my life hell.

"Guess you're not the teacher's pet anymore," Sophia whispered to me.

"What do you mean?"

"I mean, Clint has forgotten all about you. Haven't you noticed?"

We were in the studio, sitting on the couches. In the recording section, Clint and Piers were sitting inside with headsets on. They'd brought in a radio host, and we were doing two live performances. Jen was first.

We couldn't hear how she was doing, but she was putting on a show. She shook her head and her perfectly coiffed hair flew from under her headset.

"I haven't noticed anything," I said blankly.

"Ooh, someone's jealous."

"Jealous? Of what?" I couldn't help turning toward Sophia. She smirked, peering over her fake fingernails as she pretended to examine her cuticles.

"Not of what. Of *who*."

"Who, then?"

"Oh, I don't know. Someone."

I sighed and tried to ignore what Sophia was saying.

"Maybe someone in there."

"Jen?"

"I didn't say anything. But did you see how he was looking at her earlier today? And he's been staring at her tits this whole song."

"Hmm," was all I said.

I knew that Sophia was trying to get under my skin. I wasn't going to take the bait. I stared fixedly at the piece of black leather couch between my knees and tried not to lift my head. I knew I would look at Clint, and I had been trying to stay away from doing that. Watching Clint made my body react in stupid ways, like turning so hot my ears felt red, or making my tongue too thick to speak, let alone sing.

Just looking at his mouth made me blush. I couldn't help but think of how he'd put his tongue inside of me, how he'd sent me flying into ecstasy not once or twice, but three times.

One more mistake: the piano bench I'd been stretched out on, gasping for orgasmic breath, was right there inside the recording studio. I didn't know how I could go into there and sing a song in front of the guy who had been the one making me gasp. I took a breath.

Inhale, exhale. I could do this.

Sophia must be wrong. Clint hadn't stopped talking to me because he was flirting with someone else. He had stopped talking to me because I'd asked him to.

Right?

"Rachel?"

My head snapped up. Clint was standing in the doorway.

"Come on!" he said.

I flushed hard as I stood up.

"Good luck!" Sophia said, smirking at me as I walked past her to the recording studio door. Clint held it wide open, not brushing against me at all.

It was awful. Every inch of space between us was filled with the most agonizing kind of tension. It would almost have been better if he had brushed against my shoulder, or tried to pinch my ass when I wasn't looking. As it was, I was aware of all of the space between us. All of the space where he wasn't touching me.

"Go ahead and put on your headset," Clint said.

"Oh. Right. Uh, sure." I did what he said, standing in front of the microphone.

"And we're back with Rachel Ritter's first song!" The radio announcer's voice boomed in my ear, so loud that it nearly broke my eardrum.

Jeez! I fumbled with my earpiece, trying to turn down the volume. Jen must have turned the dial up to maximum when she left. It took me a second to readjust it back, and by that time I'd lost all track of what the radio show host was saying.

"Rachel?"

"Oh, sorry! Should I—" I motioned to the microphone awkwardly.

"You're already on," the radio host said, his voice clearly wearing thin with patience.

"Oh!" I cleared my throat. "Thanks. I'll be singing a piece—"

"We already announced your song," Clint interrupted. Piers smacked his forehead with his hand. I flushed. God, I was so stupid. How had I forgotten that? They'd told us that at the beginning of the contest. Of course, I knew how I'd forgotten. The piano bench was staring at me from across the room, and everything that had been in my mind had quickly slid away at the sight of it.

"Well, let's hope she has more voice than brains!" the radio host said. Piers laughed at the joke, but Clint only looked at me with a worried expression.

I gulped. Inhale, exhale. Inhale, exhale. Inhale—

The music started to play without any warning. Halfway through the deep breath, I launched into the song.

It was terrible. I started half a beat too late, and the headset wasn't playing loud enough for me to even hear the rhythm—I'd turned it down too much. I strangled my way through the first measure.

Sweat beaded on my forehead as I turned into the chorus. Piers was beaming at me with a forced smile so big I was sure that there was something else in his mug besides coffee. And Clint wasn't looking at me at all—he was staring down at the desk, his hands clasped under his chin.

The second verse kicked in, and I screwed up the high note. I'd practiced for an hour last night, and it had been fine, but with all of the tension in the room, my throat just seized up. Out came a screeching note that was at least half a note off.

I froze. The music went on, but I didn't know where I was. I couldn't get the courage to start over again, and I wasn't even sure my voice could handle it. I knew that I didn't want to try that note again.

Clint looked up at me, and now all three of them—the radio announcer, Clint, and Piers—were staring straight at me, waiting. Then the radio host faded the music out.

"And that was Rachel Ritter!" he said. "The next contestant we have comes from the Upper East Side—"

I ripped off my headset and stumbled out of the recording studio. Clint was right behind me.

"Sophia, you're up," he said.

"That was fast," she said.

"What did you do, sing *Twinkle Twinkle*?" Annette asked, sneering at me.

"Don't go away," Clint said. His hand was on my arm. It was the first time he had touched me since I'd asked him to leave me alone. His fingers burned my skin, or maybe that was just me—I was burning hot all over. I tried to breathe to calm myself down.

Inhale.

But there was no air in the room. Even breathing in as

deeply as I could, I felt like I was being smothered by the stares of all the girls around me.

"What the hell is *wrong* with you?" Vivian asked.

I didn't answer her. I walked to the hallway.

"Hey, Clint said not to leave," Annette called after me.

"I'm not leaving," I snapped. I couldn't do a second song. Even if I wanted to, it wouldn't make any difference. I had lost this contest already, irrevocably.

I stood in the hallway, trying desperately to pull oxygen into my lungs. I had just fucked up a song majorly, and it had been broadcast live on radio for anyone to hear. I thought of Lacey and Steph—were they listening? Was Rose listening? My mom, my dad?

Was Derrick listening?

That seemed the worst of all the possibilities. I thought of him hearing me mess up, and how satisfied he would be that I had confirmed his idea—that I wasn't cut out to be a singer. Tears burned the backs of my eyes, and I bit down on my knuckles to keep them from coming out. I was done. I wasn't going to win.

"Rachel?"

Clint was in the hallway. He looked so concerned, I almost asked him what was wrong. Then I realized: he was concerned about me. My heart sank even further.

"Guess I lost, huh?" I asked. I tried to make it sound light, like I didn't care, but I choked on a sob.

Instead of answering, though, he pulled me away from the door and behind one of the white marble columns.

"Clint, what are you doi—"

He kissed me.

His mouth seized mine roughly and I felt his arm encircle my waist, pull me close. Not tenderly, not how he had kissed me before. No, this was a hard kiss, a kiss meant to tear all my other thoughts away and leave only a hot burning desire.

It worked. I melted in his arms as his mouth pressed hot against mine. My whole body surged with desire.

Then he pulled away. I couldn't believe it. Two days after I'd asked him to leave me alone, and he hadn't touched me.

Until now.

"Clint— wait—"

"No."

"You promised—"

"Nobody is watching right now. They're all in there."

"But—"

He gripped my wrists in his hands. Strong hands. The veins bulged in the backs of his arms.

"Listen. You can do this. I believe you can do this. But you can't hold back like you're doing. I can hear it in your breath."

I stared at him agog. Was that what this was about? My *singing*? My head shook slowly back and forth.

"Clint."

"You have to stop holding up the air in your larynx. It's stifling your vocal cords."

"Clint, I don't know what that means. I don't know anything about breath, or singing, or… or…"

"Okay. Quick lesson."

He kissed me again, hard. He kissed me and kissed me, and I could see the black spots coming up at the bottom of my eyes. One hand pressed between my thighs, and I almost came right then and there against his fingers. But then he let go.

I gasped, sucking in lungfuls of air.

"Clint!"

"That gasp? That's what I want in between stanzas." He pointed at me, his finger grazing my lips. "Because you've got to give every note of it your all. One hundred percent. Understood?"

"Understood. Now stay away from me."

"Only if you win."

I let out a hard chuckle.

"Win? You mean if I don't lose?"

"Every one of those girls has fucked up a part of their song. Every one. And the voting isn't until after the second song. Wow them with that one and you'll win. Trust me."

Again, he was telling me to trust him.

And again, my heart told me to listen.

CHAPTER THIRTY-THREE
Clint

I almost wanted Rachel to lose. Her kiss was so damn sweet, and I could feel her body hot and ready underneath my hand. I wanted to tell her to forget the contest, to forget everything, to come into the studio with me and I would hand her the recording contract and then fuck her until she forgot why she ever came to New York City in the first place.

But I couldn't. She was proud, and determined, and I wanted to see her win this on her own.

Well, almost on her own.

I pushed her back into the studio. The other contestants swiveled their heads to look at us. Rachel tensed beneath my hand.

"Forget about them," I whispered. "Just go in and sing like you're alone in the shower."

"Okay."

"Stand here. Don't sit, you'll tense up."

She gave an almost imperceptible nod. I could sense that she didn't want me to encourage her in front of the other contestants. I left her and went back in to sit at the table. Sophia was finishing up her song and I heard her tremble into the last few notes as I put on the headset.

I thought I was almost more nervous than Rachel. As we ran through the contestants again for their second song, I glanced out the window out into the studio. Rachel was standing next to the couch, her eyes closed. I hoped she was practicing her breathing.

When I went out to get her, she opened her eyes and came in quickly, avoiding my touch. She stood at the microphone and adjusted the volume before putting on the headset. Then she gave a firm nod.

The music started, and Rachel took a deep breath before starting to sing.

The song was a relatively recent pop song that had gone platinum last year. Unlike the first one she'd tried to sing today, though, this song was much more soulful. The original part was lower, and her contralto voiced matched it perfectly. I only hoped that the audience for this radio station would appreciate her take on the hit.

Stay with me, stay with me tomorrow.
Not forever, just for now, just for me.

Her voice slid along the notes, playing up the sultry undertones. The original had been all serious—a sad song about a breakup. But when Rachel sang it now, she added nuances of playfulness turning to wistfulness. It made the song more mature—less a song about a teenager who'd just been broken up with, more about a woman who has lost something that once made her happy. It was bittersweet, and as I watched, Rachel closed her eyes.

You won't see me in the springtime,
I'll be lost and you'll be finding someone else to see
But just tomorrow
Just tomorrow
Stay with me.

She sang the final stanza perfectly. It was only when she opened her eyes that the tears rolled down her cheeks. And I realized how much this competition was hurting her.

How much I was hurting her.

CHAPTER THIRTY-FOUR
Rachel

I didn't win the radio contest, but I did tie with Annette for first place. Our prize was a free pass to see *Talismen* play their last tour show in New York City. Vivian had thrown a fit when she'd been voted out, but Clint told me afterward that she had forgotten half of the lyrics to her second song.

"Everyone messes up," he says. "That's part of a live performance."

"But none of them said that they had messed up," I said, confused. "They all pretended that they'd sung perfectly."

"That's how you do it when you're a star," Clint said. "You fuck up and you pretend like you never fucked up. That's how you recover."

I was astonished. I had never considered that everyone else had messed up as badly as I had. It was a strange kind of philosophy, not something I was used to. But if that was how I was going to be a singer, I would have to try.

For the show, I dressed up in one of the more demure dresses Clint had bought me, a dark green sheath. It was still tight around my hips, but the collar draped loosely around my neck, covering more of my cleavage. I invited Lacey and Steph to the show, and it was great to have my friends back.

"I'm sorry that I fought with you about Derrick," I said. "I should have realized how much of a jerk he was."

"Hey, don't worry," Lacey said. "We've all done stupid stuff for a guy."

"I haven't," Steph said.

"You haven't *yet*."

"Never. I'm too busy to date, anyway."

"Oh? What about that guy Lucas?"

"Lucas?" I asked, my eyes flashing between Steph and Lacey. "The guy from the party? What about him? What did I miss?"

"You missed a lot," Lacey said.

"You didn't miss anything!"

Steph blushed so hard I thought her hair was going to catch on fire.

"Steph has a crush," Lacey explained.

"I do not!"

"Well, he has a crush on you."

"He does not!"

I laughed at their bickering as we made our way down the club to the front of the stage. We had special wristbands Clint had given us, and the security guard let us through into a small section right at the lip of the stage.

"Wow," Lacey said, looking back out at the crowd. "This place is huge."

"Yeah, I think their last performance was in a stadium," I said. I turned to look out into the club. The place was packed from wall to wall, the dim lights overhead flashing colored spotlights over the crowd. Then the crowd began to cheer, their voices rising to a din that made me clap my hands over my ears.

"What's going on?" I shouted. Everybody in the club was going crazy. Lacey said something, but I couldn't hear.

"What?"

"Turn around!" both Lacey and Steph yelled at me.

I turned around. Clint had walked onstage. He was wearing jeans, a black shirt, and a black jacket, and his hair was styled up in a messy dark tousle. He gave a brief wave to the crowd, who went bananas. The floor was shaking with the noise of it.

"Wow," I said. I couldn't imagine anyone cheering for me tuning an instrument, but it seemed like all the fans in the crowd were going insane. Clint wasn't even singing yet, for goodness' sakes. It was weird to see him as the rock star I knew he was.

Clint fiddled with the guitar onstage for a second, then turned back around to the audience. There was another burst of cheering. His eyes scanned the front row and landed on me. He smiled and walked over to the edge of the stage. I thought my eardrums were going to pop from all the screaming girls behind me. He knelt down and called out to me.

"Hey, Rachel! Having fun yet?"

I smiled shyly and nodded.

"First band is up in five. If you need anything, let that guy know." He pointed over to the security guard who had escorted us in.

"Thanks!" I said, not sure if he could hear me over all the noise.

He gave me a thumbs up and headed back to his guitar. The crowd cheers rose and fell in waves behind us.

"Wow." Lacey said. "He's totally into you."

"Maybe," I said. That was all I was ready to admit.

"Maybe? Did you see how he came over to you?"

"I'm in his competition," I said. "Of course he would come say hi."

"He's madly in love with you," Lacey said firmly. "I guarantee it."

"See what I've been dealing with?" Steph said.

I shook my head at Lacey.

"He doesn't love me. He just likes a challenge." It was what I'd been telling myself for the past few days. "And a virginal farm girl? That's the biggest challenge there is."

"How does he know you're a virgin?" Steph asked.

I scrambled for an answer, but didn't come up with anything fast enough.

"I knew it!" Lacey said. "Oh. My. God. He's one hundred percent into you."

"No!"

"His dick is a virgin magnet, and you're the next

target."

"Please don't say it like that. Steph, help me out here!"

"Are you kidding me? I don't want her starting on me and Lucas again!"

"What's it like?" Lacey asked breathlessly.

"The contests?"

"No, his dick."

I flushed.

"I have no idea!"

"You haven't… done anything with him?"

"Well… I mean… I don't…"

"*AHHHHH!*" Lacey screamed, just as loudly as any of the fans behind us. "You are in love with him!"

"Are you kidding me? He's a playboy."

"A playboy with eyes for you."

I glanced back up at the stage. Clint looked straight out at me and winked.

"Maybe," I said.

"OH MY GOD!"

"Don't say anything, okay?" I said, glancing around. I didn't know where Annette was. "I don't want anyone to know there's anything at all between us. Not that there's anything between us. But definitely not during the competition."

"My lips are sealed, babe," Lacey said, giving me an exaggerated wink.

The opening band was great. While I wasn't a huge rock fan, the singer was pretty good and the energy pumping from crowd had me dancing before the end of the set. But when *Talismen* came on stage, the whole audience went insane.

Clint looked like the epitome of a hard rocker. A glinting silver belt buckle at his waist, tight jeans, and messy hair. The band didn't spend any time with introductions; they burst right into their first number. Clint stood up at the edge of the stage, strumming his guitar and singing into the microphone.

I was stunned. As he sang, his whole body changed, moving with the music.

It's the hard way
To make it easy
It's the wrong way
To make you leave me

His voice was... incredible. I hadn't realized how talented he was before. I mean, I'd heard *Talismen* on the radio, but I hadn't given it a second thought. Hearing Clint sing live, though, was a whole other experience. The notes came out growling and rough, but in perfect melody.

I could see too, now, what he had meant by breathing. He leaned away between lines so that the microphone wouldn't catch his breath. At other points, I could see him sucking in air for a long stretch without pauses. Every word was sung with such power that I was amazed he could keep going through an entire song.

His hair, already dark, went black with sweat under the bright lights onstage. Between songs, he ripped off his jacket, and the resultant scream echoed from wall to wall in the club.

"My god," I heard Steph say. "That is... quite a man."

Was it weird that I hadn't quite realized how beautiful Clint's body was? I mean, I'd had his hands all over me, but he'd never made it about himself, and while I knew he was fit, I had never really *looked* at him.

Now I did. And he looked absolutely incredible.

His muscles bulged, slick with sweat, his veins beginning to stand out on his arms. His face was creased with emotion as he sang, eyes closed. His chest was broad and the guitar was cradled in his hands like it was another part of his body. As he sang, his hair fell in front of his face, and he whipped it back with a snap of his head between stanzas.

But it was his voice that made me melt inside. His voice that thrummed through my body, sending waves of emotion through me. It was his voice that brought together all of the instruments, made everything work. With his voice, he took the entire audience and made them scream, made them cry, made them tremble.

After they had finished their set, though, I was left feeling empty.

This... this was what he had done to me in the studio. He had played the crowd tonight the same way that he'd played me. He was a master at it. It was his job. He made love to every fan out there.

Was he just manipulating me to get what he wanted?

I cheered and clapped through the encore, but inside my heart was twisting. How could I have let myself fall for someone who was like this? It wasn't right. I didn't want to be another girl in the crowd cheering, another fan who fell over herself to fall into his bed. I didn't want to be just one more girl screaming "I love you!" at the rock star.

Clint waved over at us before the band left the stage. The club lights came up and the crowd began to empty out.

"Want to get some drinks?" I asked Lacey and Steph.

"Sorry," Steph said. "I'm opening tomorrow at four am, and I don't want to leave Andy by himself in the kitchen again. I swear, my little brother would kill himself with a cake froster if I wasn't watching him."

"Okay, then it'll just be me and you, Lacey."

"Oh. Don't hate me, Rachel," Lacey said.

"What? You have to leave too?"

"Jake is kind of possessive. Like, weirdly possessive. He'll spank me if I don't get home by midnight."

"Please tell me you don't mean literally."

Lacey's eyes flashed with delight. I was shocked.

"Are you for real? Lacey, you were the only other virgin left in New York City! I thought I could count on you for support!"

"You're the only one now, babe. Go get 'em!"

I shook my head doubtfully.

"Rachel." She put her hands on my shoulders.

"Lacey."

"Don't listen to me, I'm crazy. And I'm crazy about this guy Jake."

"Yeah, I can tell."

"But I wouldn't tell you to go for something unless I thought it would be good for you. And this guy Clint looks like he's into you. Back me up on this, Steph."

"You should totally date the rock star," Steph said with a grin.

I looked up at the stage where the stagehands were already taking down the music equipment.

"Stay and talk with him, at least," Lacey insisted. "Gotta go! Good luck!"

I hugged them both goodbye and then waited around by the side of the stage to wait for Clint. A gaggle of groupies was waiting. They all looked ridiculously young and beautiful. I didn't want to feel that way, but I was jealous as hell of all the girls primping themselves so they could flirt with Clint when he came out.

Minutes passed, and Clint wasn't out yet. The girls were clustered in groups, laughing and chattering happily. None of them so much as looked at me, and I felt completely out of place.

This was supposed to be good for me? Lacey had no idea what she was talking about. I wasn't that kind of girl. And Clint wasn't my kind of guy.

What kind of guy is that, anyway? The complete jerk kind of guy? Remember how his dad treated you?

My brain couldn't stop reminding me of my past bad decisions. I wasn't about to throw myself headlong into another bad decision.

I turned and walked away. And when I got outside the club, I began to run.

CHAPTER THIRTY-FIVE
Clint

I looked for Rachel everywhere after the show, but she was nowhere to be found. The next day, most of the contestants headed out for some shopping trip or something. Piers tagged along with the camera crew to follow them. He said it was to get filler footage, but I thought he just wanted to have three girls flirting with him all day.

I found Rachel in the recording studio.

She was singing a song I'd never heard before. It sounded like a lullaby, but it was in a minor key. A very strange song. I had only been listening for a minute when she finished. I opened the door as quietly as I could, but she was still startled.

"What are you doing here?" she asked.

"Well, this is my recording studio," I said.

Her eyes flickered over my shoulder.

"Is your dad here?"

"No."

She still looked uneasy.

"He's in Paris, doing some marketing business. Don't worry," I said.

My dad had left me with strict orders not to choose a star before he got back. He was supposed to be there for the live taping of the finale, but I hoped that he wouldn't make it back in time.

Her shoulders relaxed slightly.

"Did you—did he talk to you?"

"You mean, did he chew me out about finding us together? Yeah."

"And?"

"And? He's yelled at me worse. Like the time I was twelve and took his Ferrari for a joy ride."

"Twelve years old?! Are you kidding me?"

I chuckled, remembering the way his ears had turned red with anger.

"I learned how to drive stick from Youtube videos. Yeah. He had to replace the clutch after that one."

"Wow."

"So all in all, you're not the worst. Not by a long shot."

A smile quirked at the corner of her mouth.

"Not the worst? That's quite the ringing endorsement."

"You know what I mean."

"Sure, sure."

"How's your mom, by the way? Have you talked with her?"

Rachel's face turned anxious. Maybe I shouldn't have brought it up.

"She's fine," she said. "I called Rose this morning, and she said everything was okay. But…"

"But what?"

"I miss her."

Tears misted her eyes. I could see her trying to fight back against them.

"Was that what you were singing?" I asked quickly. "One of her lullabies?"

"Yeah," Rachel said, sniffing slightly and quickly recomposing herself. "I'm working on the breathing thing."

"Let me help you."

"Oh, no. I know *exactly* how you want to help me, and it's not going to happen."

"Come on. You think I don't know anything about singing?" I paused. "Jesus, you think that I'm famous for being a shit singer? Was I that bad last night?"

"No! You were awesome!"

"Really? You think I'm awesome?" I grinned at her.

"Fine," she said, crossing her arms. "You can help

me—"

"Good. Uncross those arms."

Her jaw dropped open. I came around behind her and wrapped my hands around her waist, standing her up and kicking the bench out of the way.

"Hey!"

"Easy, there. I'm going to help you breathe."

She scoffed.

"I've been breathing for twenty-two years without anyone's assistance, you know."

"Are you going to listen to me, or are you going to be stubborn about it?"

She breathed in, then out. Under my fingers, I could feel her muscles relax.

"Alright," I said. I reached down and took her hands in mine.

"Clint—"

"Touch the very top of your collarbone." I moved her hands to the spot I wanted her to touch. Her hands were small and warm in mine. I slid them down slowly.

"Here," I said. "This is where your lungs start. Breathe in."

She breathed.

"See how your lungs move upward when you inhale? Now exhale."

Her fingers lowered as her lungs moved down.

"Now further." Our hands slid down past her breasts. It took all my willpower not to cup those beautiful soft curves. "Here. Past your sternum. This is where your diaphragm is. This is where you want to be breathing from."

"How—how do I breathe from there?"

"Okay. First, close your eyes."

Rachel tilted her head back and gave me a doubtful look.

"I'm serious. You can't focus on your body if you're looking around. You need to feel this, not see it."

253

"Okay," she said nervously. "Eyes closed."

"Now I want you to breathe down lower. Pretend you're breathing in water, and it's falling to the bottom of your lungs."

She followed my instructions. Her hands were so soft under mine.

"Exhale. Now again, but breathe more quickly this time. Suck that air into the very bottom of your lungs, past your belly button. Right here. Feel it?"

"Yeah, I feel it," she whispered.

She squirmed under my hand. My palm was against her lower belly, so close to that perfect spot. I swallowed hard.

"You want your chest to stay still. Down here is where you should be breathing in and out. Got it?"

"Got it."

"Now sing."

She breathed in deeply, quickly. Her voice spun out like golden thread through the air.

The nightingale was born to sing, the clouds were born to rain

"Perfect," I whispered as she sung. "And now!"

She inhaled, a half beat too late, but she had the right idea. Her chest stayed still, and I could feel the breath filling up her lungs from the bottom. My hands rested over hers, feeling the swelling and contracting of her body.

The thorns impaled her downy breast, the thorns pierced through her heart

"Again."

I didn't have to remind her, though. She breathed in right on beat for the rest of the song. It gave her notes a power that I hadn't heard before.

"Use all the air when you sing," I whispered in her ear, as she inhaled another breath between lines. The chorus came out loud, perfectly pitched, with more power than I'd ever heard her use before while singing.

Sing, little bird,
Sing until the break of dawn.
Sing, little bird,

Sing on, sing on.

Her voice was so beautiful, so sad, and my arms were wrapped around her. Before I could think to stop myself, I was lowering my lips to her neck.

She didn't stop singing. She didn't miss a beat. As I kissed her skin from under her ear down to her shoulder, her arm, she kept on going. My body ached to nestle into her, to have her softness under me. As I sucked softly at her wrist, she faltered. Her breath caught.

"Sing." It was an order, and she obeyed. Catching her next breath, she plunged back into the song. I kissed her hands, her fingertips. I let my tongue slide along the inside of her wrist, tasting her salty skin. I was in front of her now, and as the final notes of her song wound down, I grazed her lips with my thumb.

She bent her head slightly, kissed the pad of my thumb. It was like a bolt of energy shooting through my body. Without thought, I pulled her into my arms and kissed her completely, kissed her how I had always wanted to kiss her. It was a kiss that said *You're mine,* and she kissed me back, letting me take her. My tongue slipped against her sweet lips and she moaned slightly. My heartbeat thudded, and I swear I could hear the echoes of her song in the room as our kiss went on.

Then the door burst open. We tore apart from each other, but it was too late. Sophia was in the doorway. The camera crew was right behind her.

"There they are! I knew it!"

CHAPTER THIRTY-SIX
Rachel

I wrapped my arms around myself, drawing away from Clint. He looked absolutely furious when he saw Piers come out from behind the camera crew.

"Piers, you goddamn asshole—"

"Some of these girls told me that they had seen sparks between you two," Piers said, giving a meaningful look to Clint. "I didn't believe them, so we decided to investigate."

"She's a dirty whore," Sophia said, thrusting her finger at me. "Cheater! She was fucking him this whole time to win the contest!"

I could have cried. I was so close to the final competition - so close! And here I was going to lose it all, just because of a stupid kiss. I was shaking with anger.

"No. It was my fault."

I turned to Clint, my mouth falling open. He had a serious expression on his face, and his eyes glinted with anger.

"It was all my fault," he repeated. "I cornered Rachel in here. I kissed her. She didn't start anything. She was just in here practicing."

"Clint—" I started to protest, but he shut me up with a hard look. I could tell that he didn't want me to interfere.

"You expect us to believe that?" Sophia cried out.

"She's sleeping with him!" Annette chimed in.

"Is that true?" Piers asked. The camera men moved around, getting a closer shot. I looked away. I could already feel my cheeks burning.

"It's absolutely not true. One hundred percent false," Clint insisted. "We never had sex."

"Rachel?"

My head snapped up. Piers was pointing a microphone at me. I looked at Clint; he looked like he wanted to smash the microphone through Piers' head.

"It's true," I managed to squeak out. "We didn't."

"And the kiss?"

I shook my head, trying to find the words.

"He—he kissed me," I said. I didn't want to lie, but I wasn't going to tell the whole truth either.

"You're not attracted to him?"

There was a pause, and in my mind I tiptoed carefully out of the trap. I took a deep breath and felt it at the bottom of my lungs, under my belly button.

"I'm not —I'm not saying I'm not attracted to him."

"See!" Sophia cried out.

"Come on," I said, letting my irritation show. "Every girl in the *world* is attracted to Clint Terrance. I'm no exception."

"She's screwing him to win the contest!" Sophia cried.

The camera men swiveled from Sophia back to me for a response. I took a deep breath, down below my belly button, and tried to stay calm.

"No. I'm a virgin. I never expected anything. And I definitely didn't expect him to kiss me in the practice room."

I breathed out the last of my air. It was true. All of it was true. They couldn't come after me for anything. Clint had taken the fall for me. I didn't know why.

"There's somebody else who wants an explanation," Piers said.

I frowned. An explanation?

"Who?" I asked.

"Your fiancé."

Derrick walked through the door of the recording studio. The camera men moved closer to me, the lens fixing on my face. Clint stepped forward, putting himself slightly between us. But I knew that he wasn't going to do anything to hurt me. Not with so many people watching.

Not on tape.

"Derrick? What are you doing here?" I asked.

He clasped his hands together lightly in front of him. He was wearing a business suit, and he looked so professional. I remembered why I'd fallen for him in the first place. He came off as so mature. But I knew that in reality, he was nothing but a jerk.

"I needed to talk with you," he said dryly. "But you weren't returning my calls."

"There's nothing I have to say to you, Derrick."

He spread his hands in front of him with a gesture of openness. The biggest liar in the world, looking like he was innocent.

"Why would you avoid your fiancé—"

"You're not my fiancé! You broke up with me! Or don't you remember?"

"That's exactly why I wanted to talk with you!"

I crossed my arms.

"Go ahead, then. Talk."

"If we're ever going to work things out, we need to have an open line of communication."

He stared at me. I stared right back.

"And we need to be able to tell each other things."

I stared without saying a word.

"Well?"

"Well what?"

"Isn't there anything you need to say to me?"

"I don't know what you're talking about, Derrick."

"Look, if you just apologize, we can start move past this."

"Apologize? *I* should apologize?"

"You ran off into some other guy's arms for comfort. And I know we were fighting, but all couples fight, and we both need to apologize. I'll go first. Rachel, I'm sorry for not wanting you to do this contest. I see now that you're really into this singing thing."

This singing thing. My eyes turned to narrow slits. Fury

was boiling in my veins.

"If you want me to forgive you—"

"Stop."

My voice was low, and so was my larynx. And I wasn't about to let Derrick have one more word in this argument.

"I *don't* want you to forgive me. I don't want to *move past this*. We are *not* a couple. And you breaking up with me was the best thing that ever happened to me."

"What? Rachel, I don't…"

Derrick looked confused. I realized that he must have thought I was at home, pining away for him all this time. Well, I was going to disabuse him of that notion very quickly.

I leaned forward.

"I don't want you back, Derrick. I will never ever *ever* marry you."

There. That should give the cameras something to film.

I pushed my way past him, and let my shoulder shove Sophia to the side as I moved between her and Piers.

"Thanks for setting all this up," I hissed to Piers. He didn't look nearly as ashamed as he should have. I didn't look back. I knew that if I saw Clint standing there, I would want nothing more than to run back and throw myself into his arms.

CHAPTER THIRTY-SEVEN
Clint

Rachel was obviously terrified—I could hear her breathing quicken and grow shallow. I was proud that she had the guts to stand up to the asshole all on her own, even if it meant blaming me for the kiss that both of us had enjoyed.

After she left, Derrick spun back toward me.

"This—this is all your fault," he sputtered. "You're trying to steal Rachel—"

"She's not a thing," I said. "And I'm not stealing her."

"What do you call that kiss?"

"A kiss."

"But—but—"

"Listen, asshole," I said, thinking of a hundred other things that I wanted to call him. "She doesn't want to be with you. End of story."

The guy looked at me, then swung toward the camera as though expecting Piers to intervene. When he didn't, his shoulders slumped slightly.

"You—you're just a playboy," he said. "You'll break her heart. You'll ruin her."

"She's not mine to ruin," I said, gritting my teeth.

"She was perfect for me!" Derrick cried. "She was going to be my wife!"

Anger trickled through my system and I clenched my fists. I didn't want to have to break this guy in half, but I would if he insisted on it.

"I'm glad she decided to throw you to the curb," I said. "And if you don't get out of here, right now, I'm going to do the same thing."

I took a step forward, and Derrick, the proud and

arrogant asshole he was, tripped over his own feet running out of the room. His suit coat flapped behind him.

"Do you think he'll come back?" Piers asked.

Before answering, I put my hand over the camera lens and forcefully lowered it.

"Hey!" the camera guy said. "What are you—"

"You get out of here too," I hissed. "Don't fucking tape me for another second."

"Clint—"

I thumped Piers in the chest. He took a stumbling step back but, to his credit, didn't even blink or turn away.

"I can't believe you fucking did this. You fucking set me up!"

"Are you kidding? That was bloody great footage. You're going to get so many views from this—"

"Don't you dare."

Piers looked at me with a sympathetic expression.

"I know you like the girl, Clint, but this is good for her too. You'll see. When it airs…"

But I was already walking away.

"Clint! Come on! Don't be pissed about this! I'm trying to make this a great show! Isn't that what you wanted?"

I didn't answer him. What I'd wanted when we started wasn't the same as what I needed now.

I was sure that Rachel was going to be crying somewhere in the apartment, but she wasn't there. I found her in the glass globe. She was standing in the middle of the globe, bare feet against the glass. She was wearing the red dress she had worn on her first audition. And she was singing.

I reached up and pressed a button on the panel, then took off my own shoes.

Her voice was soft, delicate. The notes wavered tremulously in the air. When I dropped down into the globe with her, she didn't seem surprised to see me. The song trailed off and disappeared into the air.

"Clint?" She was quiet, but she wasn't sobbing. Her eyes were bright and free of tears. She looked strong. Like a warrior standing above her army.

"Are you practicing?" I asked.

"I didn't get it. I wanted to sing until I got it." She swallowed. "What am I doing wrong?"

"You're trying to push through the song."

"I don't know what that means."

"You have to relax."

She gave a short huff.

"It's hard to relax when you're focusing on a dropped larynx and a full diaphragm and whatever the hell else you taught me."

"Don't think about all that."

"You're the one who told me to think about it!"

I chuckled.

"I know. But if you fixate on it, there won't be anything left to sing. The best part of your voice is the emotion. Keep the emotion, and just use the breathing to support it."

She looked out onto the city. I stood beside her, wrapped my arms around her waist. She was breathing deeply, her stomach pressing out against my hand as she took the air inside of her. When she exhaled, though, it was a ragged breath.

"I'm scared, Clint."

I tugged her slightly against me so that her back molded to my chest. She leaned her head back, tilting it slightly against my shoulder. Her hair glinted red and gold in the auburn waves.

"Of what?" I asked.

"The final contest."

"You'll do fine. And you have a few days to prepare."

"Remind me to breathe if I forget," she murmured.

"You won't forget," I reassured her. "After all, you've had twenty-two years of practice."

She smiled at me echoing her words back to her.

"Thanks."

"Anyway, I'm not a judge anymore. It's out of my hands."

"Yeah, I know."

"You know what that means?"

She turned around in my arms. Standing there, it felt like we were floating in the middle of the air. I ached for her. The air between us crackled with tension.

"Clint…" She trailed off, eyeing the doorway.

"I locked up. Don't worry, we aren't going to get surprised by any camera crew up here."

"Okay," she said. "But what about someone standing down on the sidewalk with a pair of binoculars?"

I only smiled and kissed her.

CHAPTER THIRTY-EIGHT
Rachel

I melted into Clint's arms. He gathered me against him, his lips gentle and probing. Then he kissed me harder, harder, each second burning hotter through my nerves. I wasn't myself anymore. I wasn't Rachel, the good girl from the farm. I was the woman in the red dress, a singer. A star.

His hands pressed against my lower back, caressing me gently even as his mouth tore my breath from my body. I went dizzy with desire.

"Rachel—"

"I want you," I said, not letting him finish.

He brushed a strand of hair back from my face and kissed me again. This time, he leaned into me, and I felt him, hard and ready against my thigh. I ached between my thighs.

"Please," I whispered on his lips. "Please take me."

"You don't have to ask twice," he said. He smiled gently, and I wondered who I was giving myself to. Who was this man, who could awaken such desire in me? Who was this rock star helping me up out of the globe, his hands touching my curves as though he already owned them?

"Are we going to your bedroom?" I asked.

"I thought that here would be fine." He grinned.

"Here?" I looked out at the globe.

"Here." He reached up, and above me I heard metal parts moving.

"I—uh— I don't think I can do this on a swing," I said, all hesitation. "Remember, I'm kind of new to this."

"Don't worry," Clint said, and his voice was so

confident that I believed him. "I'll take care of you."

He kissed me then, kissed me warmly, and as he kissed me he pulled off my dress. I raised my arms and let him disrobe me.

I'll take care of you. Why was it that this sent shivers through me? He wasn't supposed to be the safe one. He wasn't supposed to be the one who cared. Derrick had been that. Clint was...

I didn't know what he was anymore.

He took his time. It was chilly in the air, but wherever he saw goosebumps he would move his mouth, kissing and sucking at my skin until my heart beat hot blood through my veins. The goosebumps disappeared, replaced with small shivers of desire as he unhooked my bra, cupping my breasts.

"Perfect," he murmured. He took one nipple into his mouth and sucked softly. I gasped as I felt the heat shoot through me to the core. I was already soaked when he hooked his fingers into my panties and tugged.

"Ohh-ohhh," I cried out softly. He slid one hand down, his fingers splitting as they stroked me on both sides of my aching slit. He moved slowly, firmly, his hand taking possession of me with each stroke.

I glanced sideways at the glass globe. He noticed my glance.

"Here," he said. He pushed a button over my head and the bottom half of the globe went dark. "Is that better for you?"

"How—how did you do that?"

"Magic," he said, kissing my neck. I moaned as his fingers probed closer to where I ached so badly I could scream. "Or something to do with darkening lens glass. One or the other."

"Mmmm," was my only response as I lifted my head and took him again into a kiss.

"Let me look at you," he said, pulling back. Immediately, a shiver rippled through my body and I pulled my arms around myself. I was naked, completely naked. No man had ever seen me like this.

Would he still want me? I cast my eyes down, agonizing over the red weals at my ankles where the new heels had cut into them, the soft plump places that the dress had been covering up. All my blemishes, all my imperfections—

"You're so fucking gorgeous."

His voice growled through my nerves, and when I looked up I saw ravenous desire on his face. His eyes slid across my shoulders and down to my hips, so fierce a gaze that I could feel it, as tangible as fingers on my skin and just as sensual.

"Now you," I said, surprising myself.

He grinned.

"Your turn. Undress me."

I licked my lips and stepped forward boldly. Reaching up to his shirt where the first button was already undone, I saw the edges of a tattoo.

"I've been wondering what you had hidden under here," I murmured.

The buttons came undone, and, inch by inch, I uncovered the tattoo on his chest.

It started out with a few simple lines, splashing out across his neck in curves of black. My fingertips traced the lines down as I undid the next button. The lines wove back and forth, intersecting before finally resolving into...

"It's music," I said. He smiled.

"Keep going."

I did. The lines slid down, parallel to each other, lines of sheet music with a few musical notes farther down. And inside his shirt, down on his chest, the lines spread again, wrapping around a tattooed heart that lay right over his real one.

Tracing my fingers over the musical notes, I tried to hum the melody, if there was one. It took a few seconds for me to recognize the tune that it resolved into.

"*Amazing Grace?*" I tilted my head quizzically.

"That's right."

"Why? You're not—I mean, you don't seem like a religious kind of guy."

He laughed.

"No, you're right. I'm not. But I wasn't a great kid, and when my mom left, I got mixed up in the wrong kind of stuff."

"Drugs?" I ventured. He nodded.

"The alcohol was worse. But yeah, that too. And my dad wasn't exactly the best role model when it came to keeping clean. But music was what did it for me. I realized that I couldn't keep on doing that shit. It was ruining the best thing that I had."

It was the most he'd ever shared of himself with me. He swallowed, his Adam's apple moving up and then down under his stubbled neck.

"So music was your saving grace." My fingertips traced the lines back up again, where they wavered and exploded at his collarbone. His chest radiated heat.

"I wouldn't say I'm safe yet, but yeah. Something like that. It keeps me in line."

"Good to know that something can."

"Hey, easy there."

I smiled.

"You just don't seem like the kind of guy who wants to stay between the lines."

"I've never had a reason to."

"But now?"

I blushed as he looked suddenly into my eyes, a grin peeking out from the corner of his mouth.

"You still have one button left."

My fingers fumbled at the bottom of his shirt. Dark hair tufted below his bellybutton, leading down below his jeans. And now my mouth went dry. Was I really doing this? Could I really do this?

Just as I hesitated, he bent and kissed me again, gently,

saving me from thought. My hands went up and pressed his skin over his tattoo as he wrapped his arms around my waist. Pulling me in, he eased my body against his. My nipples crushed against his skin and it was warm, oh so warm in his embrace.

He didn't let me undo his jeans. Instead, he picked me up, and as he raised me in his arms I saw that he'd connected the red sashes up into a hammock.

"Lay back."

The sashes went taut as I relaxed my body back. The strips of fabric held me comfortably, cradling me. I rocked back and forth, naked, caressed by the soft red silk on all sides. It was like being in a cocoon, with only small slits between the red sashes where I could see out.

My hands slid up, gripping the sashes near my arms. He wrapped sashes around my wrists, tying me into the swing, then moved to my ankles to do the same thing. I felt the fabric tighten around me, and my heart pounded in my chest.

"Is that necessary?" I asked.

"Better safe than sorry," he said, grinning. "Wouldn't want you falling out of this. And I've never tried this before."

"You what? Wait—"

"Here you go!" he cried, and pushed the swing out. I let out a short cry of exhilaration as I swung out into the globe. The hammock slid out to the end of extension and caught, rocking me out and then back. I swayed, laughing. I never felt this way, so carefree. As though I had nothing to worry about. Even though I was naked, it felt natural. It felt right. Clint would take care of me. I knew he would.

Laying back like I was, I could see the clouds overhead and the tops of the nearby buildings. Music started to play inside the globe, a soft blues rhythm that slid through the air and over my nerves, calming me. A few snowflakes landed on the glass above my head.

"Clint, it's snowing," I said wondrously.

"That's strange for November," Clint said. His voice was right by my ear. I turned to see him hanging by one of the other sashes. His tendons stood out and his arms bulged as he swung up.

I hadn't imagined that such a big guy could be so graceful. When he sang onstage, he was all ripped muscle and sharp motions. Here, though, he was as fluid as a dancer in the air. He wove through the sashes, lifting himself over me.

His knees settled on either side of my hips and he straddled me in the air. The sashes pulled taut as he lowered himself down, sliding his hands down the sashes and letting himself bend forward until his mouth was inches from mine. The buckle on his jeans was cold against my belly, and I shivered.

"Tell me more about the weather," he said, pressing a light kiss onto my cheek.

I knew he was joking, but I replied anyway.

"It's just a light snow," I said. "It reminds me... it reminds me of the farm. I remember waking up when I was a kid and it was just starting to snow outside. Before the sun even rose, when the sky was still gray and the snowflakes were almost invisible against the clouds."

"It sounds beautiful."

It was. But the words caught in my throat as I remembered that my mom had taken me outside in the fields that day. She had played with me, and it had just been me and her—Rose was still in bed, and she didn't wake her. It was one of the last times I remember her from before she got sick.

"Rachel."

The low voice brought me back to the moment. I blinked, and then realized that Clint was unbuckling his jeans, had already slipped them down to his knees. He braced himself over me as he kicked them off his ankles.

I peeked down and saw his cock straining through his black briefs. My mouth went dry.

He was so big, so thick, the outline of his erection bulging through the fabric. I ached for him, but I didn't know if I could take him into me fully. A twinge went through my body.

"I'll try to go slow," he said. Another kiss on my neck. A hand on my hip. "But I'm not sure how long I can wait."

Clint's kisses sent heat through my skin, into my core. His hand caressed my body even as he slid down his briefs and rolled on a condom. I shivered as he shifted down, pushing my thighs apart. The music in the air turned to a jumble of notes as my mind went blank with pleasure. His thumb brushed against my hot wet slit, testing me.

"Ohhhh," I moaned. I bit my lip and felt his cock twitch between my legs. He was there, right there, positioned at my opening. I ached for him, my whole body needing to be filled, but I was still holding back, uncertain. And I knew that in a moment, everything would be different.

I closed my eyes. Focused on the slow notes of the bass guitar in the song that was playing. Everyone had told me that this was the hard part.

"Are you scared?" A whisper at my ear.

"Terrified."

He paused.

I opened my eyes and found him waiting, his dark eyes reflecting the swaths of red around us. He cupped his hand around the back of my neck, massaging my muscles slowly, and I saw him wrestling with something inside of himself.

"The good kind of terrified," I amended. "The kind of terrified when you're at the top of the roller coaster waiting to fall."

He kissed my forehead, a smile slowly making its way across his face.

"I won't let you fall."

I nodded, something swelling inside of my chest.

"I know," I said.

"Stay here," he said. "Stay with me."

And just like that, I wasn't scared anymore. His concern had driven away any terrors I had. I was in his arms, and I knew that he would keep me safe. I didn't have to worry. I didn't have to focus on anything else but him.

He kissed me again, on the forehead, the nose, the lips. Small whispers of kisses. Every one tightened the coil inside of me, pulling me closer and closer. Need swallowed my body, and I writhed under him.

"Please," I whispered.

"Yes?"

"Please, Clint. Now. I need you."

"Look at me, Rachel. I want to watch you when it happens."

I bit my lip and looked up into eyes so caring and desirous, I wanted to fall upwards into them. There was no judgment in his eyes, only want. And when he smiled, a new emotion threaded through my heart.

Was it love? It couldn't be. That wasn't part of what he'd asked from me. But there it was, terrible and wonderful, spreading through me as his lips found mine.

His arms were around me, and I felt him slide into me. A sharp piercing pain gave way almost instantly to the most beautiful sensation of being filled, filled completely.

I clenched involuntarily, and above me, he moaned. He bit his lip, his eyes rolling back with pleasure. My wrists pulled tight against the sashes, barely reaching to spread across his thick shoulders. I clenched again, the wonderful unfamiliar sensations rippling through me.

"God, Rachel, you're so tight."

He eased out slowly, and I nearly cried out with the hollow ache that he left inside of me when he withdrew. My fingers gripped his shoulder blades, pulling him toward me.

"Ohhh," he moaned through gritted teeth. I realized that he was holding back for me. Boldness seized me, and I pulled his head down to kiss him again.

This time his lips touched mine at the same time that he slid inside me, and my breath disappeared with the hot burning ache. I knew what it felt like to be on the edge of an orgasm, but this was like that feeling happening forever. My core tightened and tightened and I choked out a gasp between our lips.

"Rachel?"

"More."

There was a momentary look of surprise on his face, and then he grinned. Moving slowly, he began to rock back and forth into me. The sashes holding us up rocked too, and the sky overhead swayed in a rhythm that was at once perfect and entirely too slow.

Bursts of pleasure shocked my body with every roll of his hips. I felt his muscles tense against my swollen clit as he rippled his body against mine. Just enough pressure to heighten my need and bring me closer, closer to the edge. But as I reached for the cliff, he would roll back, easing up, sending my body into tremors of need.

I began to rock opposite him, my body lifting up to meet him with each roll of his hips. I couldn't move my arms or legs much, but I could do this.

"Oh, fuck," he groaned. "Rachel—"

But I was already on the verge of orgasm. My head tilted back against the red sashes. I couldn't tell if it was still snowing or if my vision was just exploding with white bursts of electricity from the sensation of being filled.

His mouth sucked at the skin of my neck, licking in time with his strokes. Every inch of me felt like it was pulled taut, vibrating more and more as the need inside me grew.

I began to shudder. As though I was dreaming, my body moved by itself. My legs tightened around his body, pulling him into me completely. My hand gripped his hair as it came down to where I could reach, threading through the dark strands. Our bodies were slick with sweat, and the globe felt full of warm air pressing on us from all sides.

Skin slid against skin with terrible, wonderful friction.

"*Yes*," I moaned. "Yes, yes, oh God, Clint, *yes*—"

The orgasm rolled over me, different from anything I'd ever felt before, even in the studio. This felt like I was finally whole. And as the waves of ecstasy crashed through me, I arched my body and gripped his cock inside of me, hard shivers tearing through my nerves as I struggled to hold on.

"*YES! YES! OHHHHH!*"

He held me tightly as I shook, writhing from side to side as the spasms went through me. I was glad then that he had tied me in with the sashes. I felt like I was going to thrash right out of the air.

Then his cock stiffened and he groaned. His mouth was on my skin, and I could feel him biting softly at my shoulder, holding back as his own orgasm trembled through both of our bodies.

I shivered again, one last time, feeling him hard inside of me.

This—this was what it was like? To feel so complete. To be turned inside out, utterly undone, and still feel like I was more than what I'd been before.

My whole life, I had thought that my virginity would be something that someone would take from me. I'd held onto it jealously. But Clint hadn't taken anything from me—he'd given me something deep and beautiful. I was dizzy with the thought of it.

"How do you feel?"

"I… I feel… perfect." A laugh bubbled up on my lips. My body shook slightly, already cooling. Had the air been warm? It was chilly now, and I nestled my head into the crook of Clint's neck to warm myself up. His body was still hot.

"Good. Now sing."

"What?"

He lifted his body away from mine.

"Sing that song you were practicing earlier."

I laughed.

"Now? Really?"

"Really. Use your breath." He put one hand down on my belly. His palm warmed my skin.

I laughed again, but his expression was serious.

"Okay," I said. I took a deep breath. I could feel the air traveling down through my body, down to the bottom of my lungs.

I sang.

The words echoed in the globe, but I wasn't paying attention to the lyrics. They were such a part of me that I didn't need to. Instead, I focused on the way my mouth opened and let the air flow through. I focused on opening my throat, letting the notes come out one by one. And yes, I focused on my breath.

He moved down as I sang, kissing my neck, my shoulder, my breasts. Each kiss took my focus and put it in a different place on my body.

It was like the music was flowing through me. I wasn't forcing anything, just letting the song happen. And I realized as I sang that this was how I should have been doing it all along.

When I finished, Clint kissed me on the mouth. Softly, gently. How strange. I'd expected this to be rough, but he'd been more gentle than anything I could imagine.

"Perfect," Clint said. Then he grinned. "Now let me turn the recording off."

I started to sit up in the hammock, blood draining from my face. But the ties caught me by the wrists, held me back.

"You were recording? *What*? When did you turn it on?"

"When I was adjusting the swing. This room has great acoustics."

"Wait, so you were recording it when… when we…"

My face went red.

"Don't worry," he said with a wink. "I'll delete that part."

"Delete it right now, mister!"

He laughed.

"Okay, okay! I thought you would be happy about it. Our last recording session ended way too abruptly."

"That is true."

He lifted himself out of the hammock, swinging gracefully back to the platform. I watched the snowflakes melt on the top of the globe as he untied me. Then he pulled me back out of the air. It was like coming out of the sky and landing on the ground.

Unsteady on my feet, I swayed as I pulled on my red dress while he tugged on his jeans. The dress felt tighter, clinging to my damp skin. He wrapped one arm around me and pulled me in tight for a kiss on top of the tiny platform. I felt wonderful. Light on my feet.

Everything was beautiful. More colorful. More alive. How had I been afraid of this?

"Okay, time for you to head back to the apartment."

"Okay," I said.

"Wait, no. I changed my mind." Clint kissed me again. "Let's just stay here forever."

I laughed. Even my laugh seemed different somehow.

"Sounds good to me," I said. "But I'm pretty sure we would starve to death in the globe."

"I'll order in. Pizza delivery from a helicopter. They'll lower it in from the top of the globe."

"Oh, yeah?"

"Slice by slice."

I burst out laughing again. He kissed me, then paused. Then kissed me again, deeper, so passionately that the heat began to swirl through my body again. I pushed him away teasingly.

"Hey! I thought we had to head back. What are you doing?"

"Getting my kisses in while the kissing is good. Who knows when I'll get to kiss you next?"

"It won't be that long," I said.

"It'll be way, *way* too long."

"Mmmm." I pulled him in for another one. Then, laughing, I made my way down the ladder. He followed me down.

I peeked into the apartment.

"Anyone there?"

"No, but there's cameras, and—"

He caught me around the waist, pulling me into the apartment.

"Clint! Cut it out! They're taping!"

"I'll delete the tapes. Don't worry." His mouth was hot on my neck as he pressed me against the wall.

The elevator door let out a ding.

"They're back!" I hissed. "Get out of here!"

"They already know about us," Clint said. "Come on. I'm not sneaking down the ladder of my own penthouse."

He pulled me in by the waist as I squirmed, kissing me on the cheek. I looked up at the elevator.

It was Piers. There was no camera crew behind him, and I breathed a sigh of relief.

"Thank God you're here," Piers said, looking serious. "We've been looking for you everywhere."

"Well, you caught me," Clint asked. "We were just having a music lesson, and—"

"No, *you*." He looked directly at me, and I could feel my chest tense up even before he spoke.

"Rachel, it's your mom."

CHAPTER THIRTY-NINE
Clint

"My mom? What is it? What happened?" Rachel's voice rose high in panic. Her breathing hitched in her chest. I put my hand on her back for support, but I don't think she even noticed that I was touching her.

"I don't know," Piers said. "Your dad called and said that they were in the hospital and that you should come home. Here, he left the address—"

"My phone. I—I have to call him." Rachel spun, heading back to her room. I took the slip of paper Piers had the address written on.

"Is it bad?" I asked him.

He shook his head.

"No idea. Her dad was pretty out of it when he called. I can get her a taxi."

"No," I said. "I'll take her."

"You?"

I glared at Piers.

"Yeah, me. I can drive faster than any taxi."

"We're taping the recordings tomorrow, Clint, and the day after—"

"You can tape it without me." I was already on the phone with the attendant downstairs. "Yeah, could you pull the Audi out front? The black one. Yeah." I wanted to be fast and inconspicuous. This was one time I couldn't afford to get pulled over for speeding.

"Clint. I know this is stressful, but it's not your problem!" Piers said.

I looked up to see Rachel standing in the hallway. Her face was white.

"Did you call him?" I asked.

"He left a message. It was a car accident. That's all he said, and he's not picking up his phone now."

"Come on." I put an arm around her and guided her into the elevator. I gave Piers a meaningful look. "We're leaving now."

"Clint."

"I don't want to hear it." I stabbed the button for the first floor and the elevator doors slid shut. "Rachel, I'm sorry."

I pulled her close to me, but she wasn't crying. She just stared straight ahead as the elevator eased down floor by floor.

"You don't have to drive me," she said finally. "I know the way. I can drive. If you let me borrow your car—"

"No way," I said. "I'm here for you. Okay?"

"Okay." Her voice was whisper soft, and I leaned closer to hear her. "I wasn't."

"You weren't? You weren't what?"

"I wasn't there for her."

"Rachel, don't say that. We're going to be there soon, okay? I'll drive fast."

"Not too fast."

She didn't say anything else, but I knew what she was thinking. Her mom had been in a car accident, and she wasn't trying to end up the same way.

We pulled away in the Audi and I sped through every shortcut I knew to get out of New York City. When we got to the Jersey turnpike, though, there was a jam. One of the lanes was closed off and the entire road was backed up for what looked like two miles of stop and go traffic.

"Hang on," I said. I pulled into the bus-only lane.

"What are you doing?" Rachel gripped her armrest, her fingers white. "We're not supposed to drive in this lane. They'll pull us over. Clint—"

I punched in the numbers on my steering wheel and the phone rang over the speakers. I prayed that it wouldn't go to voicemail. We were almost at the tollbooth, and I knew they would stop me there.

"Hello?"

"Hey, Rog. It's Clint Terrance. Remember me?"

There was a pause. Roger Mathison was the head of NY transit authority, and he'd been to a party of my dad's recently. He'd almost OD'ed on cocaine, and I'd been the one to take him to our private doctor.

"Sure," he said hesitantly. "What are you calling for?"

"A favor."

He paused, and I could almost see him licking his lips. I'd already sworn secrecy, but he knew he owed me one.

"What do you need?"

We were at the booth. The attendant stared at the Audi, her eyebrows already furrowing.

"Sir, you can't be in this lane," she said.

"I just need a few words from you, Rog. That's it."

The attendant leaned forward out of the window. Behind us, buses were backing up.

"Sir, you absolutely cannot—"

"I have the head of transit authority on the phone here," I told her. "Mr. Mathison, will you let this young lady know we need emergency access to get through the turnpike?"

I handed her the cell phone. She tapped on her computer screen as she talked to Roger.

In the seat next to me, Rachel shifted impatiently. I put my hand on hers and squeezed lightly. *It's okay,* I mouthed, even though I knew it wasn't. I was going to do everything I could for her.

"Alright," the attendant said finally, handing me back my phone with an air of defeat. "Go on right ahead."

I was already in first, and when the bar lifted, my tires squealed. We rushed through the turnpike, passing the lanes of stopped traffic.

"Should have taken a helicopter," I muttered. "You don't get stopped in a helicopter."

Rachel only looked out the window mutely. I had to let

go of her hand to shift gears. She didn't move at all. It was like she had turned off completely, numb to any touch I gave.

She called her father again when we got off the turnpike, but from her face I could tell it went straight to voicemail.

"Don't worry," I said. "I'm sure she'll be fine."

"I'm not."

She wasn't crying, and that scared me more than anything. I'd seen her before when she was sad, but this was much, much worse. Her creamy skin had turned almost white as the snow.

"We'll be there soon," I said lamely. The navigation system had an arrival time twenty minutes from now, but as I sped through the hills, the minutes dropped off one by one. We ended up pulling into the hospital just as the snow stopped falling.

I dropped Rachel off at the entrance and parked quickly. When I got into the hospital, though, she was still at the front desk.

The nurse at the station looked up at me with heavy lids as I walked up and stood by Rachel.

"Where is she?" I asked.

"Room two eighty," Rachel said.

"Visiting hours aren't until six," the nurse said, sounding like she'd repeated the information a hundred times already tonight.

"This is an emergency, though."

"I didn't bring my ID," Rachel said, panic in her voice. "They won't let me in—"

"The room's down this way?" I pointed to the doors.

"Yes," the nurse said. "If you can get a family member to come vouch for you—"

"I've been calling my dad, but he won't pick up!" Rachel said. "Can you go and find them."

"Let me try ringing the room," the nurse said.

Rachel looked longingly past the swinging doors into

the hallway.

"That's my sister," she said. She waved through the glass door, but she didn't see her. "Rose!"

A doctor was coming out of the doorway. I took Rachel's arm and tugged her through, shoving my foot to stop the doors from automatically closing on us.

"Go ahead," I said, giving her a small push. I didn't need to; Rachel was already running down the hall. The nurse was shouting from behind me.

I turned around and stopped the nurse from chasing Rachel, letting the doors close behind me.

"You can't—"

"It's her mom," I said, putting my hands on her shoulders. The nurse stared balefully up at me.

"Fine. And you?"

"Me?" I said. I glanced down the hall. Rachel was heading into the hospital room.

She would be fine without me. I had done enough; I didn't want to butt into family business where I wasn't wanted.

"Yes, you" the nurse said insistently. "Are you family? Do you have ID?"

"No," I said, shaking my head slowly. I turned away from the doors. Rachel needed her family now, not me. "I'm nobody."

CHAPTER FORTY
Rachel

All the way to the hospital I prayed, throwing out hope into the universe desperately. I thought of what I would say to my mom when I got there. I would tell her that I loved her. I would tell her about the singing contest. She would be proud that her other daughter was finally doing well at something. Maybe she would forgive me for leaving her.

It was so stupid of me to leave the farm while she still needed help. What had I been thinking? I wouldn't leave until she got better, I vowed. I would stay by her side and take care of her—take better care of her than I'd ever taken care of her before. Even if she never remembered me again, I would take care of her and not resent it.

Now, I ran down the hospital hallway. My sister was standing outside of the room, crying.

"Rose!" I said. "What's going on? What happened? Is Mom okay?"

Rose shook her head, still sobbing too hard to speak. Fear pulsed through me. I pushed the door open.

"Dad!"

My dad turned from where he was standing at the foot of the hospital bed. He looked older than he ever had. As my eyes moved from him to the bed, he shook his head slowly.

"She's gone," he said. "Rachel, we lost her."

My heart stopped. Or maybe it didn't, but I stopped feeling it. I couldn't feel anything. Not my breathing, not my heartbeat, not anything. There was a rush of air in my ears and I struggled to speak.

"What—what do you mean?"

"Rachel, I'm sorry. Baby—"

I couldn't believe it. I went to my mom's bedside. Her skin looked paler than normal. I took her hand and nearly dropped it. She felt so cold. I pressed both of my hands around her hand, as though I could warm her up.

"*Oh, Mom.*"

I sank down to my knees on the chair next to the bed. A fierce sorrow surged forward, washing through my entire body. I had known it. The whole trip down, I'd felt a sense of overwhelming dread, like we were rushing for no reason. And now my whole body was numb.

My dad was speaking from behind me.

"It was quick. She was in a coma the whole time. The doctors did everything they could, but she finally went."

"When—when did she die?"

"Oh, Rachel. It couldn't have been fifteen minutes ago."

A sob ripped from my throat. The tears, though, didn't come. They weren't there. I could feel the grief taking over me, but I couldn't cry.

"Baby, baby."

I shook my head. The roar in my ears grew louder.

"I should have been here. I should have gotten here faster. I should have—"

"Baby, don't."

"If I had been just a little faster..." *If I hadn't been with Clint... if I had been in my room, if I could have gotten the phone call...*

"She was already gone."

"But I should... I should..." I couldn't make myself say the words.

I should never have left.

A woman came into the room. I lifted my head. She was wearing a white coat. A doctor. Her sneakers had pink trim around the edges. I couldn't stop staring at them. They seemed so out of place, like they couldn't be real. This couldn't be real. Could it?

"We're going to need to clear the room," the doctor said softly to my dad.

At that instant, I hated her. She hadn't saved my mom. She hadn't kept her alive long enough for me to say goodbye. Fury made my skin turn hot, but I tamped it down. Of course it wasn't her fault.

"Can I have a moment alone with her?" I asked. She opened her mouth as though to protest, but I wasn't going to budge. "Please. I just got here."

The doctor nodded.

"I'll be back in a few minutes," she said.

My dad followed the doctor out of the room, and I was alone with my mom.

My dead mom.

"Mom, I'm sorry. I'm so sorry, mom." I said. The words came out choked and hoarse, but I still wasn't crying. I didn't know what to say. I picked up her hand again. Her delicate hands. Like Rose's hands, not like mine.

On the wall behind the hospital bed, the monitors still ran. I stared at them, not knowing what I was looking at. One monitor beeped softly, in even intervals every ten seconds or so. There weren't any signals coming through, no matter how hard I wished. All of the lines were flat. She was gone. Really, truly gone.

My eyes burned but I couldn't cry. I swallowed the lump in my throat.

"This was all my fault. I wish I had stayed with you. I wish I had never left. I can't—I can't even ask you to forgive me anymore."

I shook my head and looked down, brushing back her gray hair. She still looked beautiful, like a princess from a fairy tale.

"I've missed you, mom," I said. "I've missed you for a while now. But now I know you're never coming back and it hurts, and I'm sorry I wasn't here when it mattered."

The ache twisted inside of me, but as hard as I tried, I couldn't let it come out. All of my pain was stuck inside, trapped in my chest, where it pulsed dark and evil around my heart.

I bent forward and kissed my mom on the forehead, next to where the bandages started. Her eyes were closed and she looked peaceful. Maybe I was just telling myself that to make it not as awful. Everything was numb.

"Goodbye," I said. Still, the tears didn't come. I could feel them inside of me, pressing on the backs of my eyes. But I couldn't feel anything.

"Goodbye," I said again, and stood up. My mother wasn't there.

She had barely been there before, but she was gone now. I had nothing left.

In the hallway, my sister was waiting. Dried tears stained her cheeks in streaks where her foundation had washed away. As I hugged her, she burst into a fresh set of tears. What was wrong with me that I couldn't cry with her? Why was the pain all wrapped up inside, unable to come out?

"Where's dad?" I asked, once she had wiped away her tears and stopped sniffling.

"He said I should drive us home in my car. He's down signing some things for the—uh, the body." She choked on the word.

"Okay." I took a deep breath and steeled myself. Then I remembered who had brought me. "I need to find Clint."

"That guy who drove you? He's with Dad."

I let out a sigh of relief. Clint would be able to take care of my Dad. And I could take care of my sister.

"Alright, then. Let's go."

Rose stood up from where she had been leaning against the wall, and I noticed that she, too, looked older. More tired. Did I? Or had I already grown up before this? Her hand trembled as she took her car keys from her pocket.

"I can drive," I offered softly. She nodded and handed me the keys, tears leaking out the corners of her eyes. She never let me drive, especially not her car. But tonight was different.

It felt like she was broken. Of course. We all were.

But it was my job to put us back together.

I pulled out onto the highway. We drove in silence for a few minutes. The moon was rising over the low hills. Rose sniffled, her face against the window. I'd given her my last Kleenex from my purse, but I hadn't been able to cry, anyway. I felt numb. My mind was full of thoughts about things that needed to be done.

Finally, though, I couldn't wait any longer. The little pieces of doubt that had been winging their way through my brain settled down together into a mass of anxiety. I had to know.

"Rose, what happened?" I asked.

She waited a moment before answering.

"Dad told you, didn't he?"

"He said Mom was in a car accident."

"Yeah."

"She wasn't driving, was she?"

"Of course not."

"But how... how did she get hit?"

"It was my fault, okay?" Rose yelled. She slammed her hand onto the dashboard and I started in my seat.

"Rose—"

"It was me! I was supposed to watch her! It was all my fault!"

My heart pounded. I swerved off the road onto a pullout and stopped the car. There wasn't another car for miles on the dark highway. I unbuckled my seatbelt and turned to Rose.

Rose broke down into fresh tears and sputtered the words around her sobs.

"It was almost...dinner...and I went to the bathroom, and then I came back and the water...the water was boiling. It was only a minute, I swear. I swear. Then I looked into the living room—"

"—and she was gone." I finished my sister's sentence. The image was clear as a summer sky in my mind. The chair, empty. The door open.

My mom, wandering off again.

"She went to the road?" I murmured, not expecting an answer. "She never goes to the road."

"It was a truck that hit—that hit her. Dan Folton, from down the hill."

Just like that, I could see him driving his truck. An old Ford, brown and weather-beaten. And my mom—

I winced.

"It wasn't your fault, Rose," I said mechanically.

"Of course it was. You were the one who took care of her. You always took care of her, and she loved you more. And then it was my turn, and I couldn't even look after her with someone helping me."

I was agog. I didn't know what to say.

Is that what she thought?

My mother had always put Rose first. She had always let Rose do whatever she wanted to do. She'd sent her away to college, for God's sake! How could she think that mom had loved me more?

"I killed her," Rose said miserably, wailing into her hands.

I put the car in park and leaned over the seat. Pulling my sister to me, I wrapped my arms around her.

"Listen to me, Rose. It is *not* your fault."

"Yes it is."

"If it is, it's as much my fault for leaving, or Dad's for having to work."

"*No.*"

"You did the best you could."

"I could have done better."

I heard myself speaking the same words, and my heart swelled. Rose thought that I would be angry at her, but instead of being angry, there was only sorrow.

I took a deep breath before speaking.

"We could always have done better. Sometimes our best isn't good enough. But it wasn't your fault that mom walked off. She'd walked off plenty of times before when I was supposed to be watching her."

"She didn't get killed those times."

"Because I was *lucky*," I said firmly. "Listen to me, okay? It was going to happen. Sometime, it was going to happen."

"She's gone," Rose said quietly. "She's gone. And I…"

She shook her head, trailing off.

"You what?"

"Nothing," Rose said, tears dripping off the end of her nose. "Nothing."

"It's not your fault, Rose. At least she's in peace now." I knew that my words weren't helping, couldn't help. I was retreating into the same cliches that everyone did in times of grief and loss. But there was nothing else I could do.

"Can we go home?" my sister asked. Her voice was the same as it had been when she was a child.

"Sure," I said. I put my hands back on the steering wheel. If she didn't want to talk with me about it, I wasn't going to push her. "Let's go home."

CHAPTER FORTY-ONE
Clint

Rachel's dad was a strong man, and I could tell he was used to taking care of everything that needed doing. But now, he seemed fragile. The nurses were in the middle of walking him through everything, but I took over making the phone calls when he started looking like he was going to break down.

I was setting up the funeral arrangements on my cell phone, rattling off my credit card number to the funeral director, when I felt a hand on my shoulder.

"One moment. I'll call you back." I hung up. "Mr. Ritter?"

"I forgot to introduce myself properly," he said. His voice was gruff, and his palm was coarse when I reached to shake his hand. "I'm John."

"Clint," I said.

"Charlene was always the one who did the introductions," he said. His eyes were far off.

"Rachel talked about her a lot," I said. "She must have been a great woman."

"Oh, she was. She was something." John nodded. Then he raised his head again. "How do you and Rachel—ah—"

"I'm sorry," I said, realizing how it might seem. "I'm the head of the music studio. I'm sure Rachel told you about the competition she was in."

"The singing thing, right. How's she doing?"

"She's a wonderful singer," I said. "I hope she'll be able to make it back for the finals. I think she has a good chance to win."

"Really?" Rachel's father raised his eyebrows.

"Absolutely."

"Oh, Rachel would love that. I wish—I wish Charlene could see…"

He wiped his eyes roughly.

"Rachel was always singing to her. Even when she wasn't singing, she was daydreaming about singing. Ever since she was a little girl."

"Did she ever have any lessons?"

"Rachel? You mean singing lessons?" He chuckled. "No, no, we couldn't afford anything like that."

"I think—"

My phone rang, cutting me off. I picked it up—it was the funeral home.

"Yes?" I turned slightly away and checked the name on the slip of paper. "Golden Fields Chapel is the place. Mr. Ritter. White roses? Yes, that sounds nice."

John was shaking his head as I hung up. I hesitated. Had I overstepped my bounds?

"No?" I asked. "Did Charlene not like roses?"

"Not that. She loved 'em," he said. "But I don't know how we'd pay for it."

I treaded carefully. I could tell this was a man with a lot of dignity.

"Don't worry about the cost."

"Someone's gotta worry," he said, drawing his brows together in a frown.

"I'm taking care of it."

He peered at me through red-rimmed eyes.

"Please," I said. "Let me do this as a favor for Rachel."

He hesitated, then nodded, still looking at me warily. I could sense that he was uncertain about something, but I hoped he would take the favor.

"Thank you," he said finally.

I let out a breath and nodded. We headed down the hallway toward the exit. He walked slowly, carefully. The night air hit us with a chilly whoosh. There were no more snowflakes here, just the cold.

"There's something else," he said.

"What is it?" I thought I had taken care of all the arrangements.

But that wasn't what he was referring to.

"What's between you and Rachel?"

"I don't know what you mean."

He stopped, coming up short before we reached the car.

"You know exactly what I mean, young man. When you talk about her, there's a different look to you. Don't tell me there's nothing between you two."

A smile slipped out between my lips.

"You're right," I said. "Of course. The truth is…"

I didn't know what to tell him. Rachel had given up her life back here to come to New York for a shot at singing. I didn't want to be the sleazy music producer. We barely knew each other, even though I felt like she had come closer to me than any other person in the world had.

And yet here I was, already pushing for her to come back with me. My muscles went tense. But I couldn't lie to him.

"The truth is that I love your daughter, Mr. Ritter. I love her more than anyone else in the world. And I only want what's best for her."

He nodded, a serious expression on his face. It shocked me. He didn't jeer at me. He wasn't going to call me a liar. He *believed* me.

"I want what's best for her, too. But what do you think she wants?" he asked.

"I don't know," I said truthfully. "She'll have to decide that for herself."

"Thank you for bringing her back here," John said. And again he reached out his hand. When I clasped it this time, though, I had a strange feeling. Her father wasn't treating me like a kid. He was treating me as another man, with respect.

"Thank you," I said, even though I couldn't name what he had done for me.

CHAPTER FORTY-TWO
Rachel

Back home, my sister went up to our old room, sobbing all the way. I let her go and went into the kitchen to get a drink of water. Numbness shrouded my heart.

The kitchen counter top was littered with bills. I felt a stab of annoyance at my sister, but it disappeared into pity. She'd never had to take care of any of this, I remembered. It had always been me handling the household. Me who made breakfast, washed the dishes, did the laundry and hung it out when it was sunny. It was me who fed my mom when she didn't feel like eating.

As I looked around, the walls began to close in on me. The air grew hot, and I felt more and more claustrophobic. Without my mom inside, this was just a house. An old house. I noticed the cracks in the windowpanes, the bare spots on the rug.

I pushed the back door open and stepped out. I was still wearing my red dress and heels, but I didn't feel cold. My skin chilled for only a moment and then went numb.

The sun was barely beginning to rise. There was frost on the tips of the dead blades of grass. It was beautiful.

I walked over to the barn. Behind it, the sky was turning lighter, the sunrise just beginning to sear the horizon. I peered in.

The barn was empty. At the bottom of the hayloft, a half-dozen bales sat molding, exposed to the moisture. Behind the drooping rafters, the first hints of sunrise burned orange and hot in the gray sky. Twin jet streams slit the gray expanse, and when I blew out, my breath, too, was white against the sky.

Just a barn. I'd spent years and years pretending that it

was my own personal concert hall. Now, I saw it as it really was. The barn paint was peeling, curling away from the wood, and the eaves were rotting through. My secret hiding place was nothing but a dreary, empty pile of wood. I finally realized how old it was—how old everything was here. No longer Eden, but something else. The tinge of gold in the hay was gone.

I walked back to the house and stopped by the blackberry bushes. The sun's rays filtered through the briars, caressing my face.

I closed my eyes.

If I tried really hard, I could almost imagine summertime again. I could see the green leaves spread out like palms, hiding clusters of plump berries. I could see the hard little green buttons that were only starting to blush pink and the overripe blackberries that had been bored into by a bird, or maybe a wasp. Whatever it was, it had left only stringy pieces of black flesh hanging off of the stem.

"Rachel?"

I opened my eyes, and I was back in this gray world. There were no leaves anymore, no berries. It was all gone.

I turned, and tears rolled down my face. I hadn't even realized that I had started crying.

Clint stood there, waiting for me. His eyes were dark, his face solemn, and he held his arms out as I stepped forward. The pain that had been stuck inside of me unraveled and spread outward, gutting me completely. Every part of me wanted to scream in anguish, and I gasped cold air as the pain pierced through me, like thorns ripping through my heart.

As I crumpled into sobs, he drew me in and held me, not saying a word. He didn't have to. He was there, and that was all I needed to know to let myself go. There was someone there to take care of me, to hold me. I didn't have to feel this pain all by myself, and that was enough.

I slept for only a few hours. When I woke up, the house was clean. And there were two black dresses laying on the couch in my room.

"For the funeral," Clint explained, when I found him. "I wasn't sure if you or your sister had anything to wear."

He was right, of course. For me, anyway. Rose had a dress already picked out, but I was grateful for the modest black silk sheath he'd picked out.

"I can stay if you need me to," he said. And, stupidly, I told him no.

"I'll be fine," I said, panic wrapping tightly around my throat. I was scared to let him go, but I was even more scared to let him stay. The funeral was tomorrow morning—the director was worried about frost.

"The final episode taping isn't until tomorrow," he said. "And I thought you might need a ride to the funeral tomorrow morning, or…"

"Or what?"

"Anything," he said. "Anything you need, Rachel. Anything I can give."

He took my hands in his and raised my fingers to his lips. His kindness stung my eyes with tears, but I blinked them back.

"Thank you… just for being here. You don't have to stay."

He left, then. An hour later, a bouquet of white roses arrived at the doorstep. I put them in a vase and set them in the middle of the table. They looked so elegant in the middle of such shabby surroundings. I put my head in my hands and cried and wished he hadn't gone. I felt so alone.

The night passed fitfully. I dreamed about turning around and finding my mother gone. I sang to her, but everytime I thought I heard her voice it was farther away. I woke up crying, reaching out.

Tt was the morning of the funeral, and I felt utterly lost. I'd been trying to hold everything together, but my

Dad was still trying to work the ranch and I had nobody to lean on. I hadn't seen him cry at all this week. It was like he was pretending everything was still the same. I knew he couldn't keep it up.

My sister, on the other hand, was trying desperately to help me with everything. But since Clint had taken care of most of it, her assistance wasn't even needed. I had her rearrange all of the flowers and food in the living room for the reception afterward, but I was running out of meaningless tasks to give her.

When it was finally time to go to the chapel, relief surged through my grief. Soon this would be over. I could get back to the farm, back to the hundred tasks requiring my attention. I could help my dad again. I couldn't even be bitter about losing my chance at singing. It had been a dream, that was all. A silly dream that had taken me away from what mattered most.

The funeral went by in a rush of words and emotion. I greeted everyone and thanked them for coming. Both my dad and sister took turns standing by me, stepping away when they needed to cry. My own tears had dried up as soon as Clint had left—I was back in charge now, and I had to keep things together.

Then there was a commotion at the door.

I looked up to see Dan Folton and his wife at the chapel entrance. Rose hadn't told me that they were coming to the funeral, and now I knew why. Everywhere in the house, people whispered and looked at them. Dan had a guilty expression on his face.

I stepped forward.

"I'm so sorry," Dan said. His wife clenched his arm tightly. They both waited for me to speak.

I should have been angry, but it wasn't Dan's fault. He had to know that.

"Thank you," I said. "Thank you both for coming. This is hard for all of us."

"If I should leave…"

"No." I pressed my lips together firmly. "My mother loved you both. She would want you here."

Dan's face melted into relief. His white eyebrows furrowed together in sympathy.

"Rachel. Little Rachel. When did you grow up?"

"I'm still working on it," I said, pressing a weak smile onto my face and letting them wrap me in a warm hug.

The funeral started right on time, as my mom would have wanted. The pastor read my mom's favorite passages from the Bible, and I felt a weight pressing on me as I stared forward at the coffin, a wreath of white roses atop the dark wood. Then I felt Rose nudging me.

"It's your turn," she whispered.

Right. The pastor had asked me to come up to speak. I'd told him that I would be able to speak for the family, but when I got up there, I looked down at the page in front of me and the words went blurry. The tears I'd been holding back were stinging my eyes, pushing to come out.

I swallowed and blinked hard, but I couldn't read the words. I had written something last night, but I didn't remember any of it. I didn't believe everything my mom believed, and now all of my sentences rang false in my mind. I couldn't read this. I couldn't.

I looked up at the rows of people. Black suits, black dresses. A sea of darkness in front of me. I was falling into it, and the air around me choked in my throat.

Breathe.

It was Clint's voice in my mind, and as I stood there, dizzy, I could almost feel his hands touching my shoulders, giving me strength.

Breathe.

I took a deep breath, focusing on taking the air deep inside me, down to the very bottom of my lungs.

And I realized as I breathed in that I wasn't going to say anything at all.

I was going to sing.

Amazing grace! How sweet the sound
That saved a wretch like me,
I once was lost, but now am found,
Was blind, but now I see.

It wasn't until I opened my mouth that I realized what I was singing. I didn't focus on the words; I focused only on the breaths in between the lines, on the pauses that left the space open around me. I closed my eyes and sang, with all the power and strength that I could muster.

'Twas grace that taught my heart to fear,
And grace my fears relieved;
How precious did that grace appear
The hour I first believed!

Through many dangers, toils, and snares,
I have already come;
'Tis grace hath brought me safe thus far,
And grace will lead me home.

The last notes rang out, and I felt my lungs closing off. I opened my eyes and looked around. These were all of the people whom my mom had loved, who had loved her. I felt a deep love envelop me, and I knew that my mom was at peace.

"Thank you," I said to everyone. And then I stepped down. I had said goodbye to my mother, in the best way I knew how.

Afterwards, I drove home with Rose to get things ready for the reception. When I parked outside the house, though, she put a hand on mine and stopped me.

"Rachel?" Her voice was scared, lost.

"What is it, Rose?"

"I need to tell you something."

"About mom?"

I thought she was going to say something about the

funeral. About the song I'd sung, maybe. Or about how she'd left mom alone. But when I looked at her, I knew that it was something else entirely.

"No. Rachel, you can't tell anyone, okay? Especially not dad. I don't want anyone to know. But I need to talk about this with someone, and I didn't know who else to talk to."

"You can always talk to me," I said. "Rose, what is it? Are you having trouble in college?"

She shook her head, her lips white.

"Rachel," she said, her voice trembling. "I'm pregnant."

CHAPTER FORTY-THREE
Clint

Piers was furious with me when I showed up to the taping late. The girls had already recorded their songs for the final competition. After I explained what had happened, though, he softened.

"So is she coming back?" he asked.

"I don't know. I hope so."

"We can't put together the final schedule until—"

"I know. Look, assume she's not coming back." I hated to say it, but I had to face the facts. Rachel wanted to be with her family.

"It's a good story," Piers said, probing.

"It's not a story. It's her life."

"I understand. But—"

"You don't understand."

I left him standing there. I didn't need to talk to Piers right now. And definitely not about Rachel.

I didn't know if she ever wanted to come back to New York. I certainly wasn't going to push her. She had her own loss to deal with. But inside, I felt like I had lost the only part of me that had ever given me any meaning.

The recordings went fine. Annette and Sophia were both good singers. I couldn't imagine any of them becoming the new face of Terrance records. One of them would get a deal, though.

My dad took me aside after the last recording. We went into his office and he sat down on his leather chair. I remembered him telling me how much it had cost—over five thousand dollars. I thought about Rachel and her family and how much that money would mean to them. But to him it meant nothing.

He was ruddy, bronzed from his time spent in Europe doing who knows what. As he slumped back in the leather chair, he rubbed the bottom of his nose.

"That Sophia girl is something else," he said. "You think she'll win?"

"Maybe," I said, noncommittally.

"I think you have a good selection here. Either girl would do good."

"Sure, Pops."

He looked at me, like he wasn't sure if I was joking or not. I'd always been so enthusiastic about his opinion, but now I really didn't care.

"I think we could get Sophia a contract for a skincare line. I've been talking with the people over at *Sephora*, and they really like what we have."

"What do we have?"

"What do we—why, we have the best advertising platform in the nation! Are you kidding me, kiddo? We got the ear of every twenty-something year old in the country."

"And what are we going do with that?" I pressed my hands on the table as I stood up. "Are we going to sell them moisturizer? Weight loss products? Motherfucking lip gloss?"

"Sky's the limit, kiddo," my dad said, totally oblivious. "We can sell 'em anything. If Sophia's the brand—"

"Let's wait until we do the finals," I said.

"Oh, come on. You and I both know—"

"Wait until the finals, Pops."

I stood up from his desk. I had a mad hope. More of a wild Hail Mary, if I was honest with myself. Piers had been falling all over himself to get the recordings set up for the final round. But me? I wanted Rachel back.

I knew it was a pipe dream. She hadn't returned any of my calls or texts. She was busy with taking care of her dad and sister. But maybe...

No. I couldn't let myself hope that it would come true.

But there was something else on my mind. Something

that Rachel had brought up. It had been nagging me this whole time.

"Hey, Pops. Can I ask you something?"

"Sure, kiddo," he said. "What is it?"

I knew he thought I was going to ask him about some marketing device. Or the rank we'd gotten with our latest record. But that wasn't it.

"Where did mom go?"

I hadn't ever talked about my mom with him. His face went pale, then flushed bright red. It was the first time I could remember that I'd ever seen him look so discomposed.

"Why do you want to know?"

"I got curious."

"She abandoned us, you know?" he said.

"Did she?"

His face, already red, turned even redder.

"She's gone, kid."

"Where?"

"What are you saying, huh? What are you saying, kid? You saying I did something to her?"

He was high. I could tell. And I had never pushed him about this topic. But now I realized that I shouldn't have taken his word for anything. I should have pushed back before.

"I'm saying I want to know where she is. I want to meet her."

"That no-good gold-digging bitch—"

"Where is she, Pops?"

He bit his lip so hard I could see blood welling at the spot where his teeth came together.

"I sent her back."

"Back?" My mind was whirling. "What do you mean, back?"

"Back. She was an immigrant, you know that?" He was spitting mad, now. "A dirty immigrant, didn't even have her papers."

"Pops—"

"She wanted my money, and she wasn't gonna get it. That's the only reason she had you. Low-life money-grubbing bitch. She wanted to take you, too."

"What?"

This was a story I had never heard. My mother had left us after I was born. That's what my dad had always said. Only now, he was saying something different.

"She wanted me to pay her. Fuck that, I told her. My lawyers did her up real good."

My heart twisted in my chest.

"What did you do, Pops?"

"They got her kicked out. She couldn't see you, they said, couldn't even call you or she'd be in trouble."

"Kicked her out?"

"Back to Costa Rica."

My mind was whirling, and I could feel my fists clenching at my sides. My nails dug into my flesh as I tensed. I spoke slowly, carefully.

"You sent her away?"

"What? You never liked her anyway. You always took after your old man. You know—"

"Stop."

My dad looked up at me, the cocaine dilating his pupils. He licked his lips, his face twitching nervously. I could tell he knew he had fucked up. But he didn't know how badly.

"Listen, kiddo, you're better off without her anyway. She wouldn't have been a good mom anyway."

"And you were a good dad, right? Is that it?"

He blinked hard.

"I gave you everything," he said, licking his lips again with a violent thrust of his tongue. He pushed himself up out of the chair, leaned over his desk. Anger simmered up, twisted his tone.

"I gave you a job. I gave you a fucking music career. I made you a rock star. I gave you *everything.*"

I shook my head. I couldn't believe what I was hearing.

All he was saying—everything he had done—it made me sick.

"I can't believe you would lie to me about this, Pops."

"You ungrateful little *fuck*. Who's getting you all riled up about this? Is it that girl?"

"Pops—"

"You stay away from her, because she'll be just as much of a bitch as your mother was. And—"

I didn't know what he was going to say, and I never got to hear it. I punched him. I punched him, hard. And as he whirled away from me, his arms flailing up in the air, I lost all my anger. It was like every part of my fury had vented through my arm into his face. Blood ran down from one nostril on his face.

He didn't feel it, I knew. That was another part of the cocaine—it dulled the pain. He was still mad at me, but punching him wasn't going to solve anything. All it did was get the hate out of me and out into the world.

He landed backwards in his chair with a thud. His fingers touched the blood on his upper lip. He looked at it wondrously. Like he couldn't have imagined me ever hitting him. I don't think I ever had. He had always seemed untouchable, like a god. Now, though, all he was to me was an empty, pitiable man.

"What'd you go and do that for, kiddo?"

I swallowed the lump in my throat. I had a lot to do. And a lot of new decisions to make. But one thing was at the top of my mind.

"Pops," I said carefully. "If you ever insult Rachel again, I'll kill you. Got it?"

I didn't even know if I would ever see Rachel again. It might have been too late for my threat to mean anything. But if I had fucked up before, I had to make it right.

Maybe it was the coke in his system, or maybe it was the venom in my voice. But he only nodded, once, slowly.

"I've got to get ready for the final round," I said. "See you there."

I closed his office door behind me without letting him get in another word. I had enough to think about without thinking about how much time I'd wasted looking up to him.

CHAPTER FORTY-FOUR
Rachel

"I have something for you."

It was afternoon, and the last visitor had just left the funeral reception. I'd gone upstairs to pack. Now, though, my dad was in the doorway. He closed the door behind me.

"What's up?" I asked. I was still distracted by what Rose had told me. We hadn't had much time to talk before the reception started. She'd told me she was pregnant, and that the father wasn't anyone I knew. *Just a guy*, she said, like she didn't want to talk about it. *Just a guy*. I couldn't imagine her sleeping with someone and not being careful. It was so unlike her.

She wanted to keep the baby, and I told her that I would support her no matter what. In my mind, though, I couldn't help but worry about how our family could handle a baby when Rose wasn't even going to be able to get a job after college. She didn't want to be a stay at home mom, did she? But I kept my lips shut. She had obviously thought it out, and I was going to be the best sister I could. The best aunt.

I'd promised to keep her secret, but every time I saw my dad I wanted to blurt it out. I wasn't prepared to handle something so important all by myself. I swallowed hard as he came into my room.

"Here. Take this," he said.

He held out a video tape, the old VHS kind. On the side of it, there was a single label: Rachel. My breath caught in my throat as I recognized the handwriting.

"This is from Mom?"

"She made a video for you," he said.

"When?" I turned the tape over in my hands, looking at it like it was a strange treasure, something made of gold and gems instead of a dusty old tape.

"A long time ago. When you were a kid, before…" My dad swallowed hard. "Before things got bad. She knew that she wasn't going to last forever, and I think she wanted you to have something to remember her by. She made one for Rose, too, and one for me."

"Did you watch them?"

"Only mine, yesterday. If you want to share yours with me, I'd sure be grateful, but not right now. Right now, that tape is for you."

I looked down at the tape. The white cardboard box was yellowing at the edges.

"You've had this for years?"

"She told me not to give it to you until she passed. In the last few years, I don't think she even remembered she'd made it. But I remembered."

My dad looked up, and to my surprise, his eyes spilled over with tears.

"She was so smart," he said. "Just like you, oh, honey. So smart and beautiful."

I didn't know what to do. I'd never seen my dad cry. I'd never seen him be emotional. None of the ranchers around here wore their feelings on their sleeves, but Dad had always been one of the most stoic. Now that he was breaking down, I felt my own defenses give way.

"I'm sorry she's gone," I said.

"Oh, my baby. She's been gone for a while now, hasn't she?"

His face was the face of a man who had loved and lost. It made my heart break to see it. Without thinking, I stepped forward and wrapped my arms around his barrel chest. He clutched me close, like a drowning man who didn't know if he would ever breathe air again. His body shook with great heaving sobs.

I'd spent the second half of my life being a parent to

my mother, and now I felt as though I would never be a child again.

My relationship with my dad had always been friendly but unemotional, but today we had turned another corner. As I held him and he held me, a deep warmth spread through me. He had finally shared himself with me, and it was okay. We were family, and we would hang on together. Whatever happened with me, whatever happened with Rose. We would always be there for each other.

It wasn't long that we stood there, but it seemed like an eternity before he pulled away and swiped one gnarled hand across his eyes.

"You watch that tape," he said. "I've got to move the cows back; it's been too long since they were rotated."

Just like that, he switched back into work mode. But I'd seen him at his deepest hurt, and I knew that our relationship had changed.

"Goodbye, baby," he said, and he gave me a rough hug.

"Bye, dad," I said.

I went downstairs. Rose was gone; there was nobody in the house. Maybe my dad had asked her to leave me alone. I sat down in my mom's chair in front of the small TV and slipped in the video tape.

When I saw my mom on screen, I gasped a sharp breath.

She looked so young. I had forgotten how young. Her hair was dark, with only a few streaks of gray, but her face looked so much younger, so *alive*. So beautiful.

Like a princess.

My mom sat down in a chair, the same chair that I was sitting in now, I realized. The sun was coming in through the window, and it lit her hair from behind like an angel. She adjusted the angle of the videotape, and I swallowed as she looked straight into the camera.

Her eyes seemed laced with gold, and her face was fierce with emotion.

"Hello, Rachel," she said. Her voice was rich and full

and strong, but I leaned forward in the chair anyway.

"Right now you're twelve years old. Both you and Rose are growing up to be such wonderful young women. When I look at you, I'll always see my baby, but I know that you're getting older. So am I.

"I wanted to say I'm sorry, Rachel. This disease…I feel it inside of me, eating me away in pieces. Sometimes I'll look around and I won't even know where I am anymore. I can see it hurting your dad most of all.

"And you… you're already taking care of me. It's so hard to look at you and see that I'm going to let you down."

I was shaking my head, tears spilling down my cheeks.

"I don't want you to end up like I am. I don't want you to stay on the farm and take care of me and your dad forever. Rachel, you have a gift. You know it. There's a little piece of beauty in all of us, but in you it's like a burning spark. You are truly special, and I know you'll do great things."

"So much of what I have to tell you comes down to love. I want you to do what you love. I want you to follow your dreams, Rachel. Find your passion and live it, because there's never… there's never enough time."

"I love you, my precious, wonderful baby. I love you so much. Remember that I'll always be with you, no matter what. I'll always be in your heart. I love you."

With that, she leaned forward, reaching with one slim arm toward the camera. The screen went dark. It was the end of the tape.

I sat there crying for a while. Slowly, surely, a sense of peace came over me. My mom hadn't let me down. She had lived a beautiful life, and she'd had it harder than most people ever do. But she had survived, and she had raised her family, and that was what I would remember from her.

I stood up, feeling stronger than before. *There's never enough time.* I wasn't going to give up now.

I knew what I had to do.

CHAPTER FORTY-FIVE
Clint

It was the night of the final competition, but my mind was elsewhere. I'd hired the best private investigators I could find to track down my mom in Costa Rica. My dad hadn't answered any more of my questions, and I wasn't sure that he was even going to come to the last episode taping.

Hell, if Piers hadn't convinced me, I wouldn't be there either.

"Welcome to *Sing and Win*!" Piers said. "We have our two finalists on stage right now, so let's introduce them!"

We were sitting in Times Square, on a makeshift stage in front of the stadium seating. Piers had somehow gotten access to half of the screens, and we were broadcasting live over a huge crowd of people. The lights of New York City sparkled brightly, too brightly. I wanted it to be dark.

He shoved the microphone in front of my face.

"I'm Clint Terrance, and it's great to be here!" I said. My training as a performer took over. My smile was forced and fake, but nobody could tell as I waved.

I looked over the stage. Sophia and Annette were sitting primly on two chairs across from me and Piers. They were wearing dresses so short I thought they would get hypothermia on stage. It had gotten so cold out here, I thought it had to snow.

Sophia actually had the gall to wink at me as I eyed her dress. She thought I was checking her out now that Rachel was gone. The thought made my stomach turn, and I looked away.

Rachel should be here. She should be the winner. I didn't even know what I was doing here.

"All this week, you've been following the contestants through a battle of songs," Piers was saying. "Through all the ups and downs, we've ended up with our finalists—the best singers we could find."

Except one, I thought. Rachel wasn't here. I scanned the crowd. Screams of girls reached me from over the mob. They loved me, of course. All the girls loved Clint Terrance.

All except the one girl who mattered.

"And now you'll get to vote on the final champion! It's your chance to make a dream come true, America. Who will be our winner?"

Piers passed me the mike.

"*Have some bloody enthusiasm,*" he hissed in my ear. I guess I hadn't been faking it as well as I'd thought I was. I raised my hand, and the crowd went wild. High-pitched shrieks reached my ears. They were cheering for me, and I didn't even care. It all felt empty.

"Let's hear our finalists!" I cried out, and the crowd roared. I passed the mike back to Piers, who shrugged as if to say *That was a little better.*

Then I saw my dad. He wasn't on stage like he'd said he would be. He was in the crowd, wearing sunglasses even though it was an overcast, windy day.

I pinched my lips tight. I wasn't going to give him the satisfaction of letting him know he could get to me. I'd said my piece to him already. If he wanted a singer for his studio, he could have one. I wasn't going to be part of any of it. I'd decided—this was the end. I wasn't going to be part of a studio I didn't believe in anymore.

Annette sang a pop song for her final piece. It was upbeat and high-energy and utterly forgettable. She finished to a smattering of applause.

I couldn't help glancing toward my dad. He looked as non-enthused as I felt, and I was somewhat relieved to know that I hadn't been completely off the mark. Annette was a girl just like any other girl. A Britney Spears wanna-be who had missed the boat.

Then Sophia strutted across the stage. I watched carefully. Not her, but the audience. All of the girls who had been cheering for me went quiet when Sophia took the mike. As she sang, I could see them tuning out.

My dad had been wrong. She wasn't going to be a star.

I had known it from the beginning, but I hadn't known why. Sophia was too stand-offish. Too elegant and prissy. She wasn't the kind of girl who you could be friends with. She was the head cheerleader at your high school. And while you might look up to her with a sort of frightened respect, you could never love her.

It was a victory for me, but it was a hollow victory. I'd proved my dad wrong, but I hadn't gained anything from it. Instead, I had lost everything that had ever mattered to me.

"Thank you, Sophia," Piers said. I realized that she had finished her song.

"Yes, thanks so much!" I said cheerfully. "Great job, Sophia!"

I had lost my music career—there was no way my dad would let me stay on at the studio after this fiasco. I had lost my family and the person I had thought was my role model. And worst of all, I had lost Rachel.

Rachel. Piers was talking about her now, a somber look on his face. I couldn't even tell if he was acting or if he actually felt sorry for her.

"There was one more finalist. Rachel Ritter left the competition this week after a tragic accident took her mother's life."

Around the stage, I saw Rachel's face projected up on Times Square, bigger than life. The ache in my heart threatened to show itself in my expression, but I shoved the feeling back down.

She was gone, and I would have to move on without her. I had never deserved her anyway.

"Rachel isn't here tonight, and so we go now to—"

"I'm here!"

I heard the familiar voice, but Piers didn't. He kept on talking into the mike.

"Now, America, it's time for you to vote for the next star!"

"Wait," I said. The screen flashed up with the number to text, but the camera guy swung over to me as I spoke. I stood up out of my chair and scanned the crowd. Piers glanced over at me, then did a second take.

"What is it?" he whispered, away from the mike.

"She's here."

"What?"

I saw a commotion in the front row, and then Rachel burst forward out of the crowd. She was wearing the black dress I'd bought her and she looked up at the stage, her face flushed. Her hair lay in a simple braid over one shoulder.

"I'm here!" she cried out. "Am I too late?"

CHAPTER FORTY-SIX
Rachel

I pushed forward through the crowd toward Clint and the rest of the people on stage. This wasn't what I'd planned. I only wanted to see the last show. But now that I was here, I couldn't stand aside. I thought of what my mom had told me in the video.

Follow your dreams.

This was my dream, and I was going to chase it for as long as I could. Piers was still talking, and I thought I would be too late.

"—and so we go now—"

"I'm here!"

Clint was standing up, his eyes fierce and dark. I paused for only a second. Would he be angry with me for bursting into the middle of the taping? But then his face softened as he recognized me in the crowd.

"Rachel!"

"Am I too late?" I asked breathlessly. The lights of Times Square flickered all around me. Piers stood silently as Clint came over to the edge of the stage. He looked like what he was—a rock god—and his presence was like a force field around him. Everyone seemed to be holding their breath along with me for his answer.

Then, he smiled.

"Never," Clint said. "You're never too late, Rachel."

The people around me cheered as Clint knelt down and gave me a hand. His strong arms plucked me up from the crowd and lifted me onto the stage.

Behind Piers, Sophia was sitting next to Annette. Her jaw dropped as Clint led me over to the microphone.

"Just remember to breathe," he whispered in my ear.

His hand was warm on the small of my back, and I felt utterly comforted. I nodded, letting my lungs open up as I took a deep breath.

Then I turned to the audience.

It was insane. There must have been a hundred thousand people out there, watching me. My face was all over the screens in front of me. I could see my red-rimmed eyes, the circles underneath where I hadn't put on any makeup. I looked so plain compared to the other girls on stage.

For a moment, I choked. I hadn't warmed up at all, and as I stood nervously on stage, my throat began to tense up.

But then my mom's words echoed through my mind, and I thought of Clint's hands on me, guiding my breath. I began to relax.

I was going to do this. I was going to follow my dreams. Even if I crashed and burned, it would be better than not trying.

"Hello," I said. "I'm Rachel Ritter." My voice boomed through the huge speakers, echoing off of the skyscrapers all around us. It made me even more nervous. I licked my lips. I could do this. Forget everything else.

"I'm going to sing a song my mom used to sing to me," I said. "It's a lullaby called *The Thorn Bird*."

I took a deep breath.

Long ago, so long ago, a young bird left her nest…

The words came out shaky at first. I could hear my voice wavering. I hadn't warmed up, hadn't even decided that I would be singing this until I was on stage. I hadn't thought I would make it in time. But now, as I sang, the familiar lyrics wrapped around me, as comforting as the blanket my mom had knitted for me when I was a little girl.

Fly, little bird,

Fly until the break of dawn.
Fly, little bird,
Fly on, fly on.

I could feel myself holding back, not breathing completely. I needed to do what Clint had told me. I needed to sing from the bottom of my lungs. But right now, in the middle of a huge crowd of people, under the bright lights of the stage, I couldn't focus.

So I closed my eyes, and instantly I was back home. Back in the barn, singing to cows and cats. Singing to my mom. And for the first time, I let myself go completely.

The nightingale was born to sing, the clouds were born to rain
The young bird found the tree of thorns and did not mind the pain.

In my mind, I saw my mom lying in bed on the farm. Her eyes were half-closed and her hair was smooth and silken on the pillow as she drifted to sleep. I wasn't singing for anyone else. I was singing for her.

"Thank you, Rachel," I heard her whisper. It almost hurt, how much my heart swelled when she remembered my name. And then I could hear her singing with me, singing the last few lines.

Sing, little bird,
Sing until the break of dawn.
Sing, little bird,
Sing on, sing on.

I was crying—tears were coming down my cheeks—but nothing could make me stop singing. I managed to get through to the last note. Then I opened my eyes.

The crowd was silent. The lights on the buildings around us blinked and twinkled, and the lighted tickertape kept rolling, but apart from that it was like time had stopped.

I knew I hadn't sung a normal song, and I wasn't sure how they would take it. But even if this was the last time I sung to such a large audience, I knew that I had done the right thing. I'd been true to myself.

I leaned forward to the microphone.

"Thank you," I said, my words a half-whisper.

Then, to my shock, the crowd burst into applause.

The sound rolled over me on stage and kept coming in louder and louder waves. I looked around in disbelief. Everybody was cheering, and I could see some people in the audience who were wiping away tears.

"Thank you, Rachel!" Piers was saying. "And now we'll go live to the results. Remember to text in your vote…"

I stepped back to the chairs where the other contestants were sitting. Sophia looked at me with an expression of pure hate. I found that I didn't even care. She had her own issues to deal with, and I wasn't going to be a part of it.

"Bitch," she hissed at me. She must have forgotten that she was miked up, because her words went out over the speaker system. Her face reddened as Piers and Clint turned to stare at her.

"Sounds like we have a little not-so-friendly competition back there," Piers said. "Do you have anything else you want to say?"

He was obviously taunting her, leading her on. I almost wanted to warn her away from taking the bait.

Almost.

"I can't believe you let her into the finals!" Sophia said, recrossing her legs. "She's obviously not a real singer. Look at her!"

The results were coming in on the screens alongside the camera focusing on Sophia's frown. Piers was a genius, I realized. Sophia's percentage of the votes was dropping every second.

"Anything else?"

"She's a fucking bitch who's fucking Clint Terrance in order to win, and—"

Her microphone cut off.

"Sorry," Piers said, an amused smile spreading on his face. "Our censor can't keep up with you. Remember, this is a live recording, no swearing allowed!"

Now the cameraman had moved up next to us and was switching focus between me and Sophia.

"You goddamn cunt!" Sophia was screaming, standing up from her chair. Her face was full of rage, her eyelid twitching at one side. "You stole this contest away from me! You stole this contest!"

She took a step toward me and I realized as she raised her hand that she was going to hit me.

The blow never landed. Clint and Piers moved quickly between us. Clint gathered me in his arms away from her, and Piers took the slap that had been meant for me. I heard the noise ring out over the speakers.

"Whoa!" he cried. "Someone get this woman out of here, am I right?"

A bodyguard quickly pulled Sophia to the side of the stage. She was still spitting curse words at the top of her lungs.

The screens switched over to Sophia's percentage, heading quickly toward zero.

"Sorry, darling," Piers said, not even fazed by her slapping him. "Looks like you're not the winner."

"You asshole! You rigged this! You rigged all of this!" She was hitting the guard on the shoulder, her face scarlet red.

The bodyguard slung Sophia over his shoulder and carried her off.

"Good riddance," Piers said. "That's one singer who won't be winning a contract with Terrance Studios!"

The crowd cheered.

"Now let's see what the final tally is. Ladies and gentlemen, your new star from *Sing and Win* is…"

There was a roar that filled my ears. I could see the mobs of people in front of me jumping, their movements like waves across Times Square. I blinked hard.

"Do you see that, Rachel?"

Clint had one arm around my waist, and he pointed at the largest screen in the square. It was my name, and next to it...

Eighty-five percent.

I had won. My head went dizzy. I'd won!

"Congratulations, Rachel Ritter!"

Piers' voice was ringing in my ears and the crowd was still shouting, but when I looked up at Clint, it felt like the whole world fell away.

"I knew you had it in you," he said. He took me in his arms and kissed me. I could hear screams from the audience, but everything was muted compared to my heartbeat. His hot lips pressed against mine and I felt the world move under my feet.

Then he broke away from the kiss, still holding me up. It was a good thing—I felt dizzy enough to tumble off the stage. His kiss had taken away the last of my breath.

Clint held up my hand in victory and the crowd went insane with noise. The floor under my feet vibrated with the sound of it.

"This is all for you," he whispered. "They love you. And so do I."

I was in a daze the whole way back. I couldn't believe that I'd won. And I couldn't believe that Clint had kissed me in front of everyone, cameras and all. When we finally left everyone and headed up to the apartment one last time, I had to ask him.

"Clint, did you mean it?"

He looked at me like he didn't know what I was talking about.

"The kiss," I said. "Saying you love me."

"What makes you think I didn't mean it?" Clint asked

with a frown.

"I mean… all the cameras…I thought you were doing it for TV. You said that we were nothing. Before. You said it was a one-time thing."

His face softened into worry.

"I didn't mean to pressure you," he said. "I got caught up in the moment. But…"

The elevator stopped, but he didn't key in the code. Instead, he turned to me and took me by the waist. I slipped into his arms as easily as if we had been made to fit together.

"Rachel," he said, his voice low. "I know I said we were nothing. I thought that's what you wanted. But I realized that I wanted more."

My heart filled my chest, and his hands tightened around my waist, pulling me close.

"I think we would make a great team," he said. "In more ways than one. And I meant it, Rachel. I haven't ever fallen for a girl before. But I know that I love you. And, since I'm never wrong—"

I laughed, and he cupped the back of my head, dipping his mouth down to catch me in a kiss.

"Clint—"

"Tell me I'm right."

"You're right!" I said, giggling as he kissed my neck just below my ear. "You're right, you're right, you're always right!"

He was right. He was right for me, and it had taken me way too long to realize it. His passion inspired me. His love of music twined with mine and deepened the desire between us. When he kissed me, it was like we were in perfect harmony, slowing and quickening together.

His hands reached down and gripped my hips, pulling me up as he spun around. He pressed me against the wall of the elevator and my legs wrapped around him.

He groaned, and I felt his cock twitch against me, sending a shudder of desire through me. I was already wet, and oh-so ready for more.

"I can't get enough of you," he growled. "Let's get out of this elevator."

When the doors opened, he carried me out, my legs still twined around his waist. I looked around in shock.

This wasn't the apartment I'd stayed in with the other girls. The furniture was all different. The walls were painted a deep, soothing green and the walls had music posters hung up all over.

"Clint, where the heck are we?"

He laughed as he carried me down the hallway.

"I had them redecorate it after the competition ended. Piers wanted a more modern look for the show, but this is how I like it."

"This is great," I said, and meant it.

"Wait. You have to see the bedroom," he said.

"Oh, do I?" My arms tightened around his neck, and I let my fingers thread through his hair.

"Yeah. We have to test it out together."

I laughed as he kicked open the door to the bedroom. Inside was a huge four-poster bed. He laid me down on the silken cream sheets, kissing me down the length of my body as he stripped the dress off of me, leaving me in only my panties. They were red silk—part of a lingerie set he had bought me at the dress shop.

I sunk back into the pillowy mattress. He stood next to the bed, loosening his tie. His tattoo peeked up from under his collar as he unbuttoned his shirt.

"My God, Rachel," he said. His hands were loose at his side, and he was looking down at the bed.

"What? What is it?"

"It's the most perfect girl in the world. How did she ever get into my bed?"

I kicked out at him playfully and he caught my ankle. He kissed the top of my foot.

"Look at these perfect toes," he said. "And these perfect calves." He kissed up to my knees.

"Perfect knees?" I teased.

"Absolutely perfect."

"Good. I've been working out."

"Oh, I can definitely tell. Very toned kneecaps." He grinned, caressing my knee with one strong hand. "And what about these?"

He moved up to my thighs with his lips, and all of a sudden I couldn't tease him anymore. I couldn't say anything. My breath hissed between my teeth as he stroked my legs up to my panties, brushing me softly there.

"Oh, this is the best part," he murmured, his lips coming close to my soaked panties, his breath warming me.

"Ohhhh," I moaned. His tongue had flicked out and pressed me *there*. Bolts of desire shot through me.

"I can't go slow this time, Rachel," he said. "I can't wait. I hope that's okay—" He was ripping off his shirt, his pants. In a second he was naked, sheathed, and kneeling again on top of me, kissing me hard.

"Are you ready? Tell me you're ready, Rachel. Fuck, I'm so hard for you." He caught his lip between his teeth as he looked down at me, and something inside me twisted, reaching for him.

"*Yes*," I breathed. "Yes, Clint, please, yes—"

His mouth was on mine and his legs shoved my thighs apart, sending flashes of desire straight to my core. His hands gripped my hips and dragged me down to meet him, hard and ready between my thighs.

"*Ohhhh.*" We both moaned simultaneously as he slid into me with a deep thrust, rocking my body into the mattress. His eyes locked onto mine, sparking with desire.

I clenched around him and his eyes went wide.

"*Fuck*," he hissed. "You drive me fucking crazy, you know that?"

"*Yes.*" I smiled, and he grinned back. He rocked back and thrust forward again, filling me. My eyes clenched shut and white explosions of lightning went off behind my eyelids.

There wasn't any more time to speak. He was on top of me, pressing his whole body against me. I felt his hands stroking me all over. My heartbeat thundered in my ears as he rocked back and forth, quicker and quicker, unable to slow. I didn't want him to. I wanted it all, wanted him inside me, wanted him to fill me.

"*Ohh*," I sighed, feeling him deep inside me. He was so thick, and I wrapped my legs around him, urging him forward.

"*Mine*," he said, and rolled his hips against me. My body leapt up instantly to the edge of climax, and I gasped for air. But his kiss stopped my mouth, taking away my breath. He rolled into me again, and I felt the shudder begin from deep inside me.

"*Mmmmm!*" Waves of orgasm rippled through me as he rocked his body against me right there, in that perfect spot. My fingers scrabbled at the sheets, trying to find purchase. I was holding on for one second, and then the next second I was gone, lost in the rolling waves of my orgasm.

Clint never stopped, not to give me breath, not to rest. His rhythm increased, and sweat slicked our bodies as he slid over me with a delicious friction. The ink on his chest blurred with my vision. He was all music, a hard pounding beat, and my body sang along with his.

The coil inside me had unraveled, but as soon as I could breathe again I could feel it tighten back up. His cock was hard as steel, and he slammed into my body, filling me over and over again.

Faster. So fast. I didn't know what my body was anymore. It seemed like something else had taken me over and was driving me to the edge of ecstasy or madness, or both. My hands slid over the hard muscles of his back, and his fingers gripped my hips tightly as he rode me hard.

I choked with pleasure when one of his hands moved to my breast. He pinched my nipple, twisting it and sending shocks through my nerves. Instead of pain, though, these were shocks of pleasure, pure pleasure. I arched up into his palm and he squeezed, still thrusting into me.

"*Ahhhhh!*" The noise came from deep in his throat.

I could feel his cock stiffen inside of me and I knew he was close. I was closer. I rocked with him, meeting him with every thrust, a wild need that took over my body and turned us both into primal creatures of desire.

As he jackhammered into me, faster and faster, stretching me to my limits, I met his rhythm. Riding him to the edge of my ecstasy, I flung myself over the cliff screaming.

"*Ohhhhhhhhhh!*"

Again and again I pulsed against him. I lost myself in the explosive orgasm, my head thrashing against the soft sheets. Wave after wave ripped through my body, searing my nerves with a white-hot energy. So powerful. So strong. I was shattered in his strong arms.

Then inside of me his cock thrust hard, and the moan came up from deep in his chest as he jerked once, then again, meeting me in ecstasy.

Once more he thrust into me, and a final shiver of bliss vibrated through my body. When he withdrew, he slid to my side and gathered me against his chest. We were both panting, the air hot between us.

In silence we lay there for a few minutes, recovering. My fingers moved to his chest, tracing the notes. Amazing grace. Yes. That was what this was. A feeling of immensity swept through me, and unbidden tears of happiness stung my eyes.

Clint's hands caressed my hair, smoothing it against the pillow.

"I love you," he whispered. In his eyes was a question. He'd said it to me before, and I hadn't answered. This time, I did.

"I love you, too." I pressed my cheek against his chest, listening to the deep thrum of his heartbeat. Here, I had lost myself and everything I had before I came to the city. I'd changed. I'd grown. I had become who I was meant to be. And in his arms, I had found myself again.

EPILOGUE
Rachel

It was spring, and the air was just starting to warm up. Back on the farm, the blackberry bushes were starting to bud green fruit and the cows were munching on newly grown grass in the pastures.

My dad was recovering from my mom's death with the help of the community. Clint had gotten him in contact with a few New York restauranteurs, and my dad was busier than ever trying to keep up with the demand. He was starting to make a few new specialty cheeses, and growing the herd at the same time. And although he still tried to maintain the stoic New Jersey farm persona, I could tell that he was thrilled that he would soon have a grandson.

Rose was starting to show, and I couldn't wait to be an aunt. She'd taken a part-time research position at a chemistry lab in New York, and the rest of the time she spent on the farm. She refused to learn any of the cows' names, but she was definitely getting better at working the milker. I hoped that she would find happiness, but for now we were all simply trying to find a new way of life.

I wasn't on the farm anymore, though. I was in New York City at Terrance Studios, and we had just finished wrapping up the final recording session. Clint wrapped me in a huge hug as the rest of the people in the studio cheered. It was a huge party—Clint had invited just about everybody who had been involved in the album.

Taylor was there, too, jumping up and down in excitement. I'd kept in touch with her after the competition, and Clint's dad had agreed to take her on as a new studio singer. She was doing a backing track for a solo project done by one of Clint's bandmates, and I couldn't have been happier for her.

"It's done!" I said, my breath coming back to normal. Someone handed me a glass of champagne and I clinked it against Clint's. "We have a record!"

"You have a record," Clint corrected. "All yours."

"I couldn't have done any of this without you," I said, shyness creeping back into my voice. It had been months of preparation, recording, re-recording. And that was just the beginning. We still had to edit all the tracks, figure out the artwork for the album, mix and master all of the songs...

I was lost in thought at all of the work we had ahead of us when Clint dipped his head and kissed me, bringing me back to the moment. His arm clasped me tightly to him and I was pink with pleasure when he finally let me get another breath.

"I cannot believe this!" Piers said, coming around to us. He clapped Clint on the back. "Billionaire bachelor Clint Terrance has managed to surprise me again!"

"Surprise?" I asked.

"The two of you together? Absolutely."

"Was it really such a surprise?" Clint asked.

"I half-thought you were pretending. For the cameras," Piers explained. "So you're really a couple now?"

I looked up at Clint, not wanting to overstep my bounds by answering for him. We had spent so much time together in the past few months, but we hadn't ever really defined our relationship. I found myself holding my breath for his response.

"Of course," he said, smiling down at me. "Hopefully she'll keep me around for a while longer. Now that she's done with the recording, though..."

"What's that supposed to mean?" I protested.

He squeezed my side.

"You're not going to use me and dump me?" he asked. His long dark brown lashes fluttered playfully.

"No, sir," I said, grinning. "You're stuck with me. At least until the record goes platinum!"

"Good to hear," Clint said, kissing the top of my head. "How's the new show coming along, Piers?"

"Great!" he said. His eyes lit up and he began to stammer. "W—wonderful, actually. Some really—ah— really good contestants."

"Really?" I asked, arching an eyebrow.

"Mmm. Ah—yes. Yes. I'm going for more champagne," he said, swiveling away from us.

"What do you think that's all about?" I asked, once he had gone.

"Huh?" Clint asked.

"You didn't notice how he got all flustered there when talking about his new show?"

"Oh. No, I didn't notice," Clint said, totally oblivious. "He was flustered?"

"Come on. He's normally the most polished Brit on television. And he was stumbling over his words like some lovesick puppy."

"You think?"

"I *know*," I said meaningfully, looking after Piers.

"Well, I'll have to keep an eye on him," Clint said. "But right now, I want to give you a present."

"A present?"

"It's upstairs."

"But the party's just started!"

"We'll be back before it's over. Trust me, Piers knows how to keep a party going."

Before I could protest any more, he'd whisked me away to the elevator. We headed up, and I tried to guess what the present could be. He'd already bought me more dresses than I knew what to do with, and it seemed like every other night he was taking me out to a fancy dinner, sometimes with Jake and Lacey or Steph and Lucas. There wasn't anything more that I wanted. But my heart still beat quickly as I followed him through the apartment and up the ladder, up to the glass globe.

He kicked off his shoes and jumped down. I sat down on the platform. He took off my heels carefully, his hands warm against the soles of my feet. He kissed the inside of my ankle tenderly.

"Come with me," he said, holding out his hands. I fell forward, trusting him to catch me. Gently, he lowered me down onto the bottom of the globe.

"Is my present out here?"

He only smiled.

"I used to come here by myself to look out on the city," he said, drawing me forward. His hand enveloped mine and I stood by his side, looking out over the glittering skyscrapers. "I used to feel like I was part of New York, and New York was part of me."

"But not anymore?"

He shook his head.

"When I found you in here, I realized that I wasn't—I wasn't part of the city at all. I locked myself up here and looked down on everyone from this glass globe. I had walled myself off from everyone, sky high above street level."

I waited. His palm was hot on mine, and I gave it a slight squeeze to comfort him. I wondered if that was the present he was giving me—the present of this secret of his. The gift of opening up to me.

"You can't get to know people that way," he continued. "You can't ever let anyone in. And before, I never wanted to let anyone in. My mom had left me, and it was just me and my dad, holed up in the studio. I thought that's what I wanted."

"And now? You don't want that?"

"No." Clint pressed his lips together firmly. "I found her, Rachel. I found my mom."

"What?" I was astonished. "What do you mean?"

"My dad sent her away. He's been lying this whole time. She never left; he sent her away."

"Your dad?"

"We've already fought about it. And talked about it. And fought some more." Clint looked down, a hard expression steeling his jaw. "And it's not over and done with yet. But I'm trying to keep things together. I've already lost my mom once and it's not going to happen again. I had a private investigator track her down. It took all this time, but he finally found her."

My mind was a whirl of questions. Where was she? Why hadn't she gotten in touch? And what did this mean for the two of us? But the most important thing to me was that Clint had regained the other half of his family.

"Are you going to go visit her?" I asked.

"Soon," Clint said. He turned to me and took my hands. "That's part of why I asked you up here. Rachel, I want to thank you."

"For what?"

"For showing me that there's more out there than I knew existed. I wouldn't have ever found out about my mother if you hadn't pushed me to realize it. I always thought my Pops was a perfect dad. The coolest guy. I should have seen that he wasn't leading me down the right path."

"As long as you're happy now," I murmured.

"I am. I'm so happy. Are you?"

It was a strange question, I thought.

"I couldn't be any happier than I am," I said. "Look at this. All of my dreams have come true."

His expression was hesitant, like it never was. I didn't know why he was acting so nervous. He licked his lips.

"Do you still think I'm bad for you, Rachel?"

I laughed, but he was serious. I paused for a second, as though to consider the question.

"No," I said. "Definitely not."

His face relaxed a bit.

"Rachel—"

"Yes?"

"I want to go visit my mom. And I want you to come with me."

"Me?" I blinked hard. I didn't understand. "I know why you want to go. But… why me?"

"Because," he said, "I want her to meet the woman I'm going to marry."

My heart seemed to jump from one beat to the next, and there was a rush in my ears. I couldn't hear the music anymore, only the echo of his words.

The woman I'm going to marry.

Clint knelt in front of me at the bottom of the globe, the lights of New York sparkling all around us. Then he was holding a ring up to my hand, a serious look on his face.

"I want you to be mine forever, Rachel Ritter. I want your voice to be the last thing I hear at night and the first thing I hear in the morning. You're a better woman than I deserve, and these past few months have been a dream. I want to make it real. Marry me."

I finally found my breath.

"Clint…"

My voice trailed off as he looked up at me, pure love in his eyes, and for a moment I thought I would faint. It couldn't be real. It wasn't. And yet there he was, the love of my life, the man who had made me happier than anyone else possibly could. I swallowed the lump in my throat and nodded happily, choking out the words.

"Yes! Yes, yes. Forever, yes!"

My hand trembled as he slipped the ring on. It sparkled, a perfect circle diamond ringed by rubies. Tears of happiness streamed down my eyes and the jewels blurred behind the tears.

"Rubies and gold, just like your hair," he said, kissing the top of my forehead.

"Oh, Clint—"

"Rachel, my wonderful, perfect Rachel."

He kissed me, his hands slipping easily around my

waist. The familiar embrace felt as new as the first time he had kissed me, but this time I let myself fall forward. His lips seized mine, and as he kissed me passionately I kissed him back, taking as good as I got. His chest was hard as steel, and his arms pulled me protectively into the only embrace I ever wanted to know.

He had taken me to bed many times in the past months, but this was completely new, a new kind of desire that pulsed through my veins. I knew his body intimately, and as he pressed into me, I felt flashes of past pleasures race across my nerves—

—when he kissed me from top to toe, his mouth sucking and licking every inch of me, from my wrists down to the small of my back, until I begged him for more—

—after another orgasm, when he'd taken me again roughly, bringing me to climax over and over and not stopping until I was screaming his name—

—when he lowered himself between my legs, his tongue probing me deeply and giving himself entirely to my pleasure—

Now, though, it was just a kiss, but it felt like all of these put together. He wanted me—*me!*—and I thought with a dark worry that it had all been a dream, that I would wake up at any moment and realize that I was back on the farm, that I had never come to New York City at all. But the kiss went on and on, and his hands were in my hair and all over my curves, and he was utterly real and perfect and this wasn't going to end, no, he would stay with me forever.

I felt myself growing dizzy as he deepened the kiss. I tilted my head back and let him take me over, my every particle vibrating with pleasure. My body melted into his arms and I forgot the world around us. My whole body ached for him, wanted him to possess me completely.

When he finally released me from the kiss, I felt faint, the air hot around us.

"Breathe," he whispered.

I breathed. His arms encircled me, and I looked into his eyes. They reflected the lights around us, sparkling in his dark irises.

We stayed that way for a minute, maybe, or an hour. His body pressed against mine and I felt his chest rise and fall along with my own, his heartbeat matching mine in a slowing rhythm that sounded like the start of a song.

Our song.

The End

Thank you for reading Bad For Me!

If you enjoyed the story would you please consider leaving a review on Amazon?

Just a few words and some stars really does help!

-

Be sure to sign up for my mailing list to find out about new releases, deals and giveaways!

http://bit.ly/AubreyDarkNewsletter

Made in the USA
Lexington, KY
08 January 2016